In TWICE SEVEN,
Ben Bova's universe is always
more than the sum of its parts . . .

"Conspiracy Theory" reveals the startling truth about those so-called Martian canals and a patch of New Mexico know as Roswell.

In "Appointment in Sinai," the technology of virtual telepresence allows people all over the world to share the experience of the first manned Mars landing . . . with results as poignant as they are unexpected.

An amnesiac android finds himself feasting with King Hrothgar, Queen Wealhtheow and a warrior by the name of Beowulf in "Legendary Heroes."

In "Life as We Know It," the eternal question "Are we alone?" gets a startling, never-to-be-forgotten answer.

An expatriate woman with a secret fights an exclusionary bureaucracy to return to her home and son in "Re-Entry Shock."

Fiction Books by Ben Bova

TWICE SEVEN

STORIES BY

BEN BOVA

AVON · EOS

Copyright notices for the stories in this collection appear on pages 289–
290, which constitutes an extension of this copyright page.

AVON BOOKS, INC.
1350 Avenue of the Americas
New York, New York 10019

Copyright © 1998 by Ben Bova
Inside cover author photograph by Eric Strachan
Published by arrangement with the author
Visit our website at **http://www.AvonBooks.com/Eos**
Library of Congress Catalog Card Number: 97-94887
ISBN: 0-380-79741-0

First Avon Eos Printing: August 1998

AVON EOS TRADEMARK REG. U.S. PAT. OFF. AND IN OTHER COUNTRIES,
MARCA REGISTRADA, HECHO EN U.S.A.

Printed in the U.S.A.

WCD   10   9   8   7   6   5   4   3   2   1

To Judine and Terry

CONTENTS

INTRODUCTION:
THE ART OF PLAIN SPEECH

It is the secret of the artist that he does his work so superlatively well that we all but forget to ask what his work was supposed to be, for sheer admiration of the way he did it.

—E. H. GOMBRICH
THE STORY OF ART

I agree with that statement—up to a point. The esteemed Dr. Gombrich may be totally correct when speaking of painting or sculpture or even architecture, but when it comes to writing fiction, Sir Ernest and I part company.

In fiction, I believe, the true art is to engage the reader so intimately in the story that we forget about the writer, for sheer involvement in the tale that the characters are weaving before our eyes.

Maybe I feel that way because I started out in the newspaper game (it's never called a business by the workers in the field). Or maybe it's because I've

1

spent most of my adult life working with scientists and engineers. Or maybe it's because I care about my readers too much.

Whatever the reason, I have always felt that the writer should be virtually invisible in his or her fiction; the reader should be drawn into the story, rather than forced to admire the writer's brush-strokes. Only after the story is finished should the reader be able to sit up and think, "That was an enjoyable piece of writing." During the reading process, the reader should be so engrossed in the story that the writer's art (or craft) is barely noticed, if at all.

I have never felt that writing should be a contest between author and the reader, a battleground filled with obscurity and arcana. I don't want my readers to struggle with my prose. I don't want to impress them with how smart I am. I want them to enjoy what I'm writing and maybe think a little about what I'm trying to say.

Problem is, when you write clearly and simply, without stylistic frills or rococo embellishments, some people think that you are not a "deep" thinker or a "stylist."

Isaac Asimov ran into this predicament often. Critics could not fault Isaac on his knowledge or his success, or even his earnestness or political correctness, so they belittled his style, calling it "pedestrian" or "simplistic." Yet Isaac's style was the one thing that made him such a success, at least as far as his non-fiction work is concerned.

Other specialists knew their subjects in more depth than Isaac did. Isaac had a tremendous breadth of knowledge, but in any particular field— be it cosmology or poetry, biblical scholarship or even biochemistry—there were specialists who knew a lot more of the details than he did.

But it was Isaac's genius to be able to take any of those specialized fields and write about them so clearly, so naturalistically, that just about anyone who is able to read could learn the fundamentals of Isaac's subject. That took *style*! And it was definitely not intuitive, the work of unreflective genius. Isaac thought about what he did, every step of the way. He deliberately developed a writing style that was so deceptively unpretentious and naturalistic that critics thought what he did was easy.

In fiction, the academic disdain for straightforward, honest prose has led critics to dismiss Hemingway and praise Faulkner, although today we are seeing that Hemingway's work is standing the test of time better than most of his contemporaries'. Maybe Hemingway was also influenced by his early days of newspapering. We know that he deliberately developed the lean, understated style that became his hallmark. He worked hard at it, every year of his writing life.

Lord knows that no one has accused the science-fiction field of overemphasis on style. If anything, the accusations have been just the opposite, that science-fiction writing is too pedestrian, too mundane. Yet the field has produced some marvelous stylists: Fritz Leiber, for example. Alfred Bester. Ray Bradbury.

There is a good reason why most science-fiction is written in a plain, naturalistic, realistic style. Out-of-this-world settings and incredible feats may abound in science-fiction stories, yet the prose is usually unadorned and straightforward. Why? Because if you want to make the reader believe what you are saying, if you want the reader to accept those out-of-this-world backgrounds and incredible deeds, it is easier if the prose you use is as simple and realistic as you can make it.

In science there is a dictum: don't add an experiment to an experiment. Don't make things unnecessarily complicated. In writing fiction, the more fantastic the tale, the plainer the prose should be. Don't ask your readers to admire your words when you want them to believe your story.

In my own work I have tried to keep the prose clean and clear, especially when I am writing about subjects as complex as space exploration, politics, and love. Those subjects are tricky enough without trying to write about them in convoluted sentences heavy with opaque metaphors and intricate similes.

Then, too, there is the difference between the optimists and the pessimists. Somehow, somewhere in the course of time, darkly pessimistic stories got to be considered more "literary" than brightly optimistic ones. I suspect this attitude began in academia, although it is really a rather juvenile perspective: teenagers frequently see the world they face as too big and complex, too awesome for them to fathom. Healthy adults saw off a chunk of that world for themselves and do their best to cultivate it. That is the message of Voltaire's *Candide*, after all.

Even in the science-fiction field, pessimistic "downbeat" stories are often regarded as intrinsically more sophisticated than optimistic "upbeat" tales. I suspect this reveals a hidden yearning within the breasts of some science-fiction people to be accepted by the academic/literary establishment.

That's okay with me, but such yearnings should not cloud our perceptions.

It may be *de rigueur* in academic circles to moan about the myth of Sisyphus and the pointless futility of human existence, but such an attitude is antithetical to the principles of science fiction, which are based on the fundamental principles of science: that the universe is understandable, and human reason can fathom the most intricate mysteries of existence, given time.

Science fiction is a fundamentally optimistic literature. We tend to see the human race not as failed angels but as evolving apes struggling toward godhood. Even in the darkest dystopian science-fiction stories, there is hope for the future. This is the literature that can take a situation such as the Sun blowing up, and ask, "Okay, what happens next?"[1]

Does that make science-fiction silly? Or pedestrian? Or juvenile? Hell no! It's those academic thumb-suckers who are the juveniles. In science fiction we deal with the real world and try to examine honestly where in the universe we are and where we are capable of going.

In *good* science fiction, that is. As Theodore Sturgeon pointed out ages ago, ninety-five percent of science fiction (and everything else) is crap. All that bears the title "science fiction" is not in Ted's top five percent. But at its best, science fiction is wonderful. And it tends to be optimistic.

Because I try to write clearly and tend to believe that the human mind can solve the problems it faces,

---

[1] If you don't believe me, read Larry Niven's "Inconstant Moon." Or my own *Test of Fire*.

I fear that my work is often regarded as simplistic, or lacking style, or less "literary" than some others'.

Such complaints are the price to be paid for writing plainly and basing fiction on the real world and actual human behavior.

One of America's first literary giants, Nathaniel Hawthorne, responded to the accusation of writing without elegance:

> *I am glad you think my style plain. I never, in any one page or paragraph, aimed at making it anything else.... The greatest possible merit of style is, of course, to make the words absolutely disappear into the thought.*

So—here are fourteen stories that range from tragedy to buffoonery, fourteen tales from the future, the past, and even from the timelessness of eternity. One of them is an outright fantasy, coauthored with a friend and kindred soul. Another can be read as fantasy, although I don't see it as such. A few of them might make you chuckle; all of them should make you think.

Each story is written as clearly as possible, with no unnecessary stylistic adornments. They may not be "Art," in Dr. Gombrich's sense, although I think they are enjoyable.

But you'll be the judge of that.

Naples, Florida
1997

Introduction to
"Inspiration"

Where do story ideas come from?

That question, in one form or another, is the one most frequently asked by young writers. Where do you get the ideas for your stories? Often, when it's a science-fiction writer they're questioning, they ask, "Where do you get your crazy ideas?"

The "official" answer among science-fiction professionals is, "Schenectady." With as straight a face as possible we reply that we subscribe to the Crazy Idea Service of Schenectady, New York. Once a month they send us a crazy idea—in a plain brown envelope, of course.

The truth is, ideas are everywhere. The air is filled with them. Pick up a newspaper, sit in a restaurant, visit a friend, and potential stories are unfolding before your eyes. In fact, getting story ideas is the easy part of writing fiction. As Thomas Mann put it, "The task of a writer consists in being able to make something out of an idea."

I can't really tell you how I wrote the short story, "Inspiration." The creative process is so largely unconscious that it's impossible to describe the day-by-day, minute-to-minute choices and decisions that add up to a finished story. But I can tell you how "Inspiration" was, well, inspired.

Many academic papers have been written about the influence of scientific research on science fiction, and vice versa. Whole books have been written about the interplay between science and science fiction. It struck me that it might be interesting to try a story that explores that theme.

I did a bit of historical research. When H. G. Wells first published The Time Machine, Albert Einstein was sixteen. William Thomson, newly made Lord Kelvin, was the grand old man of physics, and a stern guardian of the orthodox Newtonian view of the universe. Wells' idea of considering time as a fourth dimension would have been anathema to Kelvin; but it would have lit up young Albert's imagination.

Who knows? Perhaps Einstein was actually inspired by Wells.

At any rate, there was the kernel of a story. But how could I get Wells, Einstein, and Kelvin together? And why? To be an effective story, there must be a fuse burning somewhere that will cause an explosion unless the protagonist acts to prevent it.

My protagonist turned out to be a time traveler, sent on a desperate mission to the year 1896, where he finds Wells, Einstein, and Kelvin and brings them together.

And one other person, as well.

INSPIRATION

He was as close to despair as only a lad of seventeen can be.

"But you heard what the professor said," he moaned. "It is all finished. There is nothing left to do."

The lad spoke in German, of course. I had to translate it for Mr. Wells.

Wells shook his head. "I fail to see why such splendid news should upset the boy so."

I said to the youngster, "Our British friend says you should not lose hope. Perhaps the professor is mistaken."

"Mistaken? How could that be? He is a famous man! A nobleman! A baron!"

I had to smile. The lad's stubborn disdain for authority figures would become world-famous one day. But it was not in evidence this summer afternoon in A.D. 1896.

We were sitting in a sidewalk café with a magnificent view of the Danube and the city of Linz. Delicious odors of cooking sausages and bakery pastries wafted from the kitchen inside. Despite the splendid warm sunshine, though, I felt chilled and weak, drained of what little strength I had remaining.

"Where is that blasted waitress?" Wells grumbled. "We've been here half an hour, at the least."

"Why not just lean back and enjoy the afternoon, sir?" I suggested tiredly. "This is the best view in all the area."

Herbert George Wells was not a patient man. He had just scored a minor success in Britain with his first novel and had decided to treat himself to a vacation in Austria. He came to that decision under my influence, of course, but he did not yet realize that. At age twenty-nine, he had a lean, hungry look to him that would mellow only gradually with the coming years of prestige and prosperity.

Albert was round-faced and plumpish; still had his baby fat on him, although he had started a moustache as most teenaged boys did in those days. It was a thin, scraggly black wisp, nowhere near the full white brush it would become. If all went well with my mission.

It had taken me an enormous amount of maneuvering to get Wells and this teenager to the same place at the same time. The effort had nearly exhausted all my energies. Young Albert had come to see Professor Thomson with his own eyes, of course. Wells had been more difficult; he had wanted to see Salzburg, the birthplace of Mozart. I had taken him instead to Linz, with a thousand assurances that he would find the trip worthwhile.

He complained endlessly about Linz, the city's lack of beauty, the sour smell of its narrow streets, the discomfort of our hotel, the dearth of restaurants where one could get decent food—by which he meant burnt mutton. Not even the city's justly famous *Linzertorte* pleased him. "Not as good as a decent trifle," he groused. "Not as good by half."

I, of course, knew several versions of Linz that were even less pleasing, including one in which the city was nothing more than charred radioactive rubble and the Danube so contaminated that it glowed at night all the way down to the Black Sea. I shuddered at that vision and tried to concentrate on the task at hand.

It had almost required physical force to get Wells to take a walk across the Danube on the ancient stone bridge and up the Pöstlingberg to this little sidewalk café. He had huffed with anger when we had started out from our hotel at the city's central square, then soon was puffing with exertion as we toiled up the steep hill. I was breathless from the climb also. In later years a tram would make the ascent, but on this particular afternoon we had been obliged to walk.

He had been mildly surprised to see the teenager trudging up the precipitous street just a few steps ahead of us. Recognizing that unruly crop of dark hair from the audience at Thomson's lecture that morning, Wells had graciously invited Albert to join us for a drink.

"We deserve a beer or two after this blasted climb," he said, eying me unhappily.

Panting from the climb, I translated to Albert, "Mr. Wells . . . invites you . . . to have a refreshment . . . with us."

The youngster was pitifully grateful, although he would order nothing stronger than tea. It was obvious that Thomson's lecture had shattered him badly. So now we sat on uncomfortable cast-iron chairs and waited—they for the drinks they had ordered, me for the inevitable. I let the warm sunshine soak into me and hoped it would rebuild at least some of my strength.

The view was little short of breathtaking: the brooding castle across the river, the Danube itself streaming smoothly and actually blue as it glittered in the sunlight, the lakes beyond the city and the blue-white snow peaks of the Austrian Alps hovering in the distance like ghostly petals of some immense unworldly flower.

But Wells complained, "That has to be the ugliest castle I have ever seen."

"What did the gentleman say?" Albert asked.

"He is stricken by the sight of the Emperor Friedrich's castle," I answered sweetly.

"Ah. Yes, it has a certain grandeur to it, doesn't it?"

Wells had all the impatience of a frustrated journalist. "Where is that damnable waitress? Where is our beer?"

"I'll find the waitress," I said, rising uncertainly from my iron-hard chair. As his ostensible tour guide, I had to remain in character for a while longer, no matter how tired I felt. But then I saw what I had been waiting for.

"Look!" I pointed down the steep street. "Here comes the professor himself!"

William Thomson, First Baron Kelvin of Largs, was striding up the pavement with much more bounce and energy than any of us had shown. He was seventy-one, his silver-gray hair thinner than his impressive gray beard, lean almost to the point of looking frail. Yet he climbed the ascent that had made my heart thunder in my ears as if he were strolling amiably across some campus quadrangle.

Wells shot to his feet and leaned across the iron rail of the café. "Good afternoon, Your Lordship." For a moment I thought he was going to tug at his forelock.

Kelvin squinted at him. "You were in my audience this morning, were you not?"

"Yes, m'lud. Permit me to introduce myself: I am H. G. Wells."

"Ah. You're a physicist?"

"A writer, sir."

"Journalist?"

"Formerly. Now I am a novelist."

"Really? How keen."

Young Albert and I had also risen to our feet. Wells introduced us properly and invited Kelvin to join us.

"Although I must say," Wells murmured as Kelvin came 'round the railing and took the empty chair at our table, "that the service here leaves quite a bit to be desired."

"Oh, you have to know how to deal with the Teutonic temperament," said Kelvin jovially as we all sat down. He banged the flat of his hand on the table so hard it made us all jump. "Service!" he bellowed. "Service here!"

Miraculously, the waitress appeared from the doorway and trod stubbornly to our table. She looked very unhappy; sullen, in fact. Sallow pouting face with brooding brown eyes and downturned mouth. She pushed back a lock of hair that had strayed across her forehead.

"We've been waiting for our beer," Wells said to her. "And now this gentleman has joined us—"

"Permit me, sir," I said. It *was* my job, after all. In German I asked her to bring us three beers and the tea that Albert had ordered and to do it quickly.

She looked the four of us over as if we were smugglers or criminals of some sort, her eyes lingering briefly on Albert, then turned without a word or even a nod and went back inside the café.

I stole a glance at Albert. His eyes were riveted on Kelvin, his lips parted as if he wanted to speak but could not work up the nerve. He ran a hand nervously through his thick mop of hair. Kelvin seemed perfectly at ease, smiling affably, his hands laced across his stomach just below his beard; he was the man of authority, acknowledged by the world as the leading scientific figure of his generation.

"Can it be really true?" Albert blurted at last. "Have we learned everything of physics that can be learned?"

He spoke in German, of course, the only language he knew. I immediately translated for him, exactly as he asked his question.

Once he understood what Albert was asking, Kelvin nodded his gray old head sagely. "Yes, yes. The young men in the laboratories today are putting the final dots over the i's, the final crossings of the t's. We've just about finished physics; we know at last all there is to be known."

Albert looked crushed.

Kelvin did not need a translator to understand the youngster's emotion. "If you are thinking of a career in physics, young man, then I heartily advise you to think again. By the time you complete your education there will be nothing left for you to do."

"Nothing?" Wells asked as I translated. "Nothing at all?"

"Oh, add a few decimal places here and there, I suppose. Tidy up a bit, that sort of thing."

Albert had failed his admission test to the Federal Polytechnic in Zurich. He had never been a particularly good student. My goal was to get him to apply again to the Polytechnic and pass the exams.

Visibly screwing up his courage, Albert asked, "But what about the work of Roentgen?"

Once I had translated, Kelvin knit his brows. "Roentgen? Oh, you mean that report about mysterious rays that go through solid walls? X rays, is it?"

Albert nodded eagerly.

"Stuff and nonsense!" snapped the old man. "Absolute bosh. He may impress a few medical men who know little of science, but his X rays do not exist. Impossible! German daydreaming."

Albert looked at me with his whole life trembling in his piteous eyes. I interpreted:

"The professor fears that X rays may be illusory, although he does not as yet have enough evidence to decide, one way or the other."

Albert's face lit up. "Then there is hope! We have not discovered *everything* as yet!"

I was thinking about how to translate that for Kelvin when Wells ran out of patience. "Where *is* that blasted waitress?"

I was grateful for the interruption. "I will find her, sir."

Dragging myself up from the table, I left the three of them, Wells and Kelvin chatting amiably while Albert swivelled his head back and forth, understanding not a word. Every joint in my body ached, and I knew that there was nothing anyone in this world could do to help me. The café was dark inside, and smelled of stale beer. The waitress was standing at the bar, speaking rapidly, angrily, to the stout barkeep in a low venomous tone. The barkeep was polishing glasses with the end of his apron; he looked grim and, once he noticed me, embarrassed.

Three seidels of beer stood on a round tray next to her, with a single glass of tea. The beers were getting warm and flat, the tea cooling, while she blistered the bartender's ears.

I interrupted her vicious monologue. "The gentlemen want their drinks," I said in German.

She whirled on me, her eyes furious. "The *gentlemen* may have their beers when they get rid of that infernal Jew!"

Taken aback somewhat, I glanced at the barkeep. He turned away from me.

"No use asking him to do it," the waitress hissed. "We do not serve Jews here. *I* do not serve Jews and neither will he!"

The café was almost empty this late in the afternoon. In the dim shadows I could make out only a pair of elderly gentlemen quietly smoking their pipes and a foursome, apparently two married couples, drinking beer. A six-year-old boy knelt at the far end of the bar, laboriously scrubbing the wooden floor.

"If it's too much trouble for you," I said, and started to reach for the tray.

She clutched at my outstretched arm. "No! No Jews will be served here! Never!"

I could have brushed her off. If my strength had not been drained away I could have broken every bone in her body and the barkeep's, too. But I was nearing the end of my tether and I knew it.

"Very well," I said softly. "I will take only the beers."

She glowered at me for a moment, then let her hand drop away. I removed the glass of tea from the tray and left it on the bar. Then I carried the beers out into the warm afternoon sunshine.

As I set the tray on our table, Wells asked, "They have no tea?"

Albert knew better. "They refuse to serve Jews," he guessed. His voice was flat, unemotional, neither surprised nor saddened.

I nodded as I said in English, "Yes, they refuse to serve Jews."

"You're Jewish?" Kelvin asked, reaching for his beer.

The teenager did not need a translation. He replied, "I was born in Germany. I am now a citizen of Switzerland. I have no religion. But, yes, I am a Jew."

Sitting next to him, I offered him my beer.

"No, no," he said with a sorrowful little smile. "It would merely upset them further. I think perhaps I should leave."

"Not quite yet," I said. "I have something that I want to show you." I reached into the inner pocket of my jacket and pulled out the thick sheaf of paper I had been carrying with me since I had started out on this mission. I noticed that my hand trembled slightly.

"What is it?" Albert asked.

I made a little bow of my head in Wells' direction. "This is my translation of Mr. Wells' excellent story, *The Time Machine.*"

Wells looked surprised, Albert curious. Kelvin smacked his lips and put his half-drained seidel down.

"Time machine?" asked young Albert.

"What's he talking about?" Kelvin asked.

I explained, "I have taken the liberty of translating Mr. Wells' story about a time machine, in the hope of attracting a German publisher."

Wells said, "You never told me—"

But Kelvin asked, "Time machine? What on earth would a time machine be?"

Wells forced an embarrassed, self-deprecating little smile. "It is merely the subject of a tale I have written, m'lud: a machine that can travel through time. Into the past, you know. Or the, uh, future."

Kelvin fixed him with a beady gaze. "Travel into the past or the future?"

"It is fiction, of course," Wells said apologetically.

"Of course."

Albert seemed fascinated. "But how could a machine travel through time? How do you explain it?"

Looking thoroughly uncomfortable under Kelvin's wilting eye, Wells said hesitantly, "Well, if you consider time as a dimension—"

"A dimension?" asked Kelvin.

"Rather like the three dimensions of space."

"Time as a fourth dimension?"

"Yes. Rather."

Albert nodded eagerly as I translated. "Time as a dimension, yes! Whenever we move through space we move through time as well, do we not? Space and time! Four dimensions, all bound together!"

Kelvin mumbled something indecipherable and reached for his half-finished beer.

"And one could travel through this dimension?" Albert asked. "Into the past or the future?"

"Utter bilge," Kelvin muttered, slamming his emptied seidel on the table. "Quite impossible."

"It is merely fiction," said Wells, almost whining. "Only an idea I toyed with in order to—"

"Fiction. Of course," said Kelvin, with great finality. Quite abruptly, he pushed himself to his feet. "I'm afraid I must be going. Thank you for the beer."

He left us sitting there and started back down the street, his face flushed. From the way his beard moved I could see that he was muttering to himself.

"I'm afraid we've offended him," said Wells.

"But how could he become angry over an idea?" Albert wondered. The thought seemed to stun him. "Why should a new idea infuriate a man of science?"

The waitress bustled across the patio to our table. "When is this Jew leaving?" she hissed at me, eyes blazing with fury. "I won't have him stinking up our café any longer!"

Obviously shaken, but with as much dignity as a seventeen-year-old could muster, Albert rose to his feet. "I will leave, madame. I have imposed on your so-gracious hospitality long enough."

"Wait," I said, grabbing at his jacket sleeve. "Take this with you. Read it. I think you will enjoy it."

He smiled at me, but I could see the sadness that would haunt his eyes forever. "Thank you, sir. You have been most kind to me."

He took the manuscript and left us. I saw him already reading it as he walked slowly down the street toward the bridge back to Linz proper. I hoped he would not trip and break his neck as he ambled down the steep street, his nose stuck in the manuscript.

The waitress watched him too. "Filthy Jew. They're everywhere! They get themselves into everything."

"That will be quite enough from you," I said as sternly as I could manage.

She glared at me and headed back for the bar.

Wells looked more puzzled than annoyed, even after I explained what had happened.

"It's their country, after all," he said, with a shrug of his narrow shoulders. "If they don't want to mingle with Jews, there's not much we can do about it, is there?"

I took a sip of my warm flat beer, not trusting myself to come up with a properly polite response. There was only one time line in which Albert lived long enough to make an effect on the world. There were dozens where he languished in obscurity or was gassed in one of the death camps.

Wells' expression turned curious. "I didn't know you had translated my story."

"To see if perhaps a German publisher would be interested in it," I lied.

"But you gave the manuscript to that Jewish fellow."

"I have another copy of the translation."

"You do? Why would you—"

My time was almost up, I knew. I had a powerful urge to end the charade. "That young Jewish fellow might change the world, you know."

Wells laughed.

"I mean it," I said. "You think that your story is merely a piece of fiction. Let me tell you, it is much more than that."

"Really?"

"Time travel will become possible one day."

"Don't be ridiculous!" But I could see the sudden astonishment in his eyes. And the memory. It was I who had suggested the idea of time travel to him. We had discussed it for months back when he had been working for the newspapers. I had kept the idea in the forefront of his imagination until he finally sat down and dashed off his novel.

I hunched closer to him, leaned my elbows wearily on the table. "Suppose Kelvin is wrong? Suppose there is much more to physics than he suspects?"

"How could that be?" Wells asked.

"That lad is reading your story. It will open his eyes to new vistas, new possibilities."

Wells cast a suspicious glance at me. "You're pulling my leg."

I forced a smile. "Not altogether. You would do well to pay attention to what the scientists discover over the coming years. You could build a career writing about it. You could become known as a prophet if you play your cards properly."

His face took on the strangest expression I had ever seen: he did not want to believe me, and yet he did; he was suspicious, curious, doubtful and yearning—all at the same time. Above everything else he was ambitious; thirsting for fame. Like every writer, he wanted to have the world acknowledge his genius.

I told him as much as I dared. As the afternoon drifted on and the shadows lengthened, as the sun sank behind the distant mountains and the warmth of day slowly gave way to an uneasy deepening chill, I gave him carefully veiled hints of the future. A future. The one I wanted him to promote.

Wells could have no conception of the realities of time travel, of course. There was no frame of reference in his tidy nineteenth-century English mind of the infinite branchings of the future. He was incapable of imagining the horrors that lay in store. How could he be? Time branches endlessly and only a few, a precious handful of those branches, manage to avoid utter disaster.

Could I show him his beloved London obliterated by fusion bombs? Or the entire northern hemisphere of Earth depopulated by man-made plagues? Or a devastated world turned to a savagery that made his Morlocks seem compassionate?

Could I explain to him the energies involved in time travel or the damage they did to the human body? The fact that time travelers were volunteers sent on suicide missions, desperately trying to preserve a time line that saved at least a portion of the human race? The best future I could offer him was a twentieth century tortured by world wars and genocide. That was the best I could do.

So all I did was hint, as gently and subtly as I could, trying to guide him toward that best of all possible futures, horrible though it would seem to him. I could neither control nor coerce anyone; all I could do was to offer a bit of guidance. Until the radiation dose from my trip through time finally killed me.

Wells was happily oblivious to my pain. He did not even notice the perspiration that beaded my brow despite the chilling breeze that heralded nightfall.

"You appear to be telling me," he said at last, "that my writings will have some sort of positive effect on the world."

"They already have," I replied, with a genuine smile.

His brows rose.

"That teenaged lad is reading your story. Your concept of time as a dimension has already started his fertile mind working."

"That young student?"

"Will change the world," I said. "For the better."

"Really?"

"Really," I said, trying to sound confident. I knew there were still a thousand pitfalls in young Albert's path. And I would not live long enough to help him past them. Perhaps others would, but there were no guarantees.

I knew that if Albert did not reach his full potential, if he were turned away by the university again or murdered in the coming holocaust, the future I was attempting to preserve would disappear in a global catastrophe that could end the human race forever. My task was to save as much of humanity as I could.

I had accomplished a feeble first step in saving some of humankind, but only a first step. Albert was reading the time-machine tale and starting to think that Kelvin was blind to the real world. But there was so much more to do. So very much more.

We sat there in the deepening shadows of the approaching twilight, Wells and I, each of us wrapped in our own thoughts about the future. Despite his best English self-control, Wells was smiling contentedly. He saw a future in which he would be hailed as a prophet. I hoped it would work out that way. It was an immense task that I had undertaken. I felt tired, gloomy, daunted by the immensity of it all. Worst of all, I would never know if I succeeded or not.

Then the waitress bustled over to our table. "Well, have you finished? Or are you going to stay here all night?"

Even without a translation Wells understood her tone. "Let's go," he said, scraping his chair across the flagstones.

I pushed myself to my feet and threw a few coins on the table. The waitress scooped them up immediately and called into the café, "Come here and scrub down this table! At once!"

The six-year-old boy came trudging across the patio, lugging the heavy wooden pail of water. He stumbled and almost dropped it; water sloshed onto his mother's legs. She grabbed him by the ear and lifted him nearly off his feet. A faint tortured squeak issued from the boy's gritted teeth.

"Be quiet and your do work properly," she told

her son, her voice murderously low. "If I let your father know how lazy you are . . ."

The six-year-old's eyes went wide with terror as his mother let her threat dangle in the air between them.

"Scrub that table good, Adolph," his mother told him. "Get rid of that damned Jew's stink."

I looked down at the boy. His eyes were burning with shame and rage and hatred. Save as much of the human race as you can, I told myself. But it was already too late to save him.

"Are you coming?" Wells called to me.

"Yes," I said, tears in my eyes. "It's getting dark, isn't it?"

Introduction to
"Appointment in Sinai"

❖

Although science-fiction is sometimes called the literature of prophecy, no science-fiction story predicted that the first humans to land on the Moon would send live television pictures back to a billion or so eager viewers on Earth.

Of course, there will be live TV transmissions from the first people to set foot on Mars.

And maybe something more . . .

Incidentally, this story is an example of using a "worst-case" scenario as the basis for fiction. Written before NASA's announcement in 1996 that scientists had discovered what might be fossils of ancient bacteria in a meteorite that came from Mars, this story assumes that no hint of life has been found on Mars by the time the first human expedition reaches the red planet.

That is an assumption I would be happy to see proved utterly wrong.

APPOINTMENT IN SINAI

Houston

"No, I am *not* going to plug in," Debbie Kettering said firmly. "I'm much too busy."

Her husband gave her his patented lazy smile. "Come on, Deb, you don't have anything to do that can't wait a half hour or so."

His smile had always been her undoing. But this time she intended to stand firm. "No!" she insisted. "I won't."

She was not a small woman, but standing in their living room next to Doug made her look tiny. A stranger might think they were the school football hero and the cutest cheerleader on the squad, twenty years afterward. In reality, Doug was a propulsion engineer (a real rocket scientist) and Deborah an astronaut.

An ex-astronaut. Her resignation was on the computer screen in her bedroom office, ready to be e-mailed to her boss at the Johnson Space Center.

"What've you got to do that's so blasted important?" Doug asked, still grinning at her as he headed

27

for the sofa, his favorite Saturday afternoon haunt.

"A mountain of work that's been accumulating for weeks," Debbie answered. "Now's the time to tackle it, while all the others are busy and won't be able to bother me."

His smile faded as he realized how miserable his wife really was. "Come on, Deb. We both know what's eating you."

"I won't plug in, Doug."

"Be a shame to miss it," he insisted.

Suddenly she was close to tears. "Those bastards even rotated me off the shift. They don't *want* me there!"

"But that doesn't mean—"

"No, Doug! They put everybody else in ahead of me. I'm on the bottom of their pecking order. So to hell with them! I won't even watch it on TV. And that's final!"

Los Angeles

"It's all set up, man. All we need's a guy who's good with the 'lectronics. And that's you, Chico."

Luis Mendez shifted unhappily in his desk chair. Up at the front of the room Mr. Ricardo was trying to light up some enthusiasm in the class. Nobody was interested in algebra, though. Except Luis, but he had Jorge leaning over from the next desk, whispering in his ear.

Luis didn't much like Jorge, not since first grade when Jorge used to beat him up at least once a week for his lunch money. The guy was dangerous. Now he was into coke and designer drugs and burglary to support his habit. And he wanted Luis to help him.

. "I don't do locks," Luis whispered back, out of the side of his mouth, keeping his eyes on Mr. Ricardo's patient, earnest face.

"It's all 'lectronics, man. You do one kind you can do the other. Don't try to mess with me, Chico."

"We'll get caught. They'll send us to Alcatraz."

Jorge stifled a laugh. "I got a line on a whole friggin' warehouse full of VR sets, and you're worryin' about Alcatraz? Even if they sent you there you'd be livin' better than here."

Luis grimaced. Life in the 'hood was no picnic, but Alcatraz? More than once Mr. Ricardo had sorrowfully complained, "Maybe you *bufóns* would be better off in Alcatraz. At least there they make you learn."

Yeah, Luis knew. They also fry your brains and turn you into a zombie.

"Hey," Jorge jabbed at Luis's shoulder. "I ain't askin' you, Chico. I'm tellin' you. You're gonna do the locks for me, or you're gonna be in the hospital. *¿Comprende?*"

Luis understood. Trying to fight against Jorge was useless. He had learned that lesson years ago. Better to do what Jorge wanted than to get a vicious beating.

Washington

Senator Theodore O'Hara fumed quietly as he rolled his powerchair down the long corridor to his office. The trio of aides trotting behind him were puffing too hard to speak; the only sound in the marble-walled corridor was the slight whir of the powerchair's electric motor and the faint throb of the senator's artificial heart pump. And obedient panting.

He leaned on the toggle to make the chair go a bit faster. Two of his aides fell behind but Kaiser, over-weight and prematurely balding, broke into a sprint to keep up.

Fat little yes-man, O'Hara thought. Still, Kaiser was uncanny when it came to predicting trends. O'Hara scrupulously followed all the polls, as any politician must if he wants to stay in office. But when the polls said one thing and Kaiser something else, the tubby little butterball was inevitably right.

Chairman Pastorini had recessed the committee session so everybody could plug into the landing. Set aside the important business of the Senate Ap-propriations Committee, O'Hara grumbled to him-self, so we can all see a half dozen astronauts plant their gold-plated boots on Mars.

What a waste of time, he thought. And money.

It's all Pastorini's doing. He's *using* the landing. Timed the damned committee session to meet just on this particular afternoon. Knew it all along. Thinks I'll cave in because the other idiots on the committee are going to get all stirred up.

I'll cave them in. All of them. This isn't the first manned landing on Mars, he thought grimly. It's the last.

Phoenix

Jerome Zacharias—Zack to everyone who knew him—paced nervously up and down the big room. Part library, part entertainment center, part bar, the room was packed with friends and well-wishers and media reporters who had made the trek to Phoenix to be with him at this historic moment.

They were drinking champagne already, Zack saw. Toasting our success. Speculating on what they'll find on Mars.

But it could all fail, he knew. It could be a disaster. The last systems check before breaking orbit had shown that the lander's damned fuel cells still weren't charged up to full capacity. All right, the backups are okay, there's plenty of redundancy, but it just takes one glitch to ruin everything. People have been killed in space, and those kids are more than a hundred million miles from home.

If anything happens to them, it'll be my fault, Zack knew. They're going to give me the credit if it all works out okay, but it'll be my fault if they crash and burn.

Twenty years he'd sweated and schemed and connived with government leaders, industrial giants, bureaucrats of every stripe. All to get a team of twelve men and women to Mars.

For what? he asked himself, suddenly terrified that he had no real answer. To satisfy my own ego? Is that why? Spend all this money and time, change the lives of thousands of engineers and scientists and technicians and all their support people, just so I can go to my grave saying that I pushed the human race to Mars?

Suppose somebody gets killed? Then a truly wrenching thought hit him. Suppose they don't find anything there that's worth it all? Suppose Mars is just the empty ball of rusty sand and rocks that the unmanned landers have shown us? No life, not even traces of fossils?

A wasted life. That's what I'll have accomplished. Wasted my own life and the lives of all the others. Wasted.

Houston

She was sorting through all the paperwork from her years with the agency. Letters, reports, memos, the works. Funny how we still call it paperwork, Debbie thought as she toiled through her computer files.

Her heart clutched inside her when the official notification came up on her screen. The final selection of the six astronauts who would be the American part of the Mars team. Her name was conspicuously absent.

"You know why," she remembered her boss telling her, as gently as he could. "You're not only married, Deb, you're a mother. We can't send a mother on the mission; it's too long and too dangerous."

"That's prejudice!" Debbie had shrilled. "Prejudice against motherhood."

"Buffalo chips. The mission is dangerous. We're not talking about a weekend camping trip. They're going to Mars, for chrissake! I'm not going to be the one who killed some kid's mother. Not me!"

She had railed and fumed at him for nearly half an hour.

Finally, her boss stopped her with, "Seems to me you ought to be caring more about your kid. Two and a half years is a long time for him to be without his mother—even if nothing goes wrong with the mission."

Suddenly she had nothing left to say. She stomped out of his office before she broke into tears. She didn't want him or anybody else to see her cry.

Pecking at her keyboard, Debbie pulled up the stinging memoranda she had fired off to Washington. She still felt some of the molten white heat that had boiled within her. Then she went through the lawyers' briefs and the official disclaimer from the agency's legal department: they denied prejudice against women who had children. The agency's choice had been based on "prudent, well-established assessments of risks, performances, and capabilities."

"Jeez, Deb, are you going to take this to the Supreme Court?" Doug had asked in the middle of the legal battle.

"If I have to," she had snapped at him.

Doug merely shook his head. "I wonder how the rest of the crew would feel if the Supreme Court ruled you have to go with them on the mission."

"I don't care!"

"And little Douggie. He'd sure miss his mother. Two and a half years is a long time. He won't even be five yet when the mission takes off."

She had no reply for that. Nothing except blind fury that masked a deeply hidden sense of guilt.

The Supreme Court refused to hear the case, although the news media splashed the story in lurid colors. Astronaut mother denied chance to be part of Mars crew. Space agency accused of antimother bias. Women's groups came to Debbie's aid. Other groups attacked her as an unfit mother who put her personal glory ahead of her son's needs.

Her work deteriorated. Sitting in front of her computer screen, scanning through her performance appraisals over the three years since the Mars crew selection, Debbie saw that the agency wasn't going to suffer grievously from her loss. She had gone into a tailspin, she had to admit.

They'll be happy to see me go, she thought. No wonder they don't even want me at mission control during the landing. They're afraid I'll screw up.

"Mommy?"

Douggie's voice startled her. She spun on her little typist's chair and saw her five-year-old standing uncertainly at the bedroom doorway.

"You know you're not allowed to bother me while I'm working, Douggie," she said coldly.

He's the reason I'm stuck here, she raged to herself. If it weren't for him, I'd be on Mars right now, this instant, instead of looking at the wreckage of my career.

"I'm sorry, Mommy. Daddy said I should tell you."

"Tell me what?" she said impatiently. The boy was a miniature of his father: same eyes, same sandy hair. He even had that same slow, engaging grin. But now he looked frightened, almost ready to break into tears.

"Daddy says they're just about to land."

"I'm busy," she said. "You watch the landing with Daddy."

The boy seemed to draw up all his courage. "But you said you would watch it with me and 'splain what they're doing for me so I could tell all the kids in school all about it."

A little more gently, Debbie said, "But I'm busy here, honey."

"You promised."

"But . . ."

"You *promised*, Mommy."

Debbie didn't remember making any promises. She looked into her son's trusting eyes, though, and realized that he wasn't the reason she wasn't picked to go to Mars. It's not his fault, she realized. How could it be? Whatever's happened is my responsibility and nobody else's.

Her anger dissolved. She was almost sorry to see it go; it had been a bulwark that had propped her up for the past three years.

With a reluctant sigh she shut down her computer and headed off to the living room, her son's hand clasped in hers.

Los Angeles

"Luis!" Mr. Ricardo called as the teenagers scrambled for the classroom door the instant the bell sounded.

Luis scooped up his books and made his way through the small stampede up to the front of the classroom. He walked slowly, reluctantly. Nobody wanted his friends to think that he liked talking to the teacher.

Mr. Ricardo watched Luis approaching him like a prizefighter watches the guy come out from the other corner. He looked tight around the mouth, like he was expecting trouble. Ricardo was only forty or so, but years of teaching high school had made an old man out of him. His wiry hair was all gray; there were wrinkles around his dark brown eyes.

But when Luis came up to him, the teacher broke into a friendly smile. "Have you made up your mind?" he asked.

Luis had been afraid that Ricardo would put him

on the spot. He didn't know what to say.

"I don' know, Mr. R."

"Don't you want to do it?" Ricardo asked, sounding kind of disappointed; hurt, almost. "It's the opportunity of a lifetime."

"Yeah, I know. It'd be cool, but . . ." Luis couldn't tell him the rest, of course.

Ricardo's demanding eyes shifted from Luis to Jorge, loitering at the classroom door, watching them intently.

"He's going to get into a lot of trouble, you know," the teacher said. He kept his voice low, but there was steel in it.

Luis shifted his books, shuffled his feet.

"There are only ten rigs available at the planetarium. I've reserved one. If you don't use it, I'll have to let some other student have it."

"Why's it gotta be now?" Luis complained.

"Because they're landing now, *muchacho*! They're landing on Mars today! This afternoon!"

"Yeah . . ."

"Don't you want to participate in it?"

"Yeah, sure. I'd like to."

"Then let's go. We're wasting time."

Luis shook his head. "I got other things to do, man."

"Like running off with Jorge, eh?"

"Obligations," Luis muttered.

Instead of getting angry, as Luis expected, Ricardo sat on the edge of his desk and spoke earnestly to him.

"Luis, you're a very bright student. You have the brains to make something of yourself. But only if you use the brains God gave you in the right way.

Going with Jorge is only going to get you into trouble. You know that, don't you?"

"I guess so."

"Then why don't you come with me to the planetarium. It could be the turning point of your whole life."

"Maybe," Luis conceded reluctantly. He knew for certain that if he went to the planetarium, Jorge would be furious. Sooner or later there would be a beating. Jorge had sent more than one kid to the hospital. Everybody knew that sooner or later Jorge was going to kill somebody; it was just a matter of time. He had no self-control once he started beating up on somebody.

"Are you afraid of Jorge?" Ricardo asked.

"No!" Luis said it automatically. It was a lie, and they both knew it.

Ricardo smiled benignly. "Then there's no reason for you not to come to the planetarium with me. Is there?"

Luis' shoulders sagged. If I don't go with him, he'll know I'm chicken. If I do go with him, Jorge's gonna pound the shit outta me.

Ricardo got to his feet and put one hand on Luis' shoulder. "Come on with me, Luis," he commanded. "There's a much bigger world out there, and it's time you started seeing it."

They walked past Jorge, hanging in the hallway just outside the classroom door. Mr. Ricardo went past him as if he wasn't even there. Luis saw the expression on Jorge's face, though, and his knees could barely hold him up long enough to get to Ricardo's ancient Camaro.

Washington

The outer office of Senator O'Hara's walnut-panelled suite had been turned into something of a theater. All the desks had been pushed to one side of the generous room and the central section filled with folding chairs. Almost his entire staff was seated there, facing the big hologram plate that had been set up on the wall across from the windows. On a table to one side of the screen rested a single VR helmet, a set of data gloves, and the gray box of a computer.

The staff had been buzzing with anticipation when the senator pushed in through the hallway door. Instantly, though, all their talk stopped. They went silent, as if somebody had snapped off the audio.

All excited like a bunch of pissant children, the senator grumbled to himself. Half of 'em would vote in favor of another Mars mission, the young fools.

O'Hara snorted disdainfully as he wheeled up the central aisle among the chairs. Turning his power-chair smartly to face his staffers, he saw that they were trying to look as blank and uninvolved as possible. Like kids eager to see a forbidden video trying to mask their enthusiasm as long as he was watching them.

"I know what you all think," he said, his voice a grating bullfrog's croak. "Well, I'm going to surprise you."

And with that, he guided his chair to the VR rig and the two technicians, both women, standing by it.

"I'm going to use the rig myself," he announced

to his staff. Their shock was visible. Even Kaiser looked surprised, the fat sycophant.

Chuckling, he went on, "This Mars hoopla is the biggest damned boondoggle pulled over on the American taxpayer since the days of the Apollo project. But if *anybody* in this room plugs himself into the landing, it's going to be me."

Kaiser looked especially crestfallen. He's the one who won the lottery, Senator O'Hara figured. Thought you'd be the one to plug in, did you? O'Hara chuckled inwardly at the disappointment on his aide's face.

"You all can see what I'm experiencing on the hologram screen," the senator said as the technicians began to help him worm his hands into the data gloves.

An unhappy murmuring filled the room.

"I've always said that this Mars business is hooey. I want to experience it for myself—see what these fancy astronauts and scientists are actually going to *do* up there—so's nobody can say that I haven't given the opposition every possible opportunity to show me their point of view."

One of the technicians slipped the helmet over the senator's head. He stopped her from sliding down the visor long enough to say, "I always give the other side a fair break. Then I wallop 'em!"

The visor came down and for a brief, terrifying moment he was in utter darkness.

Phoenix

For nearly half an hour the oversized TV screen had been split between a newscaster chattering away and an unmoving scene of a rusty red, rock-strewn landscape on Mars. Zacharias kept pacing back and forth in the back of the big room, while his guests seemed to edge closer and closer to the giant screen.

"We are seeing Mars as it was some eleven minutes ago," the newscaster intoned solemnly, "since the red planet is so distant from Earth that it takes that long for television signals to reach us."

"He's only told us that twenty-six times in the past five minutes," somebody in the crowd muttered.

"Hush! They should be coming down any moment now."

"According to the mission schedule," the newscaster went on, "and taking into account the lag in signal transmission time, we should be seeing the parachute of the landing craft within seconds."

The unmanned landers had been on the ground for days, Zacharias knew, automatically preparing the base camp for the ten astronauts and scientists of the landing team. Over the past half hour the news broadcast had shown the big plastic bubble of the main tent, the four unmanned landers scattered around it, and the relatively clear, level section of the Sinai plain where the crewed landing craft would put down.

If all went well.

No sonic boom, Zack knew. The Martian air's too thin, and the lander slows down too high up, anyway. The aerobrake should have deployed by now; the glow from the heat shield should be visible, if only they had programmed the cameras to look for it.

What am I saying? he asked himself, annoyed,

nervous. It all happened eleven minutes ago. They're on the ground by now. Or dead.

"There it is!" the announcer yelped.

The crowd of guests surged forward toward the TV screen. Zacharias was drawn, too, despite himself. He remembered the two launch failures that he had witnessed. Put the project back years; almost killed it. After the second he vowed never to watch a rocket launch again.

Yet now he stared like any gaping tourist at the TV image of a beautiful white parachute against the deep blue Martian sky. He was glad that the meteorologists had been able to learn how to predict the planetwide dust storms that turned the sky pink for months afterward. They had timed the landing for the calmest possible weather.

The chute grew until he could see the lander beneath it, swaying slightly, like a big ungainly cylinder of polished aluminum.

They all knew that the landing craft would jettison the chute at a preset altitude, but they all gasped nonetheless. The lander plummeted downward and Zack's heart constricted beneath his ribs.

Then the landing rockets fired, barely visible in the TV cameras, and the craft slowed. It came down gracefully, with dignity, kicking up a miniature sandstorm of its own as its spraddling legs extended and their circular footpads touched gently the iron-rust sands of Mars.

Everyone in the big rec room cheered. All except Zack, who pushed his way to the bar. He felt badly in need of fortification.

Houston

"Nuthin's happ'nin'," Douggie complained. "Can't I watch *Surfer Morphs*?"

"Wait a minute," his father said easily. "They're just waiting for the dust to settle and the rocket nozzles to cool down."

Debbie saw the two virtual-reality helmets on the coffee table in front of them. Two pairs of gloves, also. Doug and Douggie can use them, she thought. Not me.

"Look!" the child cried. "The door's open!"

That should be me, Debbie thought as she watched the twelve-person team file down the lander's impossibly slim ladder to set their booted feet on the surface of Mars. I should be with them.

Douggie was quickly bored with their pretentious speeches: men and women from nine different nations, each of them pronouncing a statement written by teams of public relations experts and government bureaucrats. Debbie felt bored, too.

But then, "Two of us have virtual-reality sensors built into our helmets and gloves," said Philip Daguerre, the astronaut who commanded the ground team.

Debbie had almost had an affair with the handsome French Canadian. Would things have worked out differently if I'd had a fling with him? Probably not. She knew of three other women who had, and all three of them were still as Earthbound as she.

"Once we activate the VR system, those of you on Earth who have the proper equipment will be able to see what we see, feel what we feel, experience what we experience as we make our first excursion onto the surface of Mars."

Doug picked up one of the VR helmets.
"Can't I watch *Surfer Morphs*?" their son whined.

Los Angeles

It wasn't until Mr. Ricardo handed him the VR
helmet that Luis realized his teacher had sacrificed
his own chance to experience the Mars team's first
excursion.

There were only ten VR rigs in the whole planetarium theater. The nine others were already taken
by adults. Maybe they were college students, Luis
thought; they looked young enough to be, even
though almost everybody else in the big circular
room was his teacher's age or older.

"Don't you want it?" Luis asked Ricardo.

His teacher made a strange smile. "It's for you,
Luis. Put it on."

He thinks he's doin' me a big favor, Luis thought.
He don' know that Jorge's gonna beat the crap outta
me for this. Or maybe he knows an' don' care.

With trembling hands, Luis slipped the helmet
over his head, then worked the bristly gloves onto
his hands. Ricardo still had that strange, almost
sickly smile as he slid the helmet's visor down, shut-
ting out Luis' view.

As he sat there in utter darkness he heard Ricardo's voice, muffled by the helmet, say, "Enjoy
yourself, Luis."

Yeah, Luis thought. Might as well enjoy myself.
I'm sure gonna pay for this later on.

Washington

Senator O'Hara held his breath. All he could hear
from inside the darkness of the helmet was the faint

chugging of his heart pump. It was beating fast, for some reason.

He didn't want to seem cowardly in front of his entire staff, but the dark and the closeness of the visor over his face was stifling him, choking him. He wanted to cry out, to yank the damned helmet off and be done with it.

With the abruptness of an eyeblink he was suddenly looking out at a flat plain of rust red. Rocks and boulders were littered everywhere, like toys scattered by an army of thoughtless children. The sky was deep blue, almost black. A soft hushing sound filled his ears, like a distant whisper.

"That's the wind," said a disembodied voice. "It's blowing a stiff ninety knots, according to our instruments, but the air here is so thin that I can't feel it at all."

I'm on Mars! the Senator said to himself. It's almost like actually being there in person.

Phoenix

It's just like we expected it to be, Jerome Zacharias thought. We could have saved a lot of money by just sending automated probes.

"Over that horizon several hundred kilometers," Valerii Mikoyan was saying in flat Midwestern American English, "lies the Tharsis Bulge and the giant shield volcanoes, which we will explore by remote-controlled gliders and balloons later in this mission. And in *this* direction . . ."

Zack's view shifted across the landscape quickly enough to make him feel a moment of giddiness.

". . . just over that line of low hills, is the Valles

Marineris. We are going to ride the rover there as soon as the vehicle is checked out."

Why don't I feel excited? Zack asked himself. I'm like a kid on Christmas morning, after all the presents have been unwrapped.

Houston

For a moment Debbie was startled when Doug solemnly picked up one of the VR helmets and put it on her, like a high priest crowning a new queen.

She was sitting in the springy little metal jump seat of the cross-country rover, her hands running along the control board, checking out all its systems. Solar panels okay. Transformers. Backup fuel cells. Sensors on and running. Communications gear in the green.

"Okay," said the astronaut driving the buggy. "We are ready to roll." It might as well have been her own voice, Debbie thought.

"Clear for canyon excursion," came the mission controller's voice in her earphones. The mission controller was up in the command spacecraft, hanging high above the Plain of Sinai in a synchronous orbit.

With transmission delays of ten to twenty minutes, mission control of the Mars expedition could not be on Earth; it had to be right there, on the scene.

"Go for sight-seeing tour," Debbie acknowledged. "The bus is leaving."

Los Angeles

Luis watched the buggy depart the base area. But only for a moment. He had work to do. He was a geologist, he heard in his earphones, and his job was to take as wide a sampling of rocks as he could and pack them away in one of the return craft.

"First we photograph the field we're going to work in." Luis felt a square object in his left hand, then saw a Polaroid camera. He held it up to the visor of his helmet, sighted and clicked.

"What we're going to be doing is to collect what's called contingency samples," the geologist was saying. "We want to get them aboard a return vehicle right away, the first few hours on the surface, so that if anything happens to force us to make an unscheduled departure, we'll have a decent sampling of surface materials to take back with us."

At first Luis had found it confusing to hear the guy's voice in his head when it looked like he himself was walking around on Mars and picking up the rocks. He could *feel* them in his hands! Feel their heft, the grittiness of their surfaces. It was like the first time he had tried acid; he'd been inside his own head and outside, looking back at himself, both at the same time. That shook him up so much he had never dropped acid again.

But this was kind of different. Fun. He was the frigging geologist. He was there on Mars. He was doing something. Something worthwhile.

Washington

Collecting rocks, Senator O'Hara growled inwardly. We've spent a hundred billion dollars so some pointy-headed scientists can add to their rock collection. Oh, am I going to crucify them as soon as the committee reconvenes!

Phoenix

Zack felt as if he were jouncing and banging inside the surface rover as it trundled across the Martian landscape. He knew he was sitting in a comfortable rocking chair in his big library/bar/entertainment room. Yet he was looking out at Mars through the windshield of the rover. His hands were on its controls and he could feel every shudder and bounce of the six-wheeled vehicle.

But there's nothing out there that we haven't already seen with the unmanned landers, Zack told himself, with mounting despair. We've even brought back samples, under remote control. What are the humans on this expedition going to be able to accomplish that will be worth the cost of sending them?

Houston

Easy now, Debbie told herself. Don't let yourself get carried away. You're *not* on Mars. You're sitting in your own living room.

Los Angeles

Luis could feel the weight of the rock. It was much lighter than a rock that size would be on Earth. And red, like rust. Holding it in his left hand, he chipped at it with the hammer in his right.

"Just want to check the interior," he heard the geologist say, as if he were saying it himself.

The rock cracked in two. Luis saw a tracery of fine lines honeycombing the rock's insides.

"Huh. Never saw anything like that before." And the geologist/Luis carefully put both halves of the split rock into a container, sealed it, then marked with a pen its location in the Polaroid photograph of the area he had taken when he had started collecting.

This is fun, Luis realized. I wish I could do it for real. Like, be a real astronaut or scientist. But reality was something very different. Jorge was reality. Yeah, Luis said to himself, I could be on Mars myself someday. If Jorge don' kill me first.

Washington

Bored with the rock-sampling task, Senator O'Hara lifted the visor of his VR helmet.

"Get me out of this rig," he told the two startled technicians. Turning to Kaiser, he said, "You can try it if you like. I'm going into my office for a drink."

Phoenix

The ground was rising slightly as the rover rolled along. "Should be at the rim in less than a minute," the driver said.

Zack felt his hand ease back on the throttle slightly. "Don't want to fall over. It's a long way down."

Nothing ahead of them but the dull, rock-strewn ground and the deep blue sky.

Houston

Debbie checked the time line on the dashboard computer screen and slowed the rover even more. "We ought to be just about . . . there!"

The rim of the grandest canyon in the solar system sliced across her field of view. Craning her neck slightly, she could see the cliffs tumbling away, down and down and down, toward the valley floor miles below.

Phoenix

Mist! The floor of the valley was wreathed in mists that wafted and undulated slowly, rising and falling as Zack watched.

It's the wrong time of the year for mists to form, he knew. We've never seen this before.

As far as the eye could see, for dozens of miles, hundreds of miles, the mist billowed softly, gently along the floor of Valles Marineris. The canyon was so wide that he could not see the opposite wall; it was beyond the horizon. Nothing but gentle, whitish mist. Clouds of mystery. Clouds of excitement.

My gosh, Zack thought, do they extend the whole three-thousand-mile length of the valley?

Los Angeles

Luis roamed across the rust-colored sandy landscape, staring at more rocks than he had ever seen in his whole life. Some the size of pebbles, a few bigger than a man. How'd they get there? Where'd they come from?

And what was over the horizon? The geologist said something about big volcanoes and mountains higher than anything on Earth. Luis thought it'd be great to see them, maybe climb them.

Houston

Debbie stared at the mists billowing along the valley floor. They seemed to be breathing, like something alive. They've got to be water vapor, she thought. Got to be! And where's there's water there could be life. Maybe. Maybe.

We've got to get down onto the valley floor. Got to!

Phoenix

Zack felt like a child, the first time his father had taken him up in a helicopter. The higher they went, the more there was to see. The more he saw, the more eager he was to see more.

Staring out at the mist-shrouded rift valley, he finally realized that this was the difference between human explorers and machines. What's beyond the horizon? What's beneath those mists? He wanted to know, to explore. He *had to* seek the answers.

He realized he was crying, tears of joy and wonder streaming down his cheeks. He was glad that none of the others could see it, inside the VR helmet, but he knew that neither embarrassment nor disapproval mattered in the slightest. What's beyond the horizon? That was the eternal question and the only thing that really counted.

Los Angeles

Yeah, this is great, Luis thought. For these guys. For scientists and astronauts. It's their life. But it's not for me. When I leave here tonight it's back to the 'hood and Jorge and all that crap.

Then a powerful surge of new emotion rose within him. Why can't I go to Mars for real someday? Mr. Ricardo says I'm smart enough to get a scholarship to college.

Fuck Jorge. Let him do what he wants to me. I'll fight him back. I'll kick the shit outta him if that's what I gotta do to get to Mars. He'll have to kill me to keep me away from this.

Washington

Senator O'Hara was mixing his third martini when Kaiser came in, looking bleary-eyed.

"You been in the VR rig all this time?" O'Hara asked. He knew Kaiser did not drink, so he didn't bother offering his aide anything.

"Mostly," the pudgy little man said. O'Hara could see his aide's bald head was gleaming with perspiration.

"Bad enough we have to waste a hundred billion on this damned nonsense. Is it going to tie up my entire staff for the rest of the day?"

"And then some," Kaiser said, heading for the bar behind the Senator's desk.

O'Hara watched, dumbfounded, as his aide poured himself a stiff belt of whiskey.

He swallowed, coughed, then swallowed again. With tears in his eyes, he went to the leather sofa along the sidewall of the office and sat down like a very tired man.

O'Hara stared at him.

Holding the heavy crystal glass in both hands, Kaiser said, "You're going to have to change your stand on this Mars business."

"What?"

"You've got to stop opposing it."

"Are you crazy?"

"No, but you'd be crazy to try to stand against it now," Kaiser said, more firmly than the senator had ever heard him speak before.

"You're drunk."

"Maybe I am. I've been on Mars, Teddy. I've stood on fuckin' *Mars!*"

Kaiser had never used the senator's first name before, let alone called him "Teddy."

"You'd just better watch your tongue," O'Hara growled.

"And you'd better watch your ass," Kaiser snapped. "Do you have any idea of how many people are *experiencing* this Mars landing? Not just watching it, but experiencing it—as if they were there."

O'Hara shrugged. "Twenty million, maybe."

"I made a couple of phone calls before I came in here. Thirty-six million VR sets in the U.S., and that's not counting laboratories and training simulators. There must be more than thirty million voters on Mars right now."

"Bullcrap."

"Yeah? By tomorrow there won't be a VR rig left in the stores. Everybody's going to want to be on Mars."

O'Hara made a sour face.

"I'll bet that half the voters in dear old Pennsylvania are on Mars right this instant. You try telling them it's all a waste of money."

"But it is!" the senator insisted. "The biggest waste of taxpayer funds since SDI."

"It might be," Kaiser said, somewhat more moderately. "You might be entirely right and everybody else totally wrong. But if you vote that way in the committee, you'll get your ass whipped in November."

"You told me just the opposite no more'n ten days ago. The polls show—"

"The polls are going to swing around one hundred and eighty degrees. Guaranteed."

O'Hara glared at his aide.

"Trust me on this, Teddy. I've never let you down before, have I? Vote for continued Mars exploration or go out and find honest work."

Houston

With enormous reluctance, Debbie pulled the helmet off and removed the data gloves. Doug was still in his rig, totally absorbed. He might as well be on Mars for real, Debbie thought.

Shakily, she got up from the living-room sofa and went to Douggie's room. Her son was watching three-dimensional cartoons.

"Come with me, young man," she said in her not-to-be-argued-with voice. The boy made a face, but turned off his 3-D set and marched into the living room with his mother.

She helped him into the gloves and helmet.

"Aw, Ma," he whined, "do I hafta?"

"Yes," she whispered to her son. "In a few years, you would never forgive yourself if you didn't."

And she left her son and her husband on Mars and went back to her computer to erase her letter of resignation.

There's a lot of work to be done, she told herself. The exploration of Mars is just beginning.

Introduction to
"Conspiracy Theory"
❖

I've been involved in the exploration of space for two years longer than NASA.

I became a space enthusiast when I was in junior high school and made my first visit to the Fels Planetarium, in Philadelphia. I got hooked on the grandeur and mystery of the vast starry universe. So much so that I began to read everything I could about exploring space. This got me into the fields of astronomy and astronautics.

I also found that there were fictional stories about going to the Moon and Mars and other worlds in space. That's how I discovered science fiction.

When the United States announced that it would attempt to place an artificial satellite in orbit, I jumped from newspaper reporting to the company that was building the launching rocket. I became a technical editor on Project Vanguard in 1956. Then came Sputnik, the Space Race, and the creation of NASA in 1958.

Most of the fiction I've written about space exploration and development has been based as solidly as possible on the known facts. When I write about factories on the Moon, as in the novels Moonrise *and* Moonwar, *you* can depend on the accuracy of the physical facts. When I wrote my novel Mars, I made it as realistic as humanly possible.

A couple of years ago, however, while I was writing an essay about the history of our exploration of Mars, I was struck by a wave of nostalgia.

Back when I was sitting in the darkened dome of the Fels Planetarium, there were still arguments raging about whether or not Mars actually was crisscrossed with canals. Most professional astronomers said no, but there were enough dissenters to allow dreamers (like me) to hope that perhaps there truly were intelligent engineers on Mars, desperately struggling to bring water from the polar ice caps to the desert cities of the planet.

Well, the pitiless advance of knowledge squelched those dreams. No canals on Mars. No cities. No intelligent Martians.

But as I sat thinking about my youthful dreams, it occurred to me that the solar system was much more interesting back before NASA started exploring it. Not only could we imagine intelligent, canal-building Martians, but there was the possibility that Venus was a steaming Mesozoic jungle beneath its perpetual cover of clouds.

Just for fun, I started tinkering with a story in which my teenaged view of the solar system was right, and NASA's data was all wrong.

Again, the bare idea was not enough to make a story. I had to figure out why NASA and the scientific establishment were feeding us wrong information. And who might be hurt by this conspiracy.

Or helped.

CONSPIRACY THEORY

❖

"I'm not exactly sure why," said Roy Huggins. "When I asked for another eye checkup, they sent me here."

"To see me," said Professor Schmidt, chuckling a bit.

"Yessir," Huggins replied. He was totally serious; he did not even notice the professor's little pun.

A silence fell over them. The athletically slim Huggins, sandy-haired and boyish-looking in his sweat shirt and jeans, seemed quite honestly puzzled. Herb Schmidt, chairman of the astronomy department, was a chunky, white-bearded Santa even down to the twinkle in his baby blue eyes. A Santa in a dark three-piece suit, sitting behind a desk covered with thick reports and scattered memos heaped high like snowdrifts.

The professor eased back in his creaking old swivel chair and studied his student thoughtfully.

How many times had they met in this stuffy little office? Ever since Huggins had taken his first class in astronomy, back when he'd been an undergraduate. Now the boy had turned into a man: a youthful, vigorous man with a fine intelligent mind that had been sharply honed.

Was he enough of a man to accept the truth? And to keep the secret? The next few minutes would decide.

"Why were you having your eyes checked?" the professor asked innocently.

Huggins had to clear his throat before he could answer, "I seem to be ... well, seeing things that aren't there."

"Ghosts?" asked the professor, smiling to show he did not mean it. "Elvis Presley, perhaps?"

The younger man shook his head. "At the telescope," he said in a low, unhappy voice.

"Let me see now." Schmidt made a pretense of searching through the papers scattered across his desk. "Your time at the facility is on ..." He let the sentence hang.

"Mars," Huggins whispered. "I've been observing Mars."

Schmidt had known that all along. He stopped leafing through the papers and leaned back in his chair again, lacing his fingers together over his ample belly.

"Mars, eh?"

"I see—" Huggins swallowed again, "—canals."

"Canals?" the professor echoed.

"Well—markings. I—I checked with some of the maps that Lowell drew—just as a lark, you know."

"Percival Lowell? Way back then?"

Huggins' answer came out as a tortured moan. "They match. My drawings match Lowell's almost perfectly. A whole network of canals, all across the face of Mars."

"But the photos you've taken don't show any canals. I've seen your photographic work."

"There aren't any canals on Mars!" Huggins blurted. "You know that! I know that! We've sent spacecraft probes to Mars, and they *proved* there are no canals there! Lowell was crazy!"

"He was—enthusiastic. That's a kinder word."

Huggins nodded unhappily and chewed on a fingernail.

Schmidt heaved a big sigh. "I can see why you're upset. But it's not so bad. So you've got a problem with your eyesight. That doesn't matter so much nowadays, what with all the electronics—"

"There's nothing wrong with my eyes! I can see perfectly well. I had an eye test back home during the Thanksgiving break and I checked out twenty-twenty."

"Yet you see nonexistent canals."

Huggins' brief flare of anger withered. "It's not my eyes. I think maybe it's my mind. Maybe I'm having hallucinations."

The professor realized the game had gone far enough. No sense tormenting the poor fellow any further.

"There's nothing wrong with your mind, my boy. Just as there is nothing wrong with your eyes."

"But I see canals! On Mars!"

Stroking his snow-white beard, Schmidt replied, "I think it was Sherlock Holmes who pointed out that when you have eliminated all the possible answers, then the impossible answer is the correct one. Or was it Arthur Clarke?"

Huggins blinked at him. "What do you mean?"

"Did you ever stop to think that perhaps there really *are* canals on Mars?"

"Wha—what are you saying?"

"I am saying that Mars is crisscrossed by an elaborate system of canals built by the solar system's finest engineers to bring precious water to the Martian cities and farmlands."

Half-rising from his chair, Huggins pointed an accusing finger at his professor. "You're humoring me. You think I'm crazy, and you're humoring me."

"Not at all, my boy. Sit down and relax. I am about to entrust you with a great and wonderful secret."

Huggins plopped back into the chair, his eyes wide, his mouth half-open, the expression on his face somewhere between despair and expectation.

"You understand that what I am about to tell you must be kept totally secret from everyone you know. Not even that young woman you intend to marry may know it."

The young man nodded dumbly.

Schmidt leaned his heavy forearms on his littered desk top. "In 1946," he began, "an experimental spacecraft crash-landed in the Sonoran Desert of New Mexico. Contrary to the rumors that have arisen every now and again, the crew was not killed, and their bodies have not been kept frozen in a secret facility at some Air Force base."

"No . . . it can't be . . ."

Smiling broadly, the professor said, "But it is true.

We have been in contact with our Martian brethren for more than half a century now—"

"We?"

"A very small, very elite group. A few university dons such as myself. The tiniest handful of military officers. Four industrial leaders, at present. The group changes slightly as people die, of course. Three of our members are living on Mars at the present moment."

"*You're* crazy!"

"Am I?" Schmidt opened his top desk drawer and drew out a slim folder. From it he pulled a single photograph and handed it wordlessly to the goggle-eyed Huggins.

Who saw three figures standing in a dripping dank jungle. Only the one in the bush hat and moustache was human. They were standing in front of the enormous dead carcass of something that looked very much like a dinosaur. Each of them was holding a rifle of some unearthly design.

"Do you recognize that man?"

Huggins shook his head as he stared hard at the photograph. The man looked vaguely familiar.

"Howard Hughes, of course. Taken in 1957. On Venus."

"Venus?" Huggins' voice was a mouse's squeak.

"Venus," repeated the professor. "Underneath those clouds it's a world of Mesozoic jungles, almost from pole to pole."

"But Venus is a barren desert! Runaway greenhouse! Surface temperatures hot enough to melt lead!"

"That's all a bit of a subterfuge, I'm afraid," said

Schmidt. "Just as our erasure of the Martian canal network. A necessary deception."

"What . . . why?"

Schmidt's expression grew serious. "When the first Martians landed, back in '46, it quickly became clear to those of us privileged to meet them that Mars was ahead of the Earth technologically—but not very far ahead. A century, perhaps. Perhaps only a few decades."

"How can that be?"

Ignoring his question, the professor went on, "They needed our help. Their own natural resources were dwindling at an alarming rate, despite their heroic efforts of engineering. And conservation, too, I might add."

"They came to take over the Earth?"

"Nonsense! Pulp-magazine twaddle! Their ethical beliefs would not allow them to step on a beetle. They came to beg for our help."

Huggins felt a tiny stab of guilt at his fear-filled gut reaction.

"It was obvious," Schmidt went on, "that the Martians were in desperate straits. It was even more obvious to the tiny group who had been brought together to meet our visitors that the people of Earth were not prepared to face the fact that their planetary neighbor was the home of a high and noble civilization."

"The emotional shock would be too much for our people?" Huggins asked.

"No," said the professor, in a sad and heavy voice. "Just the opposite. The shock would be too much for the Martians. We humans are driven by fear and greed and lust, my boy. We would have ground the

Martians into the dust, just as we did with the Native Americans and the Polynesians."

Huggins looked confused. "But you said the Martians were *ahead* of us."

"Technologically, yes. But by no more than a century. And ethically they are light-years ahead of us. Most of us, that is. It is the ethical part that would have been their downfall."

"I don't understand."

"Can you imagine a delicate, ethically bound Martian standing in the way of a real-estate developer? Or a packager of tourist trips? The average human politician? Or evangelist? To say nothing of most of the military. They would have been off to nuke Mars in a flash!"

"Oh."

"The fragile Martian civilization would have been pulverized. No, we had to keep their existence a secret. It was the only decent thing to do. We had to cover up the truth, even to the point of faking data from space probes and astronomical observatories."

"All this time . . ."

"We've had some close calls. The *National Enquirer* and those other scandal sheets keep snooping around. Every time a Martian tried to make contact with an 'ordinary' human being, as their ethical code insisted they should, the affair was totally misunderstood. Sensationalized by the tabloids and all that."

"What ordinary human beings?" Huggins asked.

"You see, the Martians are not elitists. Far from it! From time to time they have tried to establish contact with farmers and sheriff's deputies and people driving down country roads at night. You know the results. Scare headlines and ridiculous stories about abductions."

"This is getting weird."

But Schmidt was not listening. "We even had one writer stumble onto the truth, back in the late forties. Someone named Burberry or Bradbury or something like that. We had to wipe his memory."

"My god!"

"It wasn't entirely effective. We've learned how to do it better since then."

"Is that what you're going to do to me? Wipe out my memory?"

Leaning back in his chair again, Schmidt resumed his beneficent Santa expression. "I don't think we'll have to. We recruit only a very, very few young men and women. I have believed for some time that you have what it takes to be one of us."

"What does that mean—being one of you?"

Positively beaming at his student, Schmidt answered, "It means helping the Martians to use the abundant resources of Venus to maintain their own civilization. It means helping the people of Earth to gradually grow in their ethical maturity until they can meet the Martians without destroying them."

"That may take generations," said Huggins.

"Centuries, more likely. It is one of the motivations behind our starting the environmental movement. If we can only get the great masses of people to treat our own planet properly we'll be halfway to the goal of treating other worlds properly. And other people."

"And in the meantime?"

Schmidt heaved a great sigh. "In the meantime we maintain the pretense that Mars is a barren desert,

Venus is a greenhouse oven, and there's nothing out there in space to be terribly interested in—unless you're an egghead of a scientist."

Huggins began to understand. "That's why the space program was stopped after the landings on the Moon."

"Yes," the professor said. "A sad necessity. We've had to work very hard to keep the uninformed parts of the government—which is most of them—from moving our space program into high gear."

"Can—" Huggins hesitated, then seemed to straighten his spine and ask, "May I meet the Martians?"

"Of course! Of course you can, my boy. Their representative is waiting to meet you now."

Schmidt pulled himself up from his chair and came around the desk. "Right this way." He gestured toward the side door of the office.

His heart hammering beneath his ribs, Huggins got up and followed his professor's burly form.

Schmidt grasped the doorknob, then stopped and turned slightly back toward his student. "I must warn you of two things," the professor said. "First, our Martian visitor obviously cannot run around the campus in his native form. So he has disguised himself as a human. Even so, he has to be very circumspect about allowing himself to be seen."

A tingle of doubt shivered in the back of Huggins' mind. "He'll look human?"

"Completely. Of course, if you wish, he will remove his human disguise. We want you to be absolutely certain of what I've told you, after all."

"I see."

With a satisfied nod, Schmidt turned the knob and pushed the door open.

Huggins was asking, "What else did you want to warn me . . ."

Before he could finish the sentence he saw the disguised Martian sitting in the darkened little side room. Huggins' jaw fell.

"That's the other thing I meant to warn you about," said Professor Schmidt. "The Martians also have a rather odd sense of humor."

Huggins just stared. At Elvis Presley.

(With apologies to Ray Bradbury.)

Introduction to
"The Great Moon Hoax"

This one you can blame on Norman Spinrad.

Norm is one of the best writers in the science-fiction field, and a man who combines deep intelligence with a droll sense of humor.

In 1992 Norm invited me to contribute to an anthology he was putting together, Down in Flames. *In his own words, the basic idea of the anthology was to "satirize, destroy, take the piss out of, overturn the basic premises of . . . your own universe." In other words, Norm wanted a story that would be the antithesis of my usual carefully researched, scientifically accurate fiction.*

Well, I have a sense of humor, too. I immediately recalled "Conspiracy Theory" and decided to do another story in the same vein. Only this one would explain just about everything from UFOs to—well, read it and see.

THE GREAT MOON HOAX
OR
A PRINCESS OF MARS

I leaned back in my desk chair and just plain stared at the triangular screen.

"What do you call this thing?" I asked the Martian.

"It is an interociter," he said. He was half in the tank, as usual.

"Looks like a television set," I said.

"Its principles are akin to your television, but you will note that its picture is in full color, and you can scan events that were recorded in the past."

"We should be watching the president's speech," said Professor Schmidt.

"Why? We know what he's going to say. He's going to tell Congress that he wants to send a man to the Moon before 1970."

The Martian shuddered. His name was a collection of hisses and sputters that came out to something pretty close to Jazzbow. Anyhow, that's what

I called him. He didn't seem to mind. Like me, he was a baseball fan.

We were sitting in my Culver City office, watching Ted Williams' last ball game from last year. Now *there* was a baseball player. Best damned hitter since Ruth. And as independent as Harry Truman. Told the rest of the world to go to hell whenever he felt like it. I admired him for that. I had missed almost the whole season last year; the Martians had taken me on safari with them. They were always doing little favors like that for me; this interociter device was just the latest one.

"I still think we should be watching President Kennedy," Schmidt insisted.

"We can view it afterward, if you like," said Jazzbow, diplomatically. As I said, he had turned into quite a baseball fan, and we both wanted to see the Splendid Splinter's final home run.

Jazzbow was a typical Martian. Some of the scientists still can't tell one from another, they look so much alike, but I guess that's because they're all cloned rather than conceived sexually. Mars is pretty damned dull that way, you know. Of course, most of the scientists aren't all that smart outside of their own fields of specialization. Take Einstein, for example. Terrific thinker. He believes if we all scrapped our atomic bombs, the world would be at peace. Yah. Sure.

Anyway, Jazzbow is about four-foot-nine with dark leathery skin, kind of like a football that's been left out in the sun too long. The water from the tank made him look even darker, of course. Powerful barrel chest, but otherwise a real spidery build, arms and legs like pipe stems. Webbed feet, evolved for walking on loose sand. Their hands have five fingers with opposable thumbs, just like ours, but the fingers have so many little bones in them that they're as flexible as an octopus's tentacles.

Martians would look really scary, I guess, if it weren't for their goofy faces. They've got big sorrowful limpid eyes with long feminine eyelashes, like a camel; their noses are splayed from one cheek to the other; and they've got these wide lipless mouths stretched into a permanent silly-looking grin, like a dolphin. No teeth at all. They eat nothing but liquids. Got long tongues, like some insects, which might be great for sex if they had any, but they don't, and, anyway, they usually keep their tongues rolled up inside a special pouch in their cheeks so they don't startle any of us earthlings. How they talk with their tongues rolled up is beyond me.

Anyway, Jazzbow was half in the tank, as I said. He needed the water's buoyancy to make himself comfortable in earthly gravity. Otherwise, he'd have to wear his exoskeleton suit, and I couldn't see putting him through that just so we could have a face-to-face with Professor Schmidt.

The professor was fidgeting unhappily in his chair. He didn't give a rat's ass about baseball, but at least he could tell Jazzbow from the other Martians. I guess it's because he was one of the special few who'd known the Martians ever since they had first crash-landed in New Mexico back in '46.

Well, Williams socked his home run and the Fenway Park fans stood up and cheered for what seemed like an hour and he never did come out of the dugout to tip his cap for them. Good for him! I thought. His own man to the very end. That was his last time on a ball field as a player. I found I had tears in my eyes.

"*Now* can we see the president?" Schmidt asked, exasperated. Normally he looked like a young Santa Claus, round and red-cheeked, with a pale blond beard. He usually was a pretty jolly guy, but just now his responsibilities were starting to get the better of him.

Jazzbow snaked one long, limber arm out of the water and fiddled with the controls beneath the inverted triangle of the interociter's screen. JFK came on the screen in full color, in the middle of his speech to the joint session of Congress:

"I believe that this nation should commit itself to achieving the goal, before this decade is out, of landing a man on the Moon and returning him safely to the Earth. I believe we should go to the Moon."

Jazzbow sank down in his water tank until only his big eyes showed, and he started noisily blowing bubbles, his way of showing that he was upset.

Schmidt turned to me. "You're going to have to talk him out of it," he said flatly.

I had not voted for John Kennedy. I had instructed all of my employees to vote against him, although I imagine some of them disobeyed me out of some twisted sense of independence. Now that he was president, though, I felt sorry for the kid. Eisenhower had let things slide pretty badly. The Commies were infiltrating the Middle East and of course they had put up the first artificial satellite and just a couple weeks ago had put the first man into space: Yuri something-or-other. Meanwhile young Jack Kennedy had let that wacky plan for the reconquest of Cuba go through. I had *told* the CIA guys that they'd need strong air cover, but they went right ahead and hit the Bay of Pigs without even a Piper Cub over them. Fiasco.

So the new president was trying to get everybody's mind off all this crap by shooting for the Moon. Which would absolutely destroy everything we'd worked so hard to achieve since that first desperate Martian flight here some fifteen years earlier.

I knew that *somebody* had to talk the president out of this Moon business. And of all the handful of people who were in on the Martian secret, I guess that the only one who could really deal with the White House on an eye-to-eye level was me.

"Okay," I said to Schmidt. "But he's going to have to come out here. I'm not going to Washington."

It wasn't that easy. The president of the United States doesn't come traipsing across the country to see an industrial magnate, no matter how many services the magnate has performed for his country. And my biggest service, of course, he didn't know anything about.

To make matters worse, while my people were talking to his people, I found out that the girl I was grooming for stardom turned out to be a snoop from the goddamned Internal Revenue Service. I had had my share of run-ins with the Feds, but using a beautiful starlet like Jean was a low blow even for them. A real crotch shot.

It was Jazzbow who found her out, of course.

Jean and I had been getting along very nicely indeed. She was tall and dark-haired and really lovely, with a sweet disposition and the kind of wide-eyed

innocence that makes life worthwhile for a nasty old
S.O.B. like me. And she loved it, couldn't get enough
of whatever I wanted to give her. One of my hobbies
was making movies; it was a great way to meet girls.
Believe it or not, I'm really very shy. I'm more at
home alone in a plane at twenty thousand feet than
at some Hollywood cocktail party. But if you own a
studio, the girls come flocking.

Okay, so Jean and I are getting along swell. Except that during the period when my staff was dick-
ering with the White House staff, one morning I
wake up and she's sitting at the writing desk in my
bedroom, going through my drawers. The desk
drawers, that is.

I cracked one eye open. There she is, naked as a
Greek goddess and just as gorgeous, rummaging
through the papers in my drawers. There's nothing
in there, of course. I keep all my business papers in
a germtight fireproof safe back at the office.

But she had found *something* that fascinated her.
She was holding it in front of her, where I couldn't
see what was in her hand, her head bent over it for
what seemed like ten minutes, her dark hair cascad-
ing to her bare shoulders like a river of polished
onyx.

Then she glanced up at the mirror and spotted me
watching her.

"Do you always search your boyfriends' desks?"
I asked. I was pretty pissed off, you know.

"What is this?" She turned and I saw she was
holding one of my safari photos between her fore-
finger and thumb, like she didn't want to get fin-
gerprints on it.

Damn! I thought. I should've stashed those away with my stag movies.

Jean got up and walked over to the bed. Nice as pie she sat on the edge and stuck the photo in front of my bleary eyes.

"What is this?" she asked again.

It was a photo of a Martian named Crunchy, the physicist George Gamow, James Dean, and me in the dripping dark jungle in front of a brontosaurus I had shot. The Venusian version of a brontosaurus, that is. It looked like a small mountain of mottled leather. I was holding the stun rifle Crunchy had lent me for the safari.

I thought fast. "Oh, this. It's a still from a sci-fi film we started a few years ago. Never finished it, though. The special effects cost too much."

"That's James Dean, isn't it?"

I peered at the photo as if I was trying to remember something that wasn't terribly important. "Yeah, I think so. The kid wanted more money than I wanted to spend on the project. That's what killed it."

"He's been dead for five or six years."

"Has it been that long?" James Dean was alive and having the time of life working with the Martians on Venus. He had left his acting career and his life on Earth far behind him to do better work than the president's Peace Corps could even dream about.

"I didn't know he did a picture for you," she said, her voice dreamy, ethereal. Like every other woman her age she had a crush on James Dean. That's what drove the poor kid to Venus.

"He didn't," I snapped. "We couldn't agree on terms. Come on back to bed."

She did, but in the middle of it my damned private phone rang. Only five people on earth knew that number, and one of them wasn't human.

I groped for the phone. "This better be important," I said.

"The female you are with," said Jazzbow's hissing voice, "is a government agent."

Oh yeah, the Martians are long-distance telepaths, too.

So I took Jean for a drive out to the desert in my Bentley convertible. She loved the scenery, thought it was romantic. Or so she said. Me, I looked at that miserable dry Mohave scrubland and thought of what it could become: blossoming farms, spacious tracts of housing where people cooped up in the cities could raise their kids, glamorous shopping malls. But about all it was good for now was an Air Force base where guys like Chuck Yeager and Scott Crossfield flew the X-planes and the Martians landed their saucers every now and then. After dark, of course.

"Just look at that sunset," Jean said, almost breathless with excitement, maybe real, maybe pretended. She *was* an actress, after all.

I had to admit the sunset was pretty. Red and purple glowing brighter than Technicolor.

"Where are we going?" she kept on asking, a little more nervous each time.

"It's a surprise." I had to keep on going until it was good and dark. We had enough UFO sightings as it was, no sense taking a chance on somebody getting a really good look. Or even worse, a photograph.

The stars came out, big and bright and looking

close enough to touch. I kept looking for one in particular to detach itself from the sky and land on the road beside us. All that stuff about saucers shining green rays on cars or planes and sucking them up inside themselves is sheer hooey. The Martians don't have anything like that. Wish they did.

Pretty soon I saw it.

"Look!" says Jean. "A falling star!"

I didn't say anything, but a couple of minutes later the headlights picked up the saucer sitting there by the side of the road, still glowing a little from the heat of its reentry from orbit.

"Don't tell me you've driven me all the way out here to see another movie set," Jean said, sounding disappointed. "This isn't your big surprise, is it?"

"Not quite," I said, pulling up beside the saucer's spindly little ladder.

She was pretty pissed off. Even when two of the Martians came slithering down the ladder she still thought it was some kind of a movie stunt. They had to move pretty slow and awkwardly because of the gravity; made me think of the monster movies we made. Jean was definitely not impressed.

"Honestly, Howard, I don't see why—"

Then one of the Martians put its snake-fingered hands on her and she gave a yelp and did what any well-trained movie starlet would do. She fainted.

Jazzbow wasn't in the ship, of course. The Martians wouldn't risk a landing in Culver City to pick him up, not even at night. Nobody but Professor Schmidt and I knew he was in my office suite there. And the other Martians, of course.

So I got Jazzbow on the ship's interociter while his fellow Martians draped the unconscious Jean on one of their couches. Her skirt rucked up nicely, showing off her legs to good advantage.

"They're not going to hurt her any, are they?" I asked Jazzbow.

"Of course not," his image answered from the inverted triangular screen. "I thought you knew us better than that."

"Yeah, I know. You can't hurt a fly. But still, she's just a kid . . ."

"They're merely probing her mind to see how much she actually knows. It will only take a few minutes."

I won't go into all the details. The Martians are extremely sensitive about their dealings with other living creatures. Not hurt a fly? Hell, they'd make the Dalai Lama look like a bloodthirsty maniac.

Very gently, like a mother caressing her sleeping baby, three of them touched her face and forehead with those tentacle-like fingers. Probing her mind. Some writer got wind of the technique second- or thirdhand and used it on television a few years later. Called it a Velcro mind-melt or something like that.

"We have for you," the ship's science officer told me, "good news and bad news."

His name sounded kind of like Snitch. Properly speaking, every Martian is an "it," not a "him" or a "her." But I always thought of them as males.

"The good news," Snitch said to me, "is that this female knew nothing of our existence. She hadn't the faintest suspicion that Martians exist or that you are dealing with them."

"Well, she does now," I grumbled.

"The bad news," he went on, with that silly grin spread across his puss, "is that she is acting as an undercover agent for your Internal Revenue Service—while she's between acting jobs."

Aw hell.

I talked it over with Jazzbow. Then he talked in Martian with Snitch. Then all three of us talked together. We had evolved a Standard Operating Procedure for situations like this, when somebody stumbled onto our secret. I didn't much like the idea of using it on Jean, but there wasn't much else we could do.

So, reluctantly, I agreed. "Just be damned careful with her," I insisted. "She's not some hick cop who's been startled out of his snooze by one of your cockamamie malfunctioning saucers."

Their saucers were actually pretty reliable, but every once in a while the atmospheric turbulence at low altitude would get them into trouble. Most of the sightings happened when the damned things wobbled too close to the ground.

Jazzbow and Snitch promised they'd be extraspecial careful.

Very gently, the Martians selectively erased Jean's memory so that all she remembered the next morning, when she woke up a half a mile from a Mohave gas station, was that she had been abducted by aliens from another world and taken aboard a flying saucer.

The authorities wanted to put her in a nuthouse, of course. But I sent a squad of lawyers to spring her, since she was under contract to my movie studio. The studio assumed responsibility for her, and my lawyers assured the authorities that she was about to star in a major motion picture. The yokels figured it had all been a publicity stunt and turned

her loose. I actually did put her into a couple of star-
ring roles, which ended her career with the IRS, although I figured that not even the Feds would have
had anything to do with Jean after the tabloids head-
lined her story about being abducted by flying-
saucer aliens. I took good care of her, though. I even
married her, eventually. That's what comes from
hanging around with Martians.

See, the Martians have a *very* high ethical standard
of conduct. They cannot willingly hurt anybody or
anything. Wouldn't step on an ant. It's led to some
pretty near scrapes for us, though. Every now and
then somebody stumbles onto them and the whole
secret's in jeopardy. They could wipe the person's
brain clean, but that would turn the poor sucker into
a zombie. So they selectively erase only the smallest
possible part of the sucker's memory.

And they always leave the memory of being taken
into a flying saucer. They tell me they have to. That's
part of their moral code, too. They're constantly testing us—the whole human race, that is—to see if
we're ready to receive alien visitors from another
world. And to date, the human race as a whole has
consistently flunked every test.

Sure, a handful of very special people know about
them. I'm pretty damned proud to be among that
handful, let me tell you. But the rest of the human
race, the man in the street, the news reporters and
preachers and even the average university professor—they either ridicule the very idea that there
could be any kind of life at all on another world or
they get scared to death of the possibility. Take a
look at the movies we make!

"Your people are sadly xenophobic," Jazzbow

told me more than once, his big liquid eyes looking melancholy despite that dumbbell clown's grin splitting his face.

I remembered Orson Welles' broadcast of *The War of the Worlds* back in '38. People got hysterical when they thought Martians had landed in New Jersey, although why anybody would want to invade New Jersey is beyond me. Here I had real Martians zipping all over the place, and they were gentle as butterflies. But no one would believe that; the average guy would blast away with his twelve-gauge first and ask where they came from afterward.

So I had to convince the president that if he sent astronauts to the moon, it would have catastrophic results.

Well, my people and Kennedy's people finally got the details ironed out and we agreed to meet at Edwards Air Force Base, out in the Mohave. Totally secret meeting. JFK was giving a speech in LA that evening at the Beverly Wilshire. I sent a company helicopter to pick him up there and fly him over to Edwards. Just him and two of his aides. Not even his Secret Service bodyguards; he didn't care much for having those guys lurking around him, anyway. Cut down on his love life too much.

We met in Hangar Nine, the place where the first Martian crew was stashed back in '46, pretty battered from their crash landing. That's when I first found out about them. I was asked by Professor Schmidt, who looked like a very agitated young Santa Claus back then, to truck in as many refrigeration units as my company could lay its hands on. Schmidt wanted to keep the Martians comfortable, and since their planet is so cold, he figured they needed mucho refrigeration. That was before he found out that the Martians spend about half their energy budget at home just trying to stay reasonably warm. They loved Southern California! Especially the swimming pools.

Anyway, there I am waiting for the president in good old Hangar Nine, which had been so Top Secret since '46 that not even the base commander's been allowed inside. We'd partitioned it and decked it out with nice furniture and all the modern conveniences. I noticed that Jazzbow had recently had an interociter installed. Inside the main living area we had put up a big water tank for Jazzbow and his fellow Martians, of course. The place kind of resembled a movie set: nice modern furnishings, but if you looked past the ten-foot-high partitions that served as walls you saw the bare metal support beams crisscrossing up in the shadows of the ceiling.

Jazzbow came in from Culver City in the same limo that brought Professor Schmidt. As soon as he got into the hangar he unhooked his exoskeleton and dived into the water tank. Schmidt started pacing nervously back and forth on the Persian carpeting I had put in. He was really wound up tight: letting the president in on this secret was an enormous risk. Not for us, so much as for the Martians.

It was just about midnight when we heard the throbbing-motor sound of a helicopter in the distance. I walked out into the open and saw the stars glittering like diamonds all across the desert sky. How many of them are inhabited? I wondered. How many critters out there are looking at our Sun and wondering if there's any intelligent life there?

Is there any intelligent life in the White House? That was the big question, far as I was concerned.

Jack Kennedy looked tired. No, worse than that, he looked troubled. Beaten down. Like a man who had the weight of the world on his shoulders. Which he did. Elected by a paper-thin majority, he was having hell's own time getting Congress to vote for his programs. Tax relief, increased defense spending, civil rights—they were all dead in the water, stymied by a Congress that wouldn't do spit for him. And now I was going to pile another ton and a half on top of all that.

"Mr. President," I said as he walked through the chilly desert night from the helicopter toward the hangar door. I sort of stood at attention: for the office, not the man, you understand. Remember, I voted for Nixon.

He nodded at me and made a weary smile and stuck out his hand the way every politician does. I let him shake my hand, making a mental note to excuse myself and go to the washroom as soon as decently possible.

As we had agreed, he left his two aides at the hangar door and accompanied me inside all by himself. He kind of shuddered.

"It's cold out there, isn't it?" he said.

He was wearing a summer-weight suit. I had an old windbreaker over my shirt and slacks.

"We've got the heat going inside," I said, gesturing him through the door in the first partition. I led him into the living area and to the big carpeted central room where the water tank was. Schmidt followed behind us so close I could almost feel his breath on my neck. It gave me that crawly feeling I get when I realize how many millions of germs are floating through the air all the time.

"Odd place for a swimming tank," the president said as soon as we entered the central room.

"It's not as odd as you think," I said. Jazzbow had ducked low, out of sight for the time being.

My people had arranged two big sofas and a scattering of comfortable armchairs around a coffee table on which they had set up a fair-sized bar. Bottles of every description, even champagne in its own ice bucket.

"What'll you have?" I asked. We had decided that, with just the three of us humans present, I would be the bartender.

Both the president and Schmidt asked for scotch. I made the drinks big, knowing they would both need them.

"Now what's this all about?" Kennedy asked after his first sip of the booze. "Why all this secrecy and urgency?"

I turned to Schmidt, but he seemed to be petrified. So absolutely frozen that he couldn't even open his mouth or pick up his drink. He just stared at the president, overwhelmed by the enormity of what we had to do.

So I said, "Mr. President, you have to stop this Moon program."

He blinked his baggy eyes. Then he grinned. "Do I?"

"Yessir."

"Why?"

"Because it will hurt the Martians."

"The Martians, you said?"

"That's right. The Martians," I repeated.

Kennedy took another sip of scotch, then put his glass down on the coffee table. "Mr. Hughes, I had heard that you'd gone off the deep end, that you've become a recluse and something of a mental case—"

Schmidt snapped out of his funk. "Mr. President, he's telling you the truth. There *are* Martians."

Kennedy gave him a "who are you trying to kid" look. "Professor Schmidt, I know you're a highly respected astronomer, but if you expect me to believe there are living creatures on Mars you're going to have to show me some evidence."

On that cue, Jazzbow came slithering out of the water tank. The president's eyes goggled as old Jazzie made his painful way, dripping on the rug, to one of the armchairs and half collapsed into it.

"Mr. President," I said, "may I introduce Jazzbow of Mars. Jazzbow, President Kennedy."

The president just kept on staring. Jazzbow extended his right hand, that perpetual clown's grin smeared across his face. With his jaw hanging open, Kennedy took it in his hand. And flinched.

"I assure you," Jazzbow said, not letting go of the president's hand, "that I am truly from Mars."

Kennedy nodded. He believed it. He had to. Martians can make you see the truth of things. Goes with their telepathic abilities, I guess.

Schmidt explained the situation. How the Martians had built their canals once they realized that their world was dying. How they tried to bring water from the polar ice caps to their cities and farmlands. It worked, for a few centuries, but eventually even that wasn't enough to save the Martians from slow but certain extinction.

They were great engineers, great thinkers. Their technology was roughly a century or so ahead of ours. They had invented the electric lightbulb, for example, during the time of our French and Indian War.

By the time they realized that Mars was going to dry up and wither away despite all their efforts, they had developed a rudimentary form of spaceflight. Desperate, they thought that maybe they could bring natural resources from other worlds in the solar system to revive their dying planet. They knew that Venus was, beneath its clouds, a teeming Mesozoic jungle. Plenty of water there, if they could cart it back to Mars.

They couldn't. Their first attempts at spaceflight ended in disasters. Of the first five saucers they sent toward Venus, three of them blew up on takeoff, one veered off course and was never heard from again, and the fifth crash-landed in New Mexico—which is a helluva long way from Venus.

Fortunately, their saucer crash-landed near a small astronomical station in the desert. A young graduate student—who eventually became Professor Schmidt—was the first to find them. The Martians inside the saucer were pretty banged up, but three of them were still alive. Even more fortunately, we had something that the Martians desperately needed: the raw materials and manufacturing capabilities to mass-produce flying saucers for them. That's where I had come in, as a tycoon of the aviation industry.

President Kennedy found his voice. "Do you mean to tell me that the existence of Martians—living, breathing, intelligent Martians—has been kept a secret since 1946? More than fifteen years?"

"It's been touch-and-go on several occasions," said Schmidt. "But, yes, we've managed to keep the secret pretty well."

"Pretty well?" Kennedy seemed disturbed, agitated. "The Central Intelligence Agency doesn't know anything about this, for Christ's sake!" Then he caught himself, and added, "Or, if they do, they haven't told me about it."

"We have tried very hard to keep this a secret from all the politicians of every stripe," Schmidt said.

"I can see not telling Eisenhower," said the president. "Probably would've given Ike a fatal heart attack." He grinned. "I wonder what Harry Truman would've done with the information."

"We were tempted to tell President Truman, but—"

"That's all water over the dam," I said, trying to get them back onto the subject. "We're here to get you to call off this Project Apollo business."

"But why?" asked the president. "We could use Martian spacecraft and plant the American flag on the Moon tomorrow morning!"

"No," whispered Jazzbow. Schmidt and I knew that when a Martian whispers, it's a sign that he's scared shitless.

"Why not?" Kennedy snapped.

"Because you'll destroy the Martians," said Schmidt, with real iron in his voice.

"I don't understand."

Jazzbow turned those big luminous eyes on the president. "May I explain it to you . . . the Martian way?"

I'll say this for Jack Kennedy. The boy had guts. It was obvious that the basic human xenophobia was strong inside him. When Jazzbow had first touched his hand Kennedy had almost jumped out of his skin. But he met the Martian's gaze and, not knowing what would come next, solemnly nodded his acceptance.

Jazzbow reached out his snaky arm toward Kennedy's face. I saw beads of sweat break out on the president's brow, but he sat still and let the Martian's tentacle-like fingers touch his forehead and temple.

It was like jumping a car battery. Thoughts flowed from Jazzbow's brain into Kennedy's. I knew what those thoughts were.

It had to do with the Martians' moral sense. The average Martian has an ethical quotient about equal to St. Francis of Assisi. That's the *average* Martian. While they're only a century or so ahead of us technologically, they're light-years ahead of us morally, socially, ethically. There hasn't been a war on Mars in more than a thousand years. There hasn't even been a case of petty theft in centuries. You can walk the avenues of their beautiful, gleaming cities at any time of the day or night in complete safety. And since their planet is so desperately near absolute depletion, they just about worship the smallest blade of grass.

If our brawling, battling human nations discovered the fragile, gentle Martian culture, there would be a catastrophe. The Martians would be swarmed under, shattered, dissolved by a tide of politicians, industrialists, real-estate developers, evangelists wanting to save their souls, drifters, grifters, con men, thieves petty and grand. To say nothing of military officers driven by xenophobia. It would make the Spanish Conquest of the Americas look like a Boy Scout Jamboree.

I could see from the look in Kennedy's eyes that he was getting the message. "*We* would destroy *your* culture?" he asked.

Jazzbow had learned the human way of nodding. "You would not merely destroy our culture, Mr. President. You would kill us. We would die, all of us, very quickly."

"But you have the superior technology . . ."

"We could never use it against you," said Jazzbow. "We would lie down and die rather than deliberately take the life of a paramecium."

"Oh."

Schmidt spoke up. "So you see, Mr. President, why this Moon project has got to be called off. We can't allow the human race *en masse* to learn of the Martians' existence."

"I understand," he murmured.

Schmidt breathed out a heavy sigh of relief. Too soon.

"But I can't stop the Apollo project."

"Can't?" Schmidt gasped.

"Why not?" I asked.

Looking utterly miserable, Kennedy told us, "It would mean the end of my administration. For all practical purposes, at least."

"I don't see—"

"I haven't been able to get a thing through Congress except the Moon project. They're stiffing me on everything else: my economics package, my defense buildup, civil rights, welfare—everything except the Moon program has been stopped dead in Congress. If I give up on the Moon I might as well resign the presidency."

"You are not happy in your work," said Jazzbow.

"No, I'm not," Kennedy admitted, in a low voice. "I never wanted to go into politics. It was my father's idea. Especially after my older brother got killed in the war."

A dismal, gloomy silence descended on us.

"It's all been a sham," the president muttered. "My marriage is a mess, my presidency is a farce, I'm in love with a woman who's married to another man—I wish I could just disappear from the face of the earth."

Which, of course, is exactly what we arranged for him.

It was tricky, believe me. We had to get his blond *inamorata* to disappear, which wasn't easy, since she was in the public eye just about as much as the president. Then we had to fake his own assassination, so we could get him safely out of the way. At first he was pretty reluctant about it all, but then the Berlin Wall went up and the media blamed *him* for it and he agreed that he wanted out—permanently. We were all set to pull it off but the Cuban Missile Crisis hit the fan and we had to put everything on hold for more than a month. By the time we had calmed that mess down he was more than ready to leave this earth. So we arranged the thing for Dallas.

We didn't dare tell Lyndon Johnson about the Martians, of course. He would've wanted to go to Mars and annex the whole damned planet. To Texas, most likely. And we didn't have to tell Nixon; he was happy to kill the Apollo program—after taking as much credit for the first lunar landing as the media would give him.

The toughest part was hoodwinking the astronomers and planetary scientists and the engineers who built spacecraft probes of the planets. It took all of Schmidt's ingenuity and the Martians' technical skills to get the various *Mariner* and *Pioneer* probes jiggered so that they would show a barren dry Venus devastated by a runaway greenhouse effect instead of the lush Mesozoic jungle that really exists beneath those clouds. I had to pull every string I knew, behind the scenes, to get the geniuses at JPL to send their two *Viking* landers to the Martian equivalents of Death Valley and the Atacama Desert in Chile. They missed the cities and the canals completely.

Schmidt used his international connections, too. I didn't much like working with Commies, but I've got to admit the two Russian scientists I met were okay guys.

And it worked. Sightings of the canals on Mars went down to zero once our faked *Mariner 6* pictures were published. Astronomy students looking at Mars for the first time through a telescope thought they were victims of eyestrain! They *knew* there were no canals there, so they didn't dare claim they saw any.

So that's how we got to the Moon and then stopped going. We set up the Apollo program so that a small number of Americans could plant the flag and their footprints on the Moon and then forget about it. The Martians studiously avoided the whole area during the four years that we were sending missions up there. It all worked out very well, if I say so myself.

I worked harder than I ever had before in my life to get the media to downplay the space program, make it a dull, no-news affair. The man in the street, the average xenophobic Joe Six-Pack forgot about the glories of space exploration soon enough. It tore at my guts to do it, but that's what had to be done.

So now we're using the resources of the planet Venus to replenish Mars. Schmidt has a tiny group of astronomers who've been hiding the facts of the solar system from the rest of the profession since the late forties. With the Martians' help they're continuing to fake the pictures and data sent from NASA's space probes.

The rest of the world thinks that Mars is a barren lifeless desert and Venus is a bone-dry hothouse beneath its perpetual cloud cover and space in general is pretty much of a bore. Meanwhile, with the help of Jazzbow and a few other Martians, we've started an environmental movement on Earth. Maybe if we can get human beings to see their own planet as a living entity, to think of the other animals and plants on our own planet as fellow residents of this Spaceship Earth rather than resources to be killed or exploited—maybe then we can start to reduce the basic xenophobia in the human psyche.

I won't live long enough to see the human race embrace the Martians as brothers. It will take generations, centuries, before we grow to their level of morality. But maybe we're on the right track now. I hope so.

I keep thinking of what Jack Kennedy said when he finally agreed to rig Project Apollo the way we did, and to arrange his own and his girlfriend's demises.

"It is a far, far better thing I do, than I have ever done," he quoted.

Thinking of him and Marilyn shacked up in a honeymoon suite on Mars, I realized that the remainder of the quote would have been totally inappropriate: "it is a far, far better rest that I go to, than I have ever known."

But what the hell, who am I to talk? I've fallen in love for the first time. Yeah, I know. I've been married several times, but this time it's real and I'm going to spend the rest of my life on a tropical island with her, just the two of us alone, far from the madding crowd.

Well, maybe not the whole rest of my life. The Martians know a lot more about medicine than we do. Maybe we'll leave this Pacific island where the Martians found her and go off to Mars and live a couple of centuries or so. I think Amelia would like that.

Introduction to "Life As We Know It"

❖

Now we get serious again.

The scientific effort to determine if life exists elsewhere in the universe has been ridiculed by politicians, pundits, and even some scientists. When NASA established a department dedicated to the search for extraterrestrial life, for example, Harvard biologist George Gaylord Simpson quipped that it was the first time in the history of science that an organization had been put together to study a subject before evidence of its subject matter had been found.

Politicians have turned SETI (the search for extraterrestrial intelligence) into a well-publicized whipping boy. However small the funds allocated for SETI, some representative or senator loudly proclaims that it's a vast waste of money and gets Congress to cancel the appropriation. It is only through the private efforts of activist groups such as the Planetary Society that astronomers have been able to continue the search.

No extraterrestrial life has yet been found, although in 1996 NASA scientists reported that microscopic structures inside a meteorite that originated on Mars may be the fossilized remains of 3.5-billion-year-old Martian bacteria.

Radio telescopes have not detected any intelligent signals, although they have barely begun to scratch the surface of the problem. There are billions of stars and thousands of millions of wavelengths to be examined.

Our spacecraft have landed on the Moon, Mars, and Venus; others have flown past all the planets of our solar system except distantmost Pluto. The Moon is, as we expected, airless, waterless and lifeless. Mars is a frigid desert, although there is some hope that life may have arisen there, only to be extinguished by the planet's increasing aridity. Venus is an utterly barren oven, with surface temperatures hot enough to melt aluminum and a heavy choking atmosphere of carbon dioxide.

Jupiter, largest of the solar system's planets, might have the chemical ingredients for life swirling in its multicolored clouds. If I were a betting man, I'd put my money on Jupiter as the most likely place to find some form of extraterrestrial life. Not intelligent life, most likely. But you never know.

Sadly, this story contains a glaring anachronism. Carl Sagan died in late 1996, more than two years after this story was written, and a thousand years too soon. He is a living character in the story, just as his dedication and drive are still living influences in the continuing search for extraterrestrial life.

LIFE AS WE KNOW IT
❖

They were all there, all the Grand Old Men of the field: McKay, Kliest, Taranto—even Sagan, little more than an ancient withered husk in his electric wheelchair. But the fire still burned in his deep, dark eyes.

All the egos and superegos who had given their lifetimes to the search for extraterrestrial life. Often derided by the media, scorned by the politicians, even scoffed at by their fellow scientists, this was going to be their day. One way or the other.

Jupiter was going to reveal its secrets to them. Today. Life on another world at last. Make or break.

I could feel the tension in the room, like just before a thunderstorm, that electrical smell in the air that makes the hair on your arms stand on end. Careers would be made today, or broken. Mine included. That's why everyone was here, waiting impatiently, chattering nervously, staring at the display screens that still showed nothing but crackling streaks of random noise.

The mission control center was a big room, huge really, but now it was jammed with bodies, hot and sweaty, buzzing with voices in half a dozen languages. The project scientists, all the top government officials, invitees like Sagan, hangers-on who inveigled their way in, everybody who thought or hoped they'd capture some of the glory of the moment, and more than a hundred news reporters and photographers, all crammed into the mission control chamber, all talking at once. Like a tribe of apes, jabbering, gesticulating, posturing to hide their dreams and ambitions and fear.

They didn't want to miss the first images from beneath the cloud tops of Jupiter. Even if it killed them, they had to be at mission control when the probe's first pictures came in.

Most of the reporters clustered around Sagan, of course, although quite a few hung near Lopez-Oyama, the center's director. Our boss.

Beautiful Allie stayed at Lopez-Oyama's side. Allison Brandt, she of the golden hair and pendulous breasts. I dreamed about Allie, saw her flawlessly naked, smiling at me willingly. In my waking hours I thought about her endlessly, picturing myself doing things with her that not even my dreams dared to imagine.

But she stayed beside the director, next to the power and the attention. I was merely an engineer, neither powerful nor glamorous. Still, I longed for Allie. Lusted after her. Even as she smiled for the photographers I noticed how she had artfully undone an extra couple of buttons on the front of her blouse.

"Imagery systems check," droned the voice of the mission controller. The huge room fell absolutely silent. I held my breath.

"Imagery systems functioning."

We all let out a sigh of relief. Me especially. The imagery systems were my responsibility. I built them. If they failed, the mission failed, I failed, six dozen careers would go down the tubes, six dozen frustrated scientists would be seeking my blood.

Our probe into Jupiter was unmanned, of course. No astronaut could survive the crushing pressures and turbulent storms beneath the cloud deck of Jupiter. No one knew if our robotic probe was sturdy enough to reach below the cloud tops and survive.

Over the years, the earlier probes had shown that beneath those gaudy colorful swirling clouds there was an ocean ten times larger than the whole Earth. An ocean of *water*. Heavily laced with ammonia, to be sure, but water nonetheless. There was only one other world in the solar system where liquid water existed—Earth. We knew that liquid water meant life on Earth.

Did it on Jupiter?

"Jupiter represents our best chance for finding extraterrestrial life." Lopez-Oyama had said those words to the congressional committee that ruled on NASA's budget, when he went begging to them for the money to fund our mission.

"Life?" asked one of the congressmen, looking startled, almost afraid. "Like animals and trees and such?"

I watched those hearings on TV; we all did, sitting

on the edges of our chairs in the center's cafeteria while the politicians decided if we lived or died. I had picked a seat next to Allie, although she barely acknowledged my presence beside her. She stared unwaveringly at the screen.

With a tolerant little shake of his head, Lopez-Oyama replied, "It probably won't be life as we know it here on Earth, sir. That would be too much to hope for."

"Then what will it be like?"

"We just don't know. We've never found life on another world before." Then he added, "But if we don't find life on Jupiter, then I doubt that life of any form exists anywhere else in the solar system."

"Do you mean *intelligent* life?" asked the committee chairwoman sharply.

Lopez-Oyama smiled winningly at her. "No, ma'am," he said. "Intelligent life would be too much to expect. I'll be happy if we find something like bacteria."

Now, as the moment of truth approached, the scientists cramming mission control were busily spinning theories about what the cameras would find in Jupiter's global ocean. They couldn't wait for the actual pictures, they had to show how clever they were to impress the reporters and each other. A bunch of alpha male apes, preening and displaying their brains instead of their fangs. Competing for primacy and the attention of the news reporters who were clustered around them, goggle-eyed, tape recorders spinning. Even the women scientists were playing the one-upmanship game, in the name of equality.

To her credit, Allie remained quiet. She was as clever a scientist as any of them, but she refused to involve herself in the primate competition. She didn't have to. Her ranking in the hierarchy was as secure as could be.

None of them paid the slightest attention to me. I was only the engineer who had built the imaging system. I wasn't a scientist, just the guy with dirt under his fingernails who made the machinery work. I'd be ignored unless something went wrong.

To tell the truth, I paid damned little attention to them and their constant gabbling. My eyes were focused on long-legged Allie, by far the most desirable female in the pack. How could I make her notice me? How could I get her to smile in my direction instead of clinging so close to the boss? How could I get to be an alpha male in her lustrous eyes?

"Data coming through."

From nearly a thousand million kilometers away, my cameras were functioning. Had already functioned, as a matter of fact, more than eight hours ago. It took that long for the telemetry signal to travel from Jupiter to our antennas out in the desert.

Suddenly all their jabbering stopped. Mission control fell absolutely silent. The first images began to raster across the main display screens, line by line. Live, from beneath the endless cloud deck of Jupiter.

Each display screen showed imagery from a different wavelength. We had blue, green, red, infrared, and even radar imaging systems. Despite all their theories, none of the scientists had been able to tell me which wavelengths would work best beneath Jupiter's cloud deck.

I had asked them how much sunlight filtered through the clouds. None of them could tell me. Which wavelengths of sunlight penetrated the

clouds? None of them knew. I had to grope blindly
and include as broad a spectrum of instruments as
possible.

Now I swivelled my gaze from one screen to the
next. The blue system was pretty much of a washout,
nothing but a blur, as I had expected. The atmosphere must be filled with haze, a planetwide fog of
ammonia and sulfur molecules.

"That looks like wave tops!"

The infrared image indeed looked as if it was
plunging toward the surface of a turbulent ocean.
Radar showed more detail. Waves, crests and
troughs racing madly across the screen. A rough sea
down there. A very turbulent, storm-tossed ocean.

"Immersion in three minutes," said mission control. The probe was going to hit those waves. It was
designed to sink slowly to a depth of about a hundred kilometers, where it would—we hoped—attain
a neutral buoyancy and float indefinitely.

Of course, if we saw something interesting at a
shallower depth, the probe could eject some of its
ballast on command and rise accordingly. The trouble was that it took more than eight hours for any
of our commands to reach the probe. We had to pray
that whatever we found wouldn't go away in the
course of eight hours—almost a full revolution of
the planet, a whole Jovian day.

I summoned up all my courage and sidled closer
to Allie, squeezing slowly through the crush of bodies. They were all staring at the screens, ignoring me,
watching the ocean waves and the streams of low-
level clouds streaking past. Storm clouds, swirling
viciously.

I pushed between Allie and Lopez-Oyama. Not

daring to try to say anything to her, I looked down on the boss's balding pate, and half whispered, "I didn't think we'd get much from the blue at this level."

He was so short that he had to crane his neck to look at me. He said nothing, just nodded in his inscrutable way.

Allie was almost my own height. We were nearly eye to eye.

"The infrared is fabulous," she said. To me!

"It *is* working pretty well, isn't it?" Be modest in triumph. All the books of advice I had studied told me that women appreciated men who were successful, yet not boastful; strong but sensitive.

"It won't work as well once it's underwater, though, will it?" she asked.

I suppressed the urge to grab her and carry her off. Instead, I deliberately turned to look at the screens instead of her cool hazel eyes.

"That's when the blue or blue-green should come into its own," I said, trying to keep my voice from trembling.

"If the laser works," said Lopez-Oyama. It was almost a growl. He was distinctly unhappy that I had stepped between him and Allie.

Mission control announced, "Impact in ten seconds."

The whole crowd seemed to surge forward slightly, lean toward the screens, waiting.

"Impact!"

All the screens went blank for a heart-stopping instant. But before anyone could shout or groan or even take a breath, they came on again. Radar was blank, of course, and the infrared was just a smudge.

But the blue and blue-green images were clear and beautiful.

"My god, it's like scuba diving in Hawaii," Allie said.

That's how crisp and clear the pictures were. We could see bubbles from our splash-in and light filtering down from the ocean's surface. The water looked crystal clear.

And empty. No fish, no fronds of vegetation, nothing that looked like life in that ammonia-laced water, nothing at all to be seen.

"Not deep enough yet," grumbled Lopez-Oyama. If we found nothing, his career was finished, we all knew that. I caught a glimpse of the congressional committee chairwoman, up in the special VIP section behind plate-glass windows, staring hard at him.

For more than an hour we saw nothing but bubbles from the probe's descent. The faint light from the surface dwindled, as we had expected. At precisely the preprogrammed moment, the laser turned on and began sweeping its intense light through the water.

"That should attract anything that can swim," Allie said hopefully.

"Or repel anything that's accustomed to swimming in darkness," said one of the scientists, almost with a smirk.

The laser beam ballooned in the water, of course. I had expected that; counted on it, really. It acted as a bright wide searchlight for me. I wanted to tell Allie why I had chosen that specific wavelength, how proud I was that it was working just as I had planned it would.

But her attention was riveted to the screen, and

Lopez-Oyama pushed to her side again, squeezing me out from between them.

Lopez-Oyama was perspiring. I could see drops of sweat glistening on his bald spot.

"Deeper," he muttered. "We've got to go deeper. The ocean is heated from below. Life-forms must be down there."

I thought I heard a slightly desperate accent on the word "must."

"Spectrographic data coming in," announced mission control.

All eyes turned to the screen that began to show the smears and bands of colors from the probe's mass spectrometer. All eyes except mine. I kept my attention on the images from the laser-illuminated sea. They were becoming cloudy, it seemed to me.

"There's the ammonia band," someone said.

"And carbon compounds, I think."

"My god, those are *organics!*"

"Organic compounds in the water!"

"Life."

"Don't jump to conclusions," Lopez-Oyama warned. But his voice was shaking with excitement.

Allie actually clutched at my shoulder. "Can your cameras *see* anything?"

The water was cloudy, murky, even where the laser beam swept through; it looked like a thin fog, glistening but obscuring.

"The ocean's filled with organic chemicals at this level," one of the scientists said.

"Particles," corrected another scientist.

"Food," somebody quipped.

"For who?"

"Deeper," Sagan said, his voice surprisingly

strong. "The organic particles are drifting down-ward. If there's anything in that ocean that eats them, it's down at a deeper level."

The probe was designed to attain neutral buoy-ancy at a depth of a hundred kilometers. We were approaching that depth now. It might not be enough.

"How deep can we push it?" Lopez-Oyama asked no one in particular.

Immediately a dozen opinions sprang out of the eager, excited, sweaty chattering apes. Earlier probes had been crushed like soda cans by the immense pressure of the Jovian ocean. But I knew that the probe's limits were not only structural, but communications-based. The probe could not hold more than a hundred kilometers of the hair-thin op-tical fiber that carried its comm signals to the surface of the ocean. So even if it could survive lower depths, we would lose touch with it.

"What's that?"

In the hazy light, a dark shape drifted by, too dis-tant to make out any detail.

"Follow it!" Lopez-Oyama snapped.

Then his face reddened. It would take more than eight hours for his order to reach the probe. In his excitement he had forgotten.

Allie turned to me. "Are the close-up cameras working?"

They were. I gestured toward the screens that showed their imagery. The dark hulk, whatever it was, had not come within the narrow focus of either of the close-view cameras. Both screens showed nothing but the cloudy water, tinted sickly green by the laser light.

"Another one!" somebody shouted.

This time the shape drifted past the view of one of the close-up cameras, briefly. We saw a bulbous dark dome, almost spherical, with snakelike appendages dangling from its bottom.

"Tentacles!"

"It's an animal! Like an octopus!"

I scanned the numerical data on the bottom of the screen. The object, whatever it was, was three and a half kilometers from the probe. And it was 432 meters long, from the top of its dome to the tip of its tentacles. Huge. Fifteen times bigger than a blue whale. Immense.

"It's not moving."

"It's drifting in the current."

"The tentacles are just hanging there. No activity that I can see."

"Conserving energy?"

"Maybe that's the way it hunts for prey."

"Trolling?"

It looked dead to me. Inert. Unmoving. It drifted out of the close-up camera's view and all the heads in the room swivelled to the wide-angle view. The dark lump did nothing to show it might be alive.

"What's the spectrograph show?"

"Not a helluva lot."

"Absorption bands, lots of them."

"Chlorophyll?"

"Don't be a butthead!"

Allie was the only one who seemed to realize the significance of what we were seeing. "If it's an animal, it's either in a quiescent, resting phase . . . or it's dead."

"The first extraterrestrial creature we find, and it's dead," somebody groused.

"There'll be more," said Lopez-Oyama, almost cheerfully.

I looked across the room at Sagan. He was leaning forward in his wheelchair, eyes intent on the screens, as if he could make something more appear just by concentrating. The reporters were gaping, not saying a word for a blessed change, forgetting to ask questions while the underwater views of the Jovian ocean filled the display screens.

Then I looked at Allie again. Her lovely face was frozen in an expression of . . . what? Fear? Dread? Did she have the same terrible suspicion that was building in my mind?

It was almost another hour before we saw another of the tentacled creatures. The probe had reached its maximum depth and was drifting through the murky water. Particles floated past the cameras, some of them as big as dinner plates. None of them active. They all just drifted by, sinking slowly like dark chunks of soot meandering toward the bottom of that sunless sea.

Then we saw the second of the octopods. And quickly afterward, an entire school of them, hundreds, perhaps a thousand or more. The sensors on the probe went into overdrive; the automatic-analysis programs would count the creatures for us. We simply stared at them.

Different sizes. Lots of small ones—if something a dozen times the size of a whale can be called small.

"Babies," Allie murmured.

A family group, I thought. A clan. All of them dead. There was no mistaking it now. My cameras showed them clearly. Big saucer eyes clouded and unmoving. Open wounds in some of them. Tentacles hanging limply. They were just drifting along like ghosts, immense dark shadows that once had been alive.

Time lost all meaning for us. The big mission control center fell absolutely silent. Even the most assertive and egocentric of the male apes among us stopped trying to make instant theories and simply stared at a scene of devastation. A holocaust.

At last Lopez-Oyama whispered, "They're all dead. The whole fucking planet's dead."

Then we saw the city. A sort of collective gasp went through the crowded mission control room when it came into view.

It was a structure, a vast, curving structure that floated in that mighty ocean, graceful despite its immense size. Curves atop curves. Huge round ports and beautifully symmetrical archways, a gigantic city built by or for the immense creatures that floated, dead and decaying, before our camera eyes.

The numbers flickering at the bottom of the screens told us that the city was hundreds of kilometers away from our lenses, yet it filled the screens of the narrow-view cameras. We could see delicate traceries along its massive curving flank, curves and whorls etched into its structure.

"Writing," someone breathed.

A dream city, built of alien inspirations and desires. It staggered our Earthbound senses, dwarfed us with its immensity and grandeur. It was enormous yet graceful and entirely beautiful in an eerie, unearthly way. It was dead.

As it swung slowly, majestically, in the powerful

ocean currents we saw that it was only a fragment of the original structure, a piece somehow torn off from its original whole. Jagged cracks and ragged edges showed where it had been ripped away from the rest of the city. To me it looked like a fragment of a shell from an enormous Easter egg, beautifully decorated, that had been smashed by some titanic unseen malevolency.

"War?" someone's voice whispered plaintively. "Did they destroy themselves?"

But I knew better. And I couldn't stand it. I turned away from the screens, away from the views of dead Jupiter, and pushed through the crowd that was still gaping stupidly at my cameras' views. I was suffocating, strangling. I had to have fresh air or die.

I bolted out the main doors and into the corridor, empty and silent, deserted by all the people who had crammed mission control. The first outside door I could find I kicked through, heedless of the red EMERGENCY ONLY sign and the wailing alarm that hooted accusingly after me.

The brilliant late-afternoon sun surprised me, made my eyes suddenly water after the cool shadows inside the building. I took in a deep raw lungful of hot, dry desert air. It felt like brick dust, alien, as if part of me were still deeply immersed in Jupiter's mighty ocean.

"It's all ruined." Allie's voice.

Turning, I saw that she had followed me. The tears in her eyes were not from the bright sunshine.

"All dead," she sobbed. "The city . . . all of them . . . destroyed."

"The comet," I said. Shoemaker-Levy 9 had struck

Jupiter twenty years ago with the violence of a million hydrogen bombs.

"Twenty years," Allie moaned. "They were *intelligent*. We could have *communicated* with them!"

If we had only been twenty years earlier, I thought. Then the true horror of it struck me. What could we have told them, twenty years ago? That a shattered comet was going to rain destruction on them? That no matter what they had built, what they had learned or hoped for or prayed to, their existence was going to be wiped out forever? That there's absolutely nothing either they or we could do about it?

"It's cold," Allie said, almost whimpering.

She wanted me to go to her, to hold her, to comfort her the way one warm-blooded primate ape comforts another. But what was the use? What was the use of anything?

What difference did any of it make in a world where you could spend millions of years evolving into intelligence, build a civilization, reach a peak of knowledge where you begin to study and understand the universe around you, only to learn that the universe can destroy you utterly, without remorse, without the slightest shred of hope for salvation?

I looked past Allie, shivering in the last rays of the dying day. Looked past the buildings and antennas, past the gray-brown hills and the distant wrinkled mountains that were turning blood red in the inevitable sunset.

I saw Jupiter. I saw those intelligent creatures wiped away utterly and implacably, as casually as a man flicks a spot of dust off his sleeve.

And I knew that somewhere out in that uncaring sky another comet was heading inexorably for Earth to end all our dreams, all our strivings, all our desires.

Introduction to "Legendary Heroes"

❖

Depending on who you ask, the line between science fiction and fantasy is thin, blurred, or nonexistent.

To me, the line is quite distinct. Science-fiction stories are those in which some element of future science or technology is so integral to the plot that if you took away the science/technology aspect the story would collapse. The archetypical science-fiction tale, under my definition, is Mary Wollstonecraft Shelley's Frankenstein. Take away the science, and there is no story at all.

Fantasy, on the other hand, deals with magic and mysticism; in fantasy tales elves and wizards replace the scientists and computers of science fiction.

No other subject treads the shady area between fantasy and science fiction as much as the subject of time travel. Although a fascinating concept, to most people the idea of travelling into the past or the future is sheer fantasy, totally impossible, well outside the realm of science.

Yet theoretical physicists, starting with Einstein, have shown that time travel is not forbidden by their equations. To the science-fiction writer, working on the dictum that you are free to use any idea so long as no one can prove *it's wrong, what is not forbidden in physics is perfectly permissible in fiction.*

I have written five novels about Orion, a man created in the far future by humans of godlike powers, and sent to various points in time to do their bidding. In these novels Orion has visited the twentieth century, the thirteenth-century empire of the Mongols, the Trojan War of Homer, the Ice Age, the Mesozoic era of dinosaurs, Alexander the Great's ancient Macedonia, and an era of interstellar warfare.

Each of the Orion novels is based on solid historical, archeological, and paleontological evidence. The issue of time travel is handled as a problem in quantum physics. To me, Orion is science fiction.

When the editor in chief of TSR's gaming magazine, *Dragon*, asked me to write a fantasy short story for him, I replied that I don't write fantasy, I write science fiction. "What about your Orion stories?" he countered.

Rather than argue with an editor who was asking for my work, I wrote "Legendary Heroes." I consider it science fiction. You may not. The definition is not so important, though, as the enjoyment readers get from the tale.

LEGENDARY HEROES

❖

For the first time that bitterly cold winter, Heorot was bright again, ringing with song and a king's gratitude to the hero.

And then the beast roared, out in the icy darkness.

"But he's dead!" King Hrothgar bellowed, pointing to the shaggy monster's arm that now was affixed over the mead hall's entrance doorway.

"I killed him," exclaimed Beowulf, "with these bare hands."

Hrothgar turned to his queen, Wealhtheow, sitting beside him on the dais between the royal torches. She was as beautiful as a starry spring night, her raven-dark hair tumbling past her shoulders, her lustrous gray eyes focused beyond the beyond.

Wealhtheow was a seer. Gripping the carved arms of her throne, shuddering under the spell of her magic, she pronounced in a hollow voice, "The monster is truly dead. Now its mate has come to claim vengeance upon us."

Hrothgar turned as white as his beard. His thanes, who had been sloshing mead and singing their old battle songs, fell into the silence of cold terror.

The captives from Britain huddled together in sudden fear in the far corner of the hall. I could see the dread in their faces. Hrothgar had planned to sacrifice them to his gods if Beowulf had not killed the monster. For a few brief hours they had thought they would be freed. Now the horror had returned.

I turned to gaze upon the lovely Queen Wealhtheow. She was much younger than Hrothgar, yet her divine gray eyes seemed to hold the wisdom of eternity. And she was staring directly at me.

How and why I was in Heorot I had no idea. I could remember nothing beyond the day we had arrived on the Scylding shore, pulling on the oars of our longboat against the freezing spray of the tide.

My name is Orion, that much I knew. And I serve Beowulf, hero of the Geats, who had sailed to far-off Daneland to kill the monster that had turned timbered Heorot, the hall of the stag, from King Hrothgar's great pride to his great sorrow.

For months the monster had stalked Heorot, striking by night when the warriors had drunk themselves into mead-besotted dreams. At length none would enter the great hall, not even stubborn old Hrothgar himself. Until Beowulf arrived with the fourteen of us and loudly proclaimed that he would kill the beast that very night.

Beowulf was a huge warrior, two ax handles across the shoulders, with flaxen braids to his waist and eyes as clear blue as the icy water of a fiord. Strength he had, and courage. Also, he was a boaster of unparalleled brashness.

The very night he came to Heorot with his fourteen companions he swaggered so hard that narrow-eyed Unferth, the most cunning of the Scylding thanes, tried to take him down a peg. Beowulf bested him in a bragging contest and won the roars of Hrothgar's mead-soaked companions.

After midnight Hrothgar and his Scyldings left the hall. The torches were put out, the hearth fire sank to low, glowering embers. It was freezing cold; I could hear the wind moaning outside. Beowulf and the rest of us stretched out to sleep. My shirt of chain mail felt like ice against my skin. I dilated my peripheral blood vessels and increased my heart rate, to make myself warmer, without even asking myself how I knew to do this.

I had volunteered to stay awake and keep watch. I could go for days without sleep, and the others were glad to let me do it. We had all drunk many tankards of honey-sweetened mead, yet my body burned away its effects almost immediately. I felt alert, aware, strong.

Through the keening wind and bitter chill I could sense the monster shambling about in the night outside, looking for more victims to slaughter.

I sat up and grasped my sword an instant before the beast burst through the massive double doors of the mead hall, snarling and slavering. The others scattered in every direction, shrieking, eyes wide with fear.

I felt terror grip my heart, too. As I stared at the approaching monster I recalled a giant cave bear, in another time, another life. It had ripped me apart with its razor-sharp claws. It had crushed my bones in its fanged jaws. It had killed me.

Beowulf leaped to his feet and charged straight at the monster. It rose onto its hind legs, twice the height of a warrior, and knocked Beowulf aside with a swat of one mighty paw. His sword went flying out of his hand as he landed flat on his back with a thud that shook the pounded-earth floor.

Everything seemed to slow down into a dreamy, sluggish lethargy. I saw Beowulf scrambling to his feet, but slowly, languidly, as if he moved through a thick invisible quagmire. I could see the beast's eyes moving in his head, globs of spittle forming between his pointed teeth and dropping slowly, slowly to the earthen floor.

Beowulf charged again, bare-handed this time. The monster focused on him, spread its forelegs out as if to embrace this pitiful fool and then crush him. I ducked beneath those sharp-clawed paws and rammed my sword into the beast's belly, up to the hilt, and then hacksawed upward.

Blood spurted over me. The monster bellowed with pain and fury and knocked me sideways across the hall. Beowulf leaped on its back, as languidly as in a dream. The others were gathering their senses now, hacking at the beast with their swords. I got to my feet just as the brute dropped ponderously back onto all fours and started for the shattered door, my sword still jammed into its gut.

One of the men got too close and the monster snatched him in its jaws and crushed the life out of him. I shook at the memory, but I took up Beowulf's dropped sword and swung as hard as I could at the beast's shoulder. The blade hit bone and stuck. The beast howled again and tried to shake Beowulf off its back. He pitched forward, grabbed at the sword sticking in its shoulder and wormed it through the tendons of the joint like a butcher carving a roast.

Howling, the monster shook free of him again, but Beowulf clutched its leg while the rest of us hacked away. Blood splattered everywhere; men roared and screamed.

And then the beast shambled for the door, with Beowulf still clutching its leg. The leg tore off and the monster stumbled out into the night, howling with pain, its life's blood spurting from its wounds.

That was why we feasted and sang at Heorot the following night. Until the beast's mate roared its cry of vengeance against us.

"I raid the coast of Britain," Hrothgar cried angrily, "and sack the cities of the Franks. Yet in my own hall I must cower like a weak woman!"

"Fear not, mighty king," Beowulf answered bravely. "Just as I killed the monster will I slay its mate. And this time I will do it alone!"

Absolute silence fell over Heorot.

Then the king spoke. "Do this, and you can have your choice of reward. Anything in my kingdom will be yours!"

Before Beowulf could reply, sly Unferth spoke up. "You have no sword, mighty warrior."

"It was carried off by the dying monster," Beowulf said.

"Here then, take mine." Unferth unbuckled the sword at his waist and handed it to the hero.

Beowulf pulled the blade from its scabbard and whistled it through the air. "A good blade and true. I will return it you, Unferth, with the monster's blood on it."

Everyone shouted approval, even the British captives. There were an even dozen of them: eleven young boys and girls, none yet in their teens, and a wizened old man with big, staring eyes and a beard even whiter than Hrothgar's.

The monster roared outside again, and silenced the cheers.

Beowulf strode to the patched-up door of the mead hall, Unferth's sword in his mighty right hand.

"Let no one follow me!" he cried.

No one did. We all stood stunned and silent as he marched out into the dark. I turned slightly and saw that Unferth was smiling cruelly, his lips forming a single word: "Fool."

"Orion." Queen Wealhtheow called my name.

She stepped down from the royal dais and walked through the crowd toward me. The others seemed frozen, like statues, staring sightlessly at the door. Hrothgar did not move, did not even breathe, as his queen approached me. The Scylding thanes, Beowulf's other companions, even the frightened British captives—none of them blinked or breathed or twitched.

"They are in stasis, Orion," Wealhtheow said as she came within arm's reach of me. "They can neither see nor hear us."

Those infinite gray eyes of hers seemed to show me worlds upon worlds, lifetimes I had led—we had led together—in other epochs, other worldlines.

"Do you remember me, Orion?"

"I love you," I whispered, knowing it was true. "I have loved you through all of space-time."

"Yes, my love. What more do you remember?"

It was like clawing at a high smooth stone wall. I

shook my head. "Nothing. I don't even know why I'm here—why you're here."

"You remember nothing of the Creators? Of your previous missions?"

"The Creators." Vaguely I recalled godlike men and women. "Aten."

"Yes," she said. "Aten."

He created me and sent me through space-time to do his bidding. Haughty and mad with power, he called me his tool, his hunter. More often I was an assassin for him.

"I remember . . . the snow, the time of eternal cold." But it was all like the misty tendrils of a dream, wafting away even as I reached for them.

"I was with you then," she said.

"The cave bear. It killed me." I could feel the pain of my ribs being crushed, hear my own screams drowned in spouting blood.

"You've lived many lives."

"And died many deaths."

"Yes, my poor darling. You have suffered much."

She was one of the Creators, I realized. I loved a goddess. And she loved me. Yet we were destined to be torn away from each other, time and again, over the eons and light-years of the continuum.

"This beast that ravaged Heorot was not a natural animal," she told me. "It was engendered and controlled by one of the Creators."

"Which one? Aten?"

She shook her head. "It makes no difference. I am here to see that the beast does not succeed. You must help me."

Deep in my innermost memories I recalled that the Creators squabbled among themselves like spoiled children. They directed the course of human history and sent minions such as me to points in space-time to carry out their whims. Many times I have killed for Aten, and many times have I died for him. Yet he brings me back, sneering at my pains and fears, and sends me out again.

I am powerless to resist his commands—he thinks. But more than once I have defied his wishes. At Troy I helped Odysseos and his Achaians to triumph. Deep in interstellar space I led whole fleets against him.

"Has Aten sent me here, or have you?" I asked her.

She smiled at me, a smile that could warm a glacier. "I have brought you here, Orion, to help Beowulf slay both monsters."

"Is Beowulf one of your creatures?"

She laughed. "That bragging oaf? No, my darling, he is as mortal as a blade of grass."

"But why is this important?" I asked. "Why has your enemy used these beasts to attack Heorot?"

"That I will explain after you have helped Beowulf to kill the second monster."

"If I live through the ordeal," I said, feeling sullen, resentful.

"My poor darling. I ask so much of you. If I could do this myself, I would."

Then she kissed me swiftly on the lips. I would have faced an entire continent filled with monsters for her.

The tingle of her lips on mine had not yet faded when the others around us stirred to life once again. And Wealhtheow was somehow back on her throne, on the dais beside her husband, aged Hrothgar.

Her husband. The thought burned in me. Then I realized that one of the men in this timbered mead hall was one of the Creators, in disguise, controlling the monsters that killed Hrothgar's warriors. Why? What was the *purpose* of it all?

That was not for me to know. Not yet. My task was clear. The king and queen left the mead hall, heading back to Hrothgar's fortress. The others milled about for a while, then started back through the frigid winter night also.

It was easy for me to slip away from them and start down the rocky trail that led to the sea. The moon scudded in and out of low dark clouds. In its fitful light I could clearly see the spoor of dark blood that the dying monster had left from the night before. This is the track Beowulf was following. I hurried along it.

The blood spoor ended at the sea, where the waves crashed against the craggy headland. Our longboat was still tucked up on the rocks, I saw, its mast stored along the deck. No one guarded it. There was no need. The boat was under Hrothgar's protection; no Scylding would dare touch it.

Bitter cold it was, with a wind coming off the sea that sliced through my chain-mail shirt and chilled me to the bone despite my conscious control of my blood circulation.

The rocky cove stretched out to my left. In the moonlit shadows I thought I saw caves in among the rocks at the cove's far end. The den of the monster, perhaps.

A growling roar, like the rumble of distant thunder, came across the icy wind. I raced across the rocks toward the caves.

The second cave was the monster's den, half-awash with the incoming tide, dimly lit by phosphorescent patches of lichen clinging to the rock walls.

The beast was even bigger than the first one, glowing faintly white in the dimly lit cave, snarling at Beowulf as it reared up on its hind legs. Even mighty Beowulf looked like a pitiful dwarf next to its enormous size.

He was already bleeding from shoulder to waist, his chain-mail shirt in shreds from the beast's raking claws. He clutched Unferth's sword in both hands and swung mightily at the monster, to no avail. It was like hitting the brute with a tress of hair.

The monster knocked Beowulf to his knees with a blow that would have crushed a normal man. His sword blade snapped in half. And I realized that Unferth had given Beowulf a useless weapon. Crafty Unferth with his glittering reptilian eyes was the other Creator among the Scyldings.

I ran toward the beast, and again the world seemed to slow into dreamy, languid motion.

"Beowulf!" I shouted. "Here!"

I threw my own sword to him. It spun lazily through the air. He caught it in one massive hand and scrabbled away from the monster on his knees.

I circled around to the side away from Beowulf, trying to draw the brute's attention before it killed the hero of the Geats. Out of the corner of my eye I saw a gleaming horde of treasure: gold coins and jewels heaped on the dank cave floor. Swords and warriors' armor, spears and helmets were strewn in profusion. The monsters had brought their kills here for many years.

The beast ignored the kneeling Beowulf and bellowed at me, dropping to all fours as it moved to protect its horde. But it moved slowly, as if in a dream. I dashed to the pile of weapons and pulled out the first sword I could reach.

Barely in time. The monster was almost on top of me. I slashed at his slavering jaws and it howled in pain and fury. I feinted sideways, then stepped back—and tripped on a helmet lying at my feet.

Off-balance, I staggered backward. The beast swung at me; I could see those razor-sharp claws coming, but there was nothing I could do to stop them. The blow knocked me onto my back. The monster's jaws reached for me, teeth like a row of swords. I clutched my own sword in both hands and rammed it upward into the beast's open mouth, but it did no good. Its teeth closed around me. I was going to be crushed to death, just as I had been all those long eons ago.

But the monster suddenly howled and dropped me. It turned to face Beowulf, bleeding, battered, but hacking at the beast's flank with the fury of a berserker.

As the brute turned away from me, I scrambled to my feet and thrust my sword into its neck, angling it upward to find the brain or spine.

It collapsed so suddenly that it nearly smothered Beowulf. For long moments we both stood on tottering legs, gasping for breath, spattered with our own blood and the monster's, staring down at its enormous carcass.

Then Beowulf looked up and grinned at me. "Help me take off its head," he said.

It was pearly pink dawn when we staggered out

of the cave. Beowulf carried the monster's gigantic shaggy head on his shoulder as lightly as if it were a bit of gossamer.

We blinked at the morning light. Icy waves lapped at our ankles.

Beowulf turned to me, his cocky grin gone. "Orion, I told Hrothgar before all his thanes that I would kill the monster myself, with no one's help."

I nodded, but said nothing.

Suddenly his broad, strong face took on the expression of a guilty little boy's. "Will you go on ahead and say that you searched for me, but could not find me? Then I can come later with the beast's head."

I glanced down at my bloody arms. "And my wounds?"

"Say you were set upon by wolves as you searched in the night for me."

I smiled at his stupid pride, but said, "Yes, I will do it."

"Good," Beowulf said. He dropped the monster's head and sat on a rock. "I will rest here for a while. I could use some sleep."

So it was that I returned to Hrothgar's fortress and told the king that I had searched for Beowulf to no avail. All that long morning and well past noon we waited in growing gloom. Unferth said confidently that the monster had killed Beowulf.

He was considerably disheartened when the hero of the Geats finally arrived—with the monster's shaggy head on his wounded shoulder.

That night the feasting at Heorot was without stint. The torches flamed, the mead flowed, the thanes sang praises of Beowulf and the women vied for his merest glance. Hrothgar's bard began to compose a saga. The king promised the British captives that they would be ransomed and returned to their dank, dreary island.

Only Unferth seemed unhappy, slinking in the shadows and glaring at me.

Queen Wealhtheow sat on her throne, smiling graciously at the uproarious celebration. Long past midnight, the king and queen left the mead hall. Warriors and even churls paired off with women and strolled off into the darkness.

At last timbered Heorot fell silent. The torches were extinguished. The hearth fire burned low. I was left alone, so I stretched out on the earthen floor next to the fading embers and willed myself to sleep.

I dreamed, yet it was not a dream. I was standing in another place, perhaps a different universe altogether. There was no ground, no sky, only a silver glow like moonlight that pervaded everything. Wealhtheow stood before me, but now she wore a form-fitting outfit of glittering silver metal. A warrior goddess, she was.

"You did well, Orion," she said in a low voice.

"Thank you."

"Your wounds?"

"They are already healing," I said.

"Yes, accelerated self-repair was built into you."

I wanted to reach out and take her in my arms, but I could not.

Instead, I asked, "Can we be together now?"

In the deepest recess of my memory I recalled a time, a lovely woodland filled with tame, graceful animals that we called Paradise, when we were together and happy. The other Creators, especially the jealous Aten, had torn her away from me.

"Not yet, my love," she said, with a sadness in her eyes that matched my own despair. "Not yet."

"At least, can I know why I was sent to Heorot? Why was it important to slay those beasts?"

"To save the British captives, of course."

That surprised me. "The captives? Those pimply-faced youngsters and that emaciated old man?"

She smiled knowingly. "One of those pimply-faced youngsters is the son of a Roman who stayed behind after the legions left Britain. His name is Artorius."

I shrugged. It made no sense to me.

"He will be important one day. A light against the darkness." She reached out her hand to me. "The sword you found in the cave. Please give it to me."

Puzzled, I detached the scabbarded sword from my belt and handed it to her. She slowly drew out the blade, examined the inscription on it, and smiled.

"Yes," she said in a whisper, "he will need this later on."

I read the one word inscribed on the matchless steel blade.

Excalibur.

Introduction to
"The Café Coup"
❖

This tale also deals with time travel, and the intriguing question of whether history could be changed by time travelers.

One of the standard arguments against the possibility of time travel is that if time travel actually existed, time travelers would be deliberately or accidentally changing history. Since we have not seen our history changing, time travel has not happened. If it hasn't happened yet, it never will. QED.

But if time travelers were altering history, would we notice? Or would our history books and even our memories be changed each time a time traveler finagled with our past?

Leaving aside such philosophical speculations, this story originated in a panel discussion of time travel at a science-fiction convention. It occurred to me during the panel's discussion of time-travel stories that while many, many tales have been written about a world in which Nazi Germany won World War II, no one that I know of has tackled the idea of having Imperial Germany win World War I.

The Kaiser's Germany actually came very close to winning the First World War. It was the intervention of the United States, brought about by U-boat sinkings of ships with Americans aboard them, that turned the tide against Germany.

Prevent the sinking of the Lusitania, I reasoned, and Germany could win World War I. In a victorious Germany, Hitler would never have risen to power. No Hitler, no World War II. No Holocaust. No Hiroshima.

Maybe.

THE CAFÉ COUP

Paris was not friendly to Americans in the soft springtime of 1922. The French didn't care much for the English, either, and they hated the victorious Germans, of course.

I couldn't blame them very much. The Great War had been over for more than three years, yet Paris had still not recovered its gaiety, its light and color, despite the hordes of boisterous German tourists who spent so freely on the boulevards. More likely, because of them.

I sat in one of the crowded sidewalk cafés beneath a splendid warm sun, waiting for my lovely wife to show up. Because of all the Germans, I was forced to share my minuscule round table with a tall, gaunt Frenchman who looked me over with suspicious eyes.

"You are an American?" he asked, looking down his prominent nose at me. His accent was worse than mine, certainly not Parisian.

"No," I answered truthfully. Then I lied, "I'm from New Zealand." It was as far away in distance as my real birthplace was in time.

"Ah," he said with an exhalation of breath that was somewhere between a sigh and a snort. "Your countrymen fought well at Gallipoli. Were you there?"

"No," I said. "I was too young."

That apparently puzzled him. Obviously I was of an age to fight in the Great War. But in fact, I hadn't been born when the British Empire troops were decimated at Gallipoli. I hadn't been born in the twentieth century at all.

"Were you in the war?" I asked needlessly.

"But certainly. To the very last moment I fought the Boche."

"It was a great tragedy."

"The Americans betrayed us," he muttered.

My brows rose a few millimeters. He was quite tall for a Frenchman, but painfully thin. Half-starved. Even his eyes looked hungry. The inflation, of course. It cost a basketful of francs, literally, to buy a loaf of bread. I wondered how he could afford the price of an aperitif. Despite the warm afternoon he had wrapped himself in a shabby old leather coat, worn shiny at the elbows.

From what I could see there were hardly any Frenchmen in the café, mostly raucous Germans roaring with laughter and heartily pounding on the little tables as they bellowed for more beer. To my amazement, the waiters had learned to speak German.

"Wilson," my companion continued bitterly. "He had the gall to speak of Lafayette."

"I thought that the American president was the one who arranged the armistice."

"Yes, with his fourteen points. Fourteen daggers plunged into the heart of France."

"Really?"

"The Americans should have entered the war on our side! Instead they sat idly by and watched us bleed to death while their bankers extorted every gram of gold we possessed."

"But the Americans had no reason to go to war," I protested mildly.

"France needed them! When their pitiful little colonies rebelled against the British lion, France was the only nation to come to their aid. They owe their existence to France, yet when we needed them they turned their backs on us."

That was largely my fault, although he didn't know it. I averted the sinking of the *Lusitania* by the German U-boat. It took enormous energies, but my darling wife arranged it so that the *Lusitania* was crawling along at a mere five knots that fateful morning. I convinced Lieutenant Walther Schwieger, skipper of the *U-20*, that it was safe enough to surface and hold the British liner captive with the deck gun while a boarding party searched for the ammunition that I knew the English had stored aboard her.

The entire affair was handled with great tact and honor. No shots were fired, no lives were lost, and the 123 American passengers arrived safely in Liverpool with glowing stories of how correct, how chivalrous, the German U-boat sailors had been. America remained neutral throughout the Great War. Indeed, a good deal of anti-British sentiment swept the United States, especially the Midwest, when their newspapers reported that the British were transporting military contraband in secret and thus risking the lives of American passengers.

"Well," I said, beckoning to the waiter for two more Pernods, "the war is over, and we must face the future as best we can."

"Yes," said my companion gloomily. "I agree."

One group of burly Germans was being particularly obnoxious, singing bawdy songs as they waved their beer glasses to and fro, slopping the foaming beer on themselves and their neighboring tables. No one complained. No one dared to say a word. The German army still occupied much of France.

My companion's face was white with fury. Yet even he restrained himself. But I noticed that he glanced at the watch on his wrist every few moments, as if he were expecting someone. Or something.

If anyone had betrayed France, it was me. The world that I had been born into was a cesspool of violence and hate, crumbling into tribal savagery all across the globe. Only a few oases of safety existed, tucked in remote areas far from the filthy, disease-ridden cities and the swarms of ignorant, vicious monsters who raped and murdered until they themselves were raped and murdered.

Once they discovered our solar-powered city, tucked high in the Sierra Oriental, I knew that the end was near. Stupidly, they attacked us, like a wild barbarian horde. We slaughtered them with laser beams and heat-seeking bullets. Instead of driving them away, that only whetted their appetite.

Their survivors lay siege to our mountaintop. We

laughed, at first, to think their pitiful handful of ragged ignoramuses could overcome our walled city, with its high-tech weaponry and endless energy from the sun. Yet somehow they spread the word to others of their kind. Day after day we watched their numbers grow, a tattered, threadbare pack of rats surrounding us, watching, waiting until their numbers were so huge they could swarm us under despite our weapons.

They were united in their bloodlust and their greed. They saw loot and power on our mountaintop, and they wanted both. At night I could see their campfires down below us, like the red eyes of rats watching and waiting.

Our council was divided. Some urged that we sally out against the besiegers, attack them and drive them away. But it was already too late for that. Their numbers were far too large, and even if we drove them away, they would return, now that they knew we existed.

Others wanted to flee into space, to leave Earth altogether and build colonies off the planet. We had the technology to build and maintain the solar-power satellites, they pointed out. It was only one technological step farther to build habitats in space.

But when we put the numbers through a computer analysis, it showed that to build a habitat large enough to house us all permanently would be beyond our current resources—and we could not enlarge our resource base as long as we were encircled by the barbarians.

I had worked on the time translator since my student days. It took enormous energy to move objects through time, far too much for all of us to escape that way. Yet I saw a possibility of hope.

If I could find a nexus, a pivotal point in time, perhaps I could change the world. Perhaps I could alter events to such an extent that this miserable world of terror and pain would dissolve, disappear, and a better world replace it. I became obsessed with the possibility.

"But you'll destroy *this* world," my wife gasped, shocked when I finally told her of my scheme.

"What of it?" I snapped. "Is this world so delightful that you want it to continue?"

She sank wearily onto the lab bench. "What will happen to our families? Our friends? What will happen to us?"

"You and I will make the translation. We will live in an earlier, better time."

"And the others?"

I shrugged. "I don't know. The mathematics isn't clear. But even if they disappear, the world that replaces them in this time will be better than the world we're in now."

"Do you really think so?"

"We'll *make* it better!"

The fools on the council disagreed, naturally. No one had translated through time, they pointed out. The energy even for a preliminary experiment would be prohibitively high. We needed that energy for our weapons.

None of them believed I could change a thing. They weren't afraid that they would be erased from existence, their world line snuffed out like a candle flame. No, in their blind ignorance they insisted that an attempt at time translation would consume so much energy that we would be left defenseless against the besieging savages outside our walls.

"The savages will no longer exist," I told them. "*None* of this world line will exist, once I've made the proper change in the geodesic."

They voted me down. They would rather face the barbarians than give up their existence, even if it meant a better world would replace the one they knew.

I accepted their judgment outwardly. Inwardly I became the most passionate student of history of all time. Feverishly I searched the books and tapes, seeking the nexus, the turning point, the place where I could make the world change for the better. I knew I had only a few months; the savage horde below our mountaintop was growing and stirring. I could hear their murmuring dirge of hate even through the walls of my laboratory, like the growls of a pack of wild beasts. Every day it grew louder, more insistent.

It was the war in the middle of the twentieth century that started the world's descent into madness. A man called Adolph Hitler escalated the horror of war to new levels of inhumanity. Not only did he deliberately murder millions of civilian men, women and children; he destroyed his own country, screaming with his last breath that the Aryan race deserved to be wiped out if they could not conquer the world.

When I first realized the enormity of Hitler's rage I sat stunned for an entire day. Here was the model, the prototype, for the brutal, cruel, ruthless, sadistic monsters who ranged my world seeking blood.

Before Hitler, war was a senseless affront to civilized men and women. Soldiers were tolerated, at best; often despised. They were usually shunned in polite society. After Hitler, war was commonplace, genocide routine, nuclear weapons valued for the megadeaths they could generate.

Hitler and all he stood for was the edge of the precipice, the first terrible step into the abyss that my world had plunged into. If I could prevent Hitler from coming to power, perhaps prevent him from ever being born, I might save my world—or at least erase it and replace it with a better one.

For days on end I thought of how I might translate back in time to kill this madman or even prevent his birth. Slowly, however, I began to realize that this single man was not the cause of it all. If Hitler had never been born, someone else would have arisen in Germany after the Great War, someone else would have unified the German people in a lust for revenge against those who had betrayed and defeated them, someone else would have preached Aryan purity and hatred of all other races, someone else would have plunged civilization into World War II.

To solve the problem of Hitler I had to go to the root causes of the Nazi program: Germany's defeat in the First World War, the war that was called the Great War by those who had lived through it. I had to make Germany win that war.

If Germany had won World War I, there would have been no humiliation of the German people, no thirst for revenge, no economic collapse. Hitler would still exist, but he would be a retired soldier, perhaps a peaceful painter or even a minor functionary in the Kaiser's government. There would be no World War II.

And so I set my plans to make Germany the victor

in the Great War, with the reluctant help of my dear wife.

"You would defy the council?" she asked me, shocked when I revealed my determination to her.

"Only if you help me," I said. "I won't go unless you go with me."

She fully understood that we would never be able to return to our own world. To do so, we would have to bring the components for a translator with us and then assemble it in the early twentieth century. Even if we could do that, where would we find a power source in those primitive years? They were still using horses then.

Besides, our world would be gone, vanished, erased from space-time.

"We'll live out our lives in the twentieth century," I told her. "And we'll know that our own time will be far better than it is now."

"How can you be sure it will be better?" she asked me softly.

I smiled patiently. "There will be no World War II. Europe will be peaceful for the rest of the century. Commerce and art will flourish. Even the Russian communists will join the European federation peacefully, toward the end of the century."

"You're certain?"

"I've run the analysis on the master computer a dozen times. I'm absolutely certain."

"And our own time will be better?"

"It has to be. How could it possibly be worse?"

She nodded, her beautiful face solemn with the understanding that we were leaving our world forever. Good riddance to it, I thought. But it was the only world we had ever known, and she was not happy to deliberately toss it away and spend the rest of her life in the a bygone century.

Still, she never hesitated about coming with me. I wouldn't go without her, she knew that. And I knew that she wouldn't let me go unless she came with me.

"It's really quite romantic, isn't it?" she asked me, the night before we left.

"What is?"

"Translating across time together. Our love will span the centuries."

I held her close. "Yes. Across the centuries."

Before sunrise the next morning we stole into the laboratory and powered up the translator. No one was on guard, no one was there to try to stop us. The council members were all sleeping, totally unaware that one of their loyal citizens was about to defy their decision. There were no renegades among us, no rebels. We had always accepted the council's decisions and worked together for our mutual survival.

Until now. My wife silently took her place on the translator's focal stage while I made the final adjustments to the controls. She looked radiant standing there, her face grave, her golden hair glowing against the darkened laboratory shadows.

At last I stepped up beside her. I took her hand; it was cold with anxiety. I squeezed her hand confidently.

"We're going to make a better world," I whispered to her.

The last thing I saw was the pink glow of dawn rising over the eastern mountains, framed in the lab's only window.

Now, in the Paris of 1922 that I had created, victorious Germany ruled Europe with strict but civilized authority. The Kaiser had been quite lenient with Great Britain; after all, was he not related by blood to the British king? Even France got off relatively lightly, far more lightly than the unlucky Russians. Germany kept Alsace-Lorraine, of course, but took no other territory.

France's punishment was mainly financial: Germany demanded huge, crippling reparations. The real humiliation was that France was forced to disarm. The proud French army was reduced to a few regiments and forbidden modern armaments such as tanks and airplanes. The Parisian police force was better equipped.

My companion glanced at his watch again. It was the type that the army had issued to its officers, I saw.

"Could you tell me the time?" I asked, over the drunken singing of the German tourists. My wife was late, and that was quite unlike her.

He paid no attention to me. Staring furiously at the Germans who surrounded us, he suddenly shot to his feet and shouted, "Men of France! How long shall we endure this humiliation?"

He was so tall and lean that he looked like a human Eiffel Tower standing among the crowded sidewalk tables. He had a pistol in his hand. One of the waiters was so surprised by his outburst that he dropped his tray. It clattered to the pavement with a crash of shattered glassware.

But others were not surprised, I saw. More than a dozen men leaped up and shouted, "*Vive La France!*" They were all dressed in old army uniforms, as was my companion, beneath his frayed leather coat. They were all armed, a few of them even had rifles.

Absolute silence reigned. The Germans stared, dumbfounded. The waiters froze in their tracks. I certainly didn't know what to say or do. My only thought was of my beautiful wife; where was she, why was she late, was there some sort of insurrection going on? Was she safe?

"Follow me!" said the tall Frenchman to his armed compatriots. Despite every instinct in me, I struggled to my feet and went along with them.

From cafés on both sides of the wide boulevard armed men were striding purposefully toward their leader. He marched straight ahead, right down the middle of the street, looking neither to the right nor left. They formed up behind him, some two or three dozen men.

Breathlessly, I followed along.

"To the Elysée!" shouted the tall one, striding determinedly on his long legs, never glancing back to see if the others were following him.

Then I saw my wife pushing through the curious onlookers thronging the sidewalks. I called to her, and she ran to me, blond and slim and more lovely than anyone in all of space-time.

"What is it?" she asked, as breathless as I. "What's happening?"

"Some sort of coup, I think."

"They have guns!"

"Yes."

"We should get inside. If there's shooting—"

"No, we'll be all right," I said. "I want to see what's going to happen."

It was a coup, all right. But it failed miserably.

Apparently the tall one, a fanatical ex-major named de Gaulle, believed that his little band of followers could capture the government. He depended on a certain General Pétain, who had the prestige and authority that de Gaul himself lacked.

Pétain lost his nerve at the critical moment, however, and abandoned the coup. The police and a detachment of army troops were waiting for the rebels at the Petit Palace; a few shots were exchanged. Before the smoke had drifted away the rebels had scattered, and de Gaulle himself was taken into custody.

"He will be charged with treason, I imagine," I said to my darling wife as we sat that evening at the very same sidewalk café. The very same table, in fact.

"I doubt that they'll give him more than a slap on the wrist," she said. "He seems to be a hero to everyone in Paris."

"Not to the Germans," I said.

She smiled at me. "The Germans take him as a joke." She understood German perfectly and could eavesdrop on their shouted conversations quite easily.

"He is no joke."

We both turned to the dark little man sitting at the next table; we were packed in so close that his chair almost touched mine. He was a particularly ugly man, with lank black hair and the swarthy face of a born conspirator. His eyes were small, reptilian, and his upper lip was twisted by a curving scar.

"Charles de Gaulle will be the savior of France," he said. He was absolutely serious. Grim, even.

"If he's not guillotined for treason," I replied lightly. Yet inwardly I began to tremble.

"You were here. You saw how he rallied the men of France."

"All two dozen of them," I quipped.

He looked at me with angry eyes. "Next time it will be different. We will not rely on cowards and turncoats like Pétain. Next time we will take the government and bring all of France under his leadership. Then . . ."

He hesitated, glancing around as if the police might be listening.

"Then?" my wife coaxed.

He lowered his voice. "Then revenge on Germany and all those who betrayed us."

"You can't be serious."

"You'll see. Next time we will win. Next time we will have all of France with us. And then all of Europe. And then, the world."

My jaw must have dropped open. It was all going to happen anyway. The French would rearm. Led by a ruthless, fanatical de Gaulle, they would plunge Europe into a second world war. All my efforts were for nothing. The world that we had left would continue to exist—or be even worse.

He turned his reptilian eyes to my lovely wife. Although many of the German women were blond, she was far more beautiful than any of them.

"You are Aryan?" he asked, his tone suddenly menacing.

She was nonplussed. "Aryan? I don't understand."

"Yes you do," he said, almost hissing the words. "Next time it will go hard on the Aryans. You'll see."

I sank my head in my hands and wept openly.

Introduction to "Re-Entry Shock"

Normally I write my stories from a male point of view. My protagonists are almost always men. Caucasian men, at that. Chet Kinsman. Keith Stoner, of the Voyagers novels. Jamie Waterman, the protagonist of Mars.

I have written about male characters who are black or Asian; Jamie Waterman is half-Navaho, although his Navaho heritage is pretty deeply submerged beneath his white Western upbringing. I have written about women characters, some of them quite strong enough to be the protagonists of their stories.

But I've always found it difficult to see women characters (or non-Caucasian male characters, for that matter) from the inside. That's what I need to be able to do, for my protagonists. I have to be able to get inside their heads, deep into their souls, to make them work as protagonists.

So when I started writing "Re-Entry Shock," the protagonist was male. And the story wasn't working. Something in my subconscious mind was resisting the story as I was trying to write it.

Then a very conscious thought struck me. The Magazine of Fantasy & Science Fiction, *the most literate market in the field, had just acquired a new editor: Kristine Kathryn Rusch. I knew Kristine slightly; she is a fellow writer, and practically every writer in the field knows every other writer, at least slightly. It occurred to the business side of my brain that Kris might prefer stories with women protagonists. H'mm.*

Purely as an exercise in writing—and marketing—I went back to "Re-Entry Shock" and changed the protagonist to a woman. To my somewhat surprised delight, Dolores Anna Maria Alvarez de Montoya stepped onto the center of the stage and took over the story as if she had been meant to be its protagonist from the beginning of time.

Which, of course, she had been.

RE-ENTRY SHOCK

❖

"The tests are for your own protection," he said. "Surely you can understand that."

"I can understand that you are trying to prevent me from returning to my home," Dolores flared angrily. And immediately regretted her outburst. It would do her no good to lose her temper with this little man.

The two of them were sitting in a low-ceilinged windowless room that might have been anywhere on Earth or the Moon. In fact, it was on the space station that served as the major transfer point for those few special people allowed to travel from the Moon to Earth or vice versa.

"It's nothing personal," the interviewer said, looking at the display screen on his desk instead of at Dolores. "We simply cannot allow someone to return just because they announce that they want to."

"So you say," she replied.

"The tests are for your own protection," he repeated, weakly.

"Yes. Of course." She had been through the whole grueling routine for more than a week now. "I have passed all the tests. I can handle the gravity. The difference in air pressure. I am not carrying any diseases. There is no physical reason to keep me from returning."

"But you've been away nearly ten years. The cultural shock, the readjustment—the psychological problems often outweigh the physical ones. It's not simply a matter of buying a return ticket and boarding a shuttle."

"I know. I have been told time and again that it is a privilege, not a right."

The interviewer lifted his eyes from his display screen and looked directly at her for the first time. "Are you absolutely certain you want to do this?" he asked. "After ten years—are you willing to give up your whole life, your friends and all, just to come back?"

Dolores glanced at the nameplate on his desk. "Yes, Mr. Briem," she said icily. "That is precisely what I want to do."

"But why?"

Dolores Anna Maria Alvarez de Montoya leaned back in the spindly plastic chair. It creaked in complaint. She was a solidly built woman in her early forties, with a strong-boned deeply tanned face. Her dark straight hair, graying prematurely, was tied back in a single long braid. To the interviewer she looked exactly like what the computer files said she was: a journeyman construction worker with a questionable political background. A problem.

"I want to be able to breathe freely again," Dolores answered slowly. "I've lived like an ant in a hive long enough. Hemmed in by their laws and regulations. People weren't meant to live like that. I want to come back home."

For a long moment the interviewer stared at Dolores, his Nordic blue eyes locked on her deep onyx pools. Then he turned back toward the display screen on his desk as if he could see more of her through her records than by watching the woman herself.

"You say 'home.' You've been away nearly ten years."

"It is still my home," Dolores said firmly. "I was born there. My roots are there."

"Your son is there."

She had expected that. Yet she still drew in her breath at the pain. "Yes," she conceded. "My son is there."

"You left of your own volition. You declared that you never wanted to come back. You renounced your citizenship."

"That was ten years ago."

"You've changed your mind—after ten years."

"I was very foolish then. I was under great emotional stress. A divorce . . ." She let her voice trail off. She did not mention the fierce political passions that had burned within her back in those days.

"Yes," said the interviewer. "Very foolish."

C. Briem: that was all his nameplate said. He did not seem to Dolores to be a really nasty man. Not very sympathetic, naturally. But not the totally cold inhuman kind of bureaucrat she had seen so often over the years. He was quite young, she thought, for a position of such power. Young and rather attractive, with hair the color of afternoon sunshine cropped short and neat. And good shoulders beneath his severely tailored one-piece suit. It was spotless white, of course. Dolores wore her one and only business suit, gray and shabby after all the years of hanging in closets or being folded in a tight travel bag. She had worn it only at the rallies and late-night meetings she had attended; fewer and fewer, as the years passed by.

Over the past week Dolores had gone through a dozen interviews like this one. And the complete battery of physical tests. This man behind the desk had the power to recommend that she be allowed to return to her home, or to keep her locked out and exiled from her roots, her memories, her only son.

"How old is your boy now?" he suddenly asked.

Startled, Dolores answered, "Eleven—no, he'll be twelve years old next month. I was hoping to get back in time to see him on his birthday."

"We really don't want any more immigrant laborers," he said, trying to make his voice hard but not quite able to do so.

"I am not an immigrant," Dolores replied firmly. "I am a native. And I am not a laborer. I am a fluid-systems technician."

"A plumber."

She smiled tolerantly. "A plumber who works on fusion-power plants. They require excellent piping and welding. I run the machines that do such work. It is all in the dossier on your screen, I'm sure."

He conceded his point with a dip of his chin. "You've worked on fusion plants for all the ten years you were out there?"

"Most of the time. I did some work on solar-power systems as well. They also require excellent plumbing."

For long moments the interviewer said nothing, staring at the screen as if it would tell him what to do, which decision to make.

Finally he returned his gaze to Dolores. "I will have to consult the immigration board, Ms. Alvarez. You will have to wait for their decision."

"How long will that take?"

He blinked his blue eyes once, twice. "A day or so. Perhaps longer."

"Then I must remain aboard this station until they decide?"

"Of course. Your expenses will be paid by the government on its regular per diem allowance."

Dolores felt her nostrils flare. Government per diem allowances did not come anywhere near the prices charged by the station's restaurants or the hotel. And it usually took months for any government to honor the expense reports that per diem people sent in.

She got to her feet. "I hope it will be a quick decision, then."

The interviewer remained seated, but seemed to thaw just a bit. "No, Ms. Alvarez. Hope for a slow decision. The more time they take to make up their minds, the better your chances."

Dolores murmured, "Like a jury deciding a person's life or death."

"Yes," he said sadly. "Very much like that."

Dolores drifted through the rest of the day, walking through the long sloping passageways of the circular station, heading away from the administrative offices with their impersonal interviewers and computerized records of a woman's entire life.

Do they know? she asked himself silently. Do they suspect why I want to return? Of course they must have records of my old political activities, but do they know what I am trying to accomplish now?

Even when the three lunar colonies had united in declaring their independence from the World Government the separation between the peoples of Earth and those living in space had never been total. Governments might rage and threaten, corporations might cut off entire colonies from desperately needed trade, but still a trickle of people made it from space back to Mother Earth. And vice versa. The journey was often painful and always mired in red tape, but as far as Dolores knew no one had ever been flatly denied permission to go home again.

Until now.

The other people striding along the wide passageways were mostly administrative staff personnel who wore one-piece jumpsuits, as had the handsome young Mr. Briem. White, sky-blue, fire-engine red, grassy green, their colors denoted the wearers' jobs. But as Dolores neared the area where the tourist shops and restaurants were located, the people around her changed.

The tourists dressed with far more variety: men in brilliantly colored running suits or conservative business outfits such as Dolores herself wore; the younger women showing bare midriffs, long shapely legs glossy with the sheen of hosiery, startling makeup and hairdos.

The space station was huge, massive, like a small city in orbit. As she strolled aimlessly along its passageways Dolores realized that the station had grown in the ten years since she had last seen it. It was like Samarkand or Damascus or any of those other ancient cities along the old caravan trails: a center of commerce and trade, even tourism. Surely the restrictions against returning home were easier now than they had been ten years before.

Then she realized that these tourists were aboard a space station that orbited a mere five hundred kilometers above Earth's surface. They would not be allowed to go to the Moon or to one of the O'Neil habitats. They were flatlanders on vacation. And there were almost no lunar citizens or residents of O'Neil communities here in this station. At least, none that she could identify.

She caught a glance of the Earth hanging outside one of the rare windows along the passageway, huge and blue and glowing with beauty. Five hundred kilometers away. Only five hundred kilometers.

As the station swung in its stately rotation the view of Earth passed out of sight. Dolores saw the distant Moon hanging against the black background of deep space. Then even that passed, and there was nothing to see but the infinite emptiness.

Will they find out? Dolores wondered. Is there something in my record, something I might have said during the interviews, some tiny hint, that will betray me?

She stopped in mid-stride, almost stumbled as a sudden bolt of electrical surprise flashed through her. Hector Luis! Her son!

But then she saw that it was merely a curly-haired boy of ten or twelve, a stranger walking with his trusting hand firmly in the grasp of a man who must have been his father. Dolores watched them pass by without so much as a flicker of a glance at her. As if she were not there in the corridor with them. As if she did not exist.

The last hologram she had seen of her son had been more than a year ago. The boy walking past looked nothing like Hector Luis, really. The same height maybe. Not even a similar build.

You are becoming maudlin, she chided herself.

She realized that she was in the midst of the shopping area. Store windows stretched on both sides of the passageway, merchandise of all sorts glittered brightly in the attractive displays. Maybe I can find something for Hector Luis, she thought. Maybe if I buy a gift for him it will impress the immigration board. She had no doubt that they were watching her. Yet she felt slightly ashamed of her thought, using her son as a tool to pry open the board members' hearts.

She window-shopped until she lost track of the time. The more she gazed at the lush variety of merchandise the more confused she became. What would a twelve-year-old boy like? What does her son like? She had no idea.

Finally her stomach told her that she had missed lunch and it was almost time for supper. There were restaurants further up the corridor. Dolores frowned inwardly: the government's munificent per diem allowance might just cover the price of a beer.

With a shrug she moved through the meandering tourists and headed for a meal she could barely afford. She studied the menus displayed on the electronic screens outside each of the four restaurants, then entered the least expensive.

She hardly felt any surprise at all when she saw that Mr. Briem was already seated at a table by the window, alone. Yes, they are certainly watching me.

He saw Dolores as she approached his table.

"*Buenas tardes*, Mr. Briem," she said, with a gracious nod of her head.

"Ms. Alvarez!" He scrambled to his feet and pretended to be surprised. "Would you care to join me? I just came in here a few moments ago."

"I would be very happy to. It is very lonely to eat by one's self."

"Yes," he said. "It is."

Dolores sat across the little square table from him, and they studied the menu screen for a few moments. She grimaced at the prices, but Briem did not seem to notice.

They tapped out their orders on the keyboard. Then Dolores asked politely, "Do you come here often?"

He made a small shrug. "When I get tired of my own cooking. Often enough."

A young woman walked up to the table, petite, oriental-looking. "Hi, Cal. A little early for you, isn't it?"

"I'm going to the concert tonight," he answered quickly.

"Oh so?" The woman glanced at Dolores, then turned her eyes back to him. "Me too."

"I'll see you there, then."

"Good. Maybe we can have dessert or coffee together afterward."

Briem nodded and smiled. It was an innocent smile, Dolores thought. It almost made her believe that he truly was in this restaurant because he was going to a concert later in the evening and the young oriental was not an agent of the immigration department or a bodyguard assigned to watch over him while he dealt with this would-be infiltrator.

"Your first name is Calvin?" Dolores asked.

"Calvert," he replied. "I prefer Cal. It sounds less like an old British mystery story."

"I am called Dolores. My especial friends call me Dee."

His smile came back, warmer this time. The robot rolled up to their table with their trays of dinner on its flat top. They started to eat.

"I was thinking of buying my son a present," Dolores said, "but I don't know what to get him. What are twelve-year-old boys interested in these days?"

"I really don't know."

"There is so much in the store windows! It's rather overwhelming."

"You haven't gone shopping for a while?"

"Not for a long time. Where I was, there were no stores. Not gift stores. I suppose I have missed a lot of things in the past ten years."

They fell silent for a few moments. Dolores turned her attention to her broth. It was thin and delicately flavored, not like the rich heavy soups she was accustomed to.

"Ms. Alvarez—"

"Dolores."

"Dolores, then." Cal Briem looked troubled. "I suppose I shouldn't bring up the subject. It's none of my affair, really . . ."

"What is it?"

"Your political activities."

"Ah." She had known it would come up sooner

or later. At least he was bringing it out into the open.

"You were quite an activist in your younger days. But over the past few years you seem to have stopped."

"I have grown older."

He looked at her, *really* looked at her, for a long silent moment.

"I can't accept the idea that you've given up your beliefs," he said at last.

"I was never a radical. I never advocated violence. During the times of the great labor unrest I served as a mediator more than once."

"We know. It's in your record."

She put down her spoon, tired of the whole charade. "Then my political beliefs are going to be counted against me, aren't they?"

"They don't help," he said softly.

"You are going to prevent me from returning home because my political position is not acceptable to you."

"Did you marry again?" He changed the subject. "We have no record of it if you did."

"No. I did not marry again."

"For ten years you've remained unmarried?"

She recognized the unvoiced question. "After the terrible mess of my first marriage, I never allowed myself to become so attached to someone that he could cause me pain."

"I see," he said.

"Besides," Dolores added, "where I was, out on the construction jobs, there were not that many men who were both eligible and attractive."

"I find that hard to believe."

"Believe it," she said fervently.

"Your political activities broke up your marriage, didn't they?"

She fought an urge to laugh. Raoul's father owned half of the solar system's largest construction firm. "They did not help to cement us together, no," she said.

"Have you given up your political activities altogether?" he asked, his voice trembling slightly.

Dolores spooned up another sip of broth before answering. "Yes," she half lied. "But I still have my beliefs."

"Of course."

They finished the brief meal in virtual silence. When their bills appeared on the table's display screen Briem gently pushed Dolores's hand aside and tapped his own number on the keyboard.

"Let the immigration board pay for this," he said, smiling shyly. "They can afford it better than you."

"*Muchas gracias,*" said Dolores. But inwardly she asked herself, Why is he doing this? What advantage does he expect to gain?

"Would you like to go to the concert?" he asked as they got up from the table.

Dolores thought a moment. Then, "No, I think not. Thank you anyway. I appreciate your kindness."

As they walked out into the broad passageway again, Briem said, "Your son's been living all this time with his father, hasn't he?"

Again she felt the stab of pain. And anger. What is he trying to do to me? Dolores raged inwardly. "I don't think you have any right to probe into my personal affairs," she snapped.

His face went red. "Oh, I didn't mean—I was only

trying to be helpful. You had asked about what the boy might be interested in . . ."

The anger drained out of her as quickly as it had risen. "I'm sorry. I have always been too quick to lose my temper."

"It's understandable," Briem said.

"One would think that at my age I would have learned better self-control."

"*De nada*," he said, with an atrocious accent.

But she smiled at his attempt to defuse the situation. Then she caught a view of Earth again in the window across the passageway. Dolores headed toward it like a woman lured by a lover, like a sliver of iron pulled by a magnet.

Briem walked beside her. "I really should be getting to the auditorium. The concert."

"Yes," Dolores muttered, staring at the glowing blue-and-white panorama parading before her eyes. "Of course."

He grasped her sleeve, forcing her to tear her eyes away and look at him.

"Tell me what you learned in the ten years you were away," he said, suddenly urgent. "Tell me the most important thing you've learned."

She blinked at the fervor in his voice, the intensity of his expression. "The most important?"

"I know you still have a political agenda. You haven't given up all your hopes, your ideals. But what did the past ten years teach you?"

Dolores put aside all pretense. She knew she was ending all her hopes for returning home, killing her only chance to see her son once again. But she told him anyway, without evasion, without pretense.

"They need us. They cannot survive without us.

Nor can we truly survive without them. This enforced separation is killing us both."

Strangely, Briem smiled. "They need us," he echoed. "And we need them."

Dolores nodded dumbly, her eyes drawn back to the gleaming beckoning sprawl of the world she had left.

"We've changed, too," Briem said softly, almost in a whisper. "Some of us have, at least. There are a few of us who realize that we can't remain separated. A few of us who believe exactly what you believe."

"Can that be true?"

"Yes," he said. "The human race must not remain separated into the wealthy few who live in space and the impoverished billions on Earth. That way is worse than madness. It's evil."

"You know what I want to do, then. You have known it all along."

"I suspected it," said Briem. "And I'm glad that my suspicions were correct. We need people like you: people who've been there and can convince the government and the voters that we *must* reestablish strong ties with our brothers and sisters."

Dolores felt giddy, almost faint. "Then you will recommend—"

"I'm the chairman of the immigration board," Briem revealed. "Your application for return will be approved, I promise you."

Her thoughts tumbled dizzyingly in her mind, but the one that stood out most powerfully was that she would see her son again. I will see Hector Luis! I will hold him in my arms!

"Now I've really got to get to that concert," Briem

said. "I'm playing second keyboard tonight."

"Yes," Dolores said vaguely. "I am sorry to have kept you."

He flashed her a smile and dashed off down the passageway.

"And thank you!" Dolores called after him.

Then she turned back to the window. Five hundred kilometers away was the Earth she had left only a week ago. The Earth on which she had spent ten years, working in their filthy choked cities, living among the helpless and the hopeless, trying to change their world, to make their lives better, learning day by painful day that they could not long survive without the wealth, the knowledge, the skills that the space communities had denied them.

The Earth slid from her view and she saw the Moon once again, clean and cool, distant yet reachable. She would return to the world of her birth, she realized. She would work with all the passion and strength in her to make them understand the debt they owed to the people of Earth. She would reunite the severed family of humankind.

And she would see her son and make him understand that despite everything she loved him. Perhaps she would even reunite her own severed family.

Dolores smiled to herself. She was dreaming impossible dreams and she knew it. But without the dreams, she also knew, there can be no reality.

Introduction to
"In Trust"

This is one of those rare stories whose origin can be pinpointed with great exactitude.

My wife, Barbara, and I were having dinner with Dianne and Michael Bienes, two of the most gracious people in the world. Michael is a reader of science fiction, and—like many SF aficionados—enjoys intellectual puzzles.

He asked if I would want to have my body frozen after clinical death, in the hopes that sometime in the future medical science might learn how to cure whatever it was that killed me and bring me back to life. I said yes.

Then he asked who I could trust to watch over my frozen body for all the years—maybe centuries—it would take before I could be successfully revived. That started a lively conversation about insurance companies and social institutions.

By the time dessert was being served we had agreed that there was only one institution we could think of that had the "staying power" and the reputation for integrity that would lead us to trust our frozen bodies to it.

"Now why don't you write a story about it?" Michael prompted.

So I did.

159

IN TRUST

❖

Trust was not a virtue that came easily to Jason Manning.

He had clawed his way to the top of the multi-national corporate ladder mainly by refusing to trust anyone: not his business associates, not his rivals or many enemies, not his so-called friends, not any one of his wives and certainly none of his mistresses.

"Trust nobody," his sainted father had told him since childhood, so often that Jason could never remember when the old man had first said it to him.

Jason followed his father's advice so well that by the time he was forty years old he was one of the twelve wealthiest men in America. He had capped his rise to fortune by deposing his father as CEO of the corporation the old man had founded. Dad had looked deathly surprised when Jason pushed him out of his own company. He had foolishly trusted his own son.

So Jason was in a considerable quandary when it finally sank in on him, almost ten years later, that he was about to die.

He did not trust his personal physician's diagnosis, of course. Pancreatic cancer. He couldn't have pancreatic cancer. That's the kind of terrible retribution that nature plays on you when you haven't taken care of your body properly. Jason had never smoked, drank rarely and then only moderately, and since childhood he had eaten his broccoli and all the other healthful foods his mother had set before him. All his adult life he had followed a strict regimen of high fiber, low fat, and aerobic exercise.

"I want a second opinion!" Jason had snapped at his physician.

"Of course," said the sad-faced doctor. He gave Jason the name of the city's top oncologist.

Jason did not trust that recommendation. He sought his own expert.

"Pancreatic cancer," said the head of the city's most prestigious hospital, dolefully.

Jason snorted angrily and swept out of the woman's office, determined to cancel his generous annual contribution to the hospital's charity drive. He took on an alias, flew alone in coach class across the ocean, and had himself checked over by six other doctors in six other countries, never revealing to any of them who he truly was.

Pancreatic cancer.

"It becomes progressively more painful," one of the diagnosticians told him, his face a somber mask of professional concern.

Another warned, "Toward the end, even our best

analgesics become virtually useless." And he burst into tears, being an Italian.

Still another doctor, a kindly Swede, gave Jason the name of a suicide expert. "He can help you to ease your departure," said the doctor.

"I can't do that," Jason muttered, almost embarrassed. "I'm a Catholic."

The Swedish doctor sighed understandingly.

On the long flight back home Jason finally admitted to himself that he was indeed facing death, all that broccoli notwithstanding. For God's sake, he realized, I shouldn't even have trusted Mom! Her and her, "Eat all of it, Jace. It's good for you."

If there was one person in the entire universe that Jason came close to trusting, it was his brother, the priest. So, after spending the better part of a month making certain rather complicated arrangements, Jason had his chauffeur drive him up to the posh Boston suburb where Monsignor Michael Manning served as pastor of St. Raphael's.

Michael took the news somberly. "I guess that's what I can look forward to, then." Michael was five years younger than Jason, and had faithfully followed all his brother's childhood bouts with chicken pox, measles, and mumps. As a teenager he had even broken exactly the same bone in his leg as Jason had, five years after his big brother's accident, in the same way: sliding into third base on the same baseball field.

Jason leaned back in the bottle green leather armchair and stared into the crackling fireplace, noting as he did every time he visited his brother that Michael's priestly vow of poverty had not prevented him from living quite comfortably. The rectory was a marvelous old house, kept in tip-top condition by teams of devoted parishioners, and generously stocked by the local merchants with viands and all sorts of refreshments. On the coffee table between the two brothers rested a silver tray bearing delicate china cups and a fine English teapot filled with steaming herbal tea.

"There's nothing that can be done?" Michael asked, brotherly concern etched into his face.

"Not now," Jason said.

"How long ... ?"

"Maybe a hundred years, maybe even more."

Michael blinked with confusion. "A hundred years? What're you talking about, Jace?"

"Freezing."

"Freezing?"

"Freezing," Jason repeated. "I'm going to have myself frozen until medical science figures out how to cure pancreatic cancer. Then I'll have myself thawed out and take up my life again."

Michael sat up straighter in his chair. "You can't have yourself frozen, Jace. Not until you're dead."

"I'm not going to sit still and let the cancer kill me," Jason said, thinking of the pain. "I'm going to get a doctor to fix me an injection."

"But that'd be suicide! A mortal sin!"

"I won't be dead forever. Just until they learn how to cure my cancer."

There was fear in Michael's eyes. "Jace, listen to me. Taking a lethal injection is suicide."

"It's got to be done. They can't freeze me while I'm still alive. Even if they could, that would stop my heart just as completely as the injection would, and I'd be dead anyway."

"It's still suicide, Jace," Michael insisted, truly upset. "Holy Mother Church teaches—"

"Holy Mother Church is a couple of centuries behind the times," Jason grumbled. "It's not suicide. It's more like a long-term anesthetic."

"You'll be legally dead."

"But not morally dead," Jason insisted.

"Still . . ." Michael lapsed into silence, pressing his fingers together prayerfully.

"I'm not committing suicide," Jason tried to explain. "I'm just going to sleep for a while. I won't be committing any sin."

Michael had been his brother's confessor since he had been ordained. He had heard his share of sinning.

"You're treading a very fine line, Jace," the monsignor warned his brother.

"The Church has got to learn to deal with the modern world, Mike."

"Yes, perhaps. But I'm thinking of the legal aspects here. Your doctors will have to declare you legally dead, won't they?"

"It's pretty complicated. I have to give myself the injection; otherwise, the state can prosecute them for homicide."

"Your state allows assisted suicides, does it?" Michael asked darkly.

"Yes, even though you think it's a sin."

"It is a sin," Michael snapped. "That's not an opinion, that's a fact."

"The Church will change its stand on that, sooner or later," Jason said.

"Never!"

"It's got to! The Church can't lag behind the modern world forever, Mike. It's got to change."

"You can't change morality, Jace. What was true two thousand years ago is still true today."

Jason rubbed at the bridge of his nose. A headache was starting to throb behind his eyes, the way it always did when he and Michael argued.

"Mike, I didn't come here to fight with you."

The monsignor softened immediately. "I'm sorry, Jace. It's just that . . . you're running a terrible risk. Suppose you're never awakened? Suppose you finally die while you're frozen? Will God consider that you've committed suicide?"

Jason fell back on the retort that always saved him in arguments with his brother. "God's a lot smarter than either one of us, Mike."

Michael smiled ruefully. "Yes, I suppose He is."

"I'm going to do it, Mike. I'm not going to let myself die in agony if I can avoid it."

His brother conceded the matter with a resigned shrug. But then, suddenly, he sat up ramrod-straight again.

"What is it?" Jason asked.

"You'll be legally dead?" Michael asked.

"Yes. I told you—"

"Then your will can go to probate."

"No, I won't be . . ." Jason stared at his brother. "Oh my God!" he gasped. "My estate! I've got to make sure it's kept intact while I'm frozen."

Michael nodded firmly. "You don't want your money gobbled up while you're in the freezer. You'd wake up penniless."

"My children all have their own lawyers," Jason groaned. "My bankers. My ex-wives!"

Jason ran out of the rectory.

Although the doctors had assured him that it would take months before the pain really got severe, Jason could feel the cancer in his gut, growing and feeding on his healthy cells while he desperately tried to arrange his worldly goods so that no one could steal them while he lay frozen in a vat of liquid nitrogen.

His estate was vast. In his will he had left generous sums for each of his five children and each of his five former wives. Although they hated one another, Jason knew that the instant he was frozen they would unite in their greed to break his will and grab the rest of his fortune.

"I need that money," Jason told himself grimly. "I'm not going to wake up penniless a hundred years or so from now."

His corporate legal staff suggested that they hire a firm of estate specialists. The estate specialists told him they needed the advice of the best constitutional lawyers in Washington.

"This is a matter that will inevitably come up before the Supreme Court," the top constitutional lawyer told him. "I mean, we're talking about the legal definition of death here."

"Maybe I shouldn't have myself frozen until the legal definition of death is settled," Jason told him.

The top constitutional lawyer shrugged his expensively clad shoulders. "Then you'd better be prepared to hang around for another ten years or so. These things take time, you know."

Jason did not have ten months, let alone ten years. He gritted his teeth and went ahead with his plans for freezing, while telling his lawyers he wanted his last will and testament made iron-clad, foolproof, unbreakable.

They shook their heads in unison, all eight of them, their faces sad as hounds with toothaches.

"There's no such thing as an unbreakable will," the eldest of the lawyers warned Jason. "if your putative heirs have the time—"

"And the money," said one of the younger attorneys.

"Or the prospect of money," added a still younger one.

"Then they stand a good chance of eventually breaking your will."

Jason growled at them.

Inevitably, the word of his illness and of his plan to freeze himself leaked out beyond the confines of his executive suite. After all, no one could be trusted to keep such momentous news a secret. Rumors began to circulate up and down Wall Street. Reporters began sniffing around.

Jason realized that his secret was out in the open when a delegation of bankers invited him to lunch. They were fat, sleek-headed men, such as sleep of nights, yet they looked clearly worried as Jason sat down with them in the oak-panelled private dining room of their exclusive downtown club.

"Is it true?" blurted the youngest of the group. "Are you dying?"

The others around the circular table all feigned embarrassment but leaned forward eagerly to hear Jason's reply.

He spoke bluntly and truthfully to them.

The oldest of the bankers, a lantern-jawed white-haired woman of stern visage, was equally blunt.

"Your various corporations owe our various banks several billions of dollars, Jason."

"That's business," he replied. "Banks loan billions to corporations all the time. Why are you worried?"

"It's the uncertainty of it all!" blurted the youngest one again. "Are you going to be dead or aren't you?"

"I'll be dead for a while," he answered, "but that will be merely a legal fiction. I'll be back."

"Yes," grumbled one of the older bankers. "But when?"

With a shrug, Jason replied, "That, I can't tell you. I don't know."

"And what happens to your corporations in the meantime?"

"What happens to our outstanding loans?"

Jason saw what was in their eyes. Foreclosure. Demand immediate payment. Take possession of the corporate assets and sell them off. The banks would make a handsome profit, and his enemies would gleefully carve up his corporate empire among themselves. His estate—based largely on the value of his holdings in his own corporations—would dwindle to nothing.

Jason went back to his sumptuous office and gulped antacids after his lunch with the bankers. Suddenly a woman burst into his office, her hair hardly mussed from struggling past the cadres of secretaries, executive assistants, and office managers who guarded Jason's privacy.

Jason looked up from his bottle of medicine, bleary-eyed, as she stepped in and shut the big double doors behind her, a smile of victory on her pert young face. He did not have to ask who she was or why she was invading his office. He instantly recognized that Internal Revenue Service look about her: cunning, knowing, ruthless, sure of her power.

"Can't a man even die without being hounded by the IRS?" he moaned.

She was good-looking, in a feline, predatory sort of way. Reminded him of his second wife. She prowled slowly across the thickly sumptuous carpeting of Jason's office and curled herself into the hand-carved Danish rocker in front of his desk.

"We understand that you are going to have yourself frozen, Mr. Manning." Her voice was a tawny purr.

"I'm dying," he said.

"You still have to pay your back taxes, dead or alive," she said.

"Take it up with my attorneys. That's what I pay them for."

"This is an unusual situation, Mr. Manning. We've never had to deal with a taxpayer who is planning to have himself frozen." She arched a nicely curved brow at him. "This wouldn't be some elaborate scheme to avoid paying your back taxes, would it?"

"Do you think I gave myself cancer just to avoid paying taxes?"

"We'll have to impound all your holdings as soon as you're frozen."

"What?"

"Impound your holdings. Until we can get a court to rule on whether or not you're deliberately trying to evade your tax responsibilities."

"But that would ruin my corporations!" Jason yelled. "It would drive them into the ground."

"Can't be helped," the IRS agent said, blinking lovely golden brown eyes at him.

"Why don't you just take out a gun and kill me, right here and now?"

She actually smiled. "It's funny, you know. They used to say that the only two certainties in the world are death and taxes. Well, you may be taking the certainty out of death." Her smile vanished and she finished coldly, "But taxes will always be with us, Mr. Manning. Always!"

And with that, she got up from the chair and swept imperiously out of his office.

Jason grabbed the phone and called his insurance agent.

The man was actually the president of Amalgamated Life Assurance Society, Inc., the largest insurance company in Hartford, a city that still styled itself as The Insurance Capital of the World. He and Jason had been friends—well, acquaintances, actually—for decades. Like Jason, the insurance executive had fought his way to the top of his profession, starting out with practically nothing except his father's modest chain of loan offices and his mother's holdings in AT&T.

"It's the best move you can make," the insurance executive assured Jason. "Life insurance is the safest investment in the world. And the benefits, when we pay off, are not taxable."

That warmed Jason's heart. He smiled at the executive's image in his phone's display screen. The man was handsome, his hair silver, his face tanned, his skin taut from the best cosmetic surgery money could buy.

"The premiums," he added, "will be kind of steep,

Jace. After all, you've only got a few months to go."

"But I want my estate protected," Jason said. "What if I dump all my possessions into an insurance policy?"

For just a flash of a moment the executive looked as if an angel had given him personal assurance of eternal bliss. "Your entire estate?" he breathed.

"All my worldly goods."

The man smiled broadly, too broadly, Jason thought. "That would be fine," he said, struggling to control himself. "Just fine. We would take excellent care of your estate. No one would be able to lay a finger on it, believe me."

Jason felt the old warning tingle and heard his father's voice whispering to him.

"My estate will be safe in your hands?"

"Perfectly safe," his erstwhile friend assured him.

"We're talking a long time here," Jason said. "I may stay frozen for years and years. A century or more."

"The insurance industry has been around for centuries, Jace. We're the most stable institution in Western civilization."

Just then the phone screen flickered and went gray. Jason thought that they had been cut off. But before he could do anything about it, a young oriental gentleman's face came on the screen, smiling at him.

"I am the new CEO of Amalgamated Life," he said, in perfectly good American English. "How may I help you?"

"What happened to—"

"Amalgamated has been acquired by Lucky Sun Corporation, a division of Bali Entertainment and

Gambling, Limited. We are diversifying into the insurance business. Our new corporate headquarters will be in Las Vegas, Nevada. Now then, how can I be of assistance to you?''

Jason screamed and cut the connection.

Who can I trust? he asked himself, over and over again, as his chauffeur drove him to his palatial home, far out in the countryside. How can I stash my money away where none of the lawyers or tax people can steal it away from me?

He thought of Snow White sleeping peacefully while the seven dwarfs faithfully watched over her. I don't have seven dwarfs, Jason thought, almost in tears. I don't have anybody. No one at all.

The assassination attempt nearly solved his problem for him.

He was alone in his big rambling house, except for the servants. As he often did, Jason stood out on the glassed-in back porch, overlooking the beautifully wooded ravine that gave him a clear view of the sunset. Industrial pollution from the distant city made the sky blaze with brilliant reds and oranges. Jason swirled a badly needed whisky in a heavy crystal glass, trying to overcome his feelings of dread as he watched the sun go down.

He knew that there would be precious few sunsets left for him to see. Okay, so I won't really be dead, he told himself. I'll just be frozen for a while. Like going to sleep. I'll wake up later.

Oh yeah? a voice in his head challenged. Who's going to wake you up? What makes you think they'll take care of your frozen body for years, for centuries? What's to stop them from pulling the plug on

you? Or selling your body to some medical research
lab? Or maybe for meat!

Jason shuddered. He turned abruptly and headed
for the door to the house just as a bullet smashed
the curving glass where he had been standing an
instant earlier.

Pellets of glass showered him. Jason dropped his
glass and staggered through the door into the library.

"A sniper?" he yelped out loud. "Out here?"

No, he thought, with a shake of his head. Snipers
do their sniping in the inner city or on college cam-
puses or interstate highways. Not out among the
homes of the rich and powerful. He called for his
butler.

No answer.

He yelled for any one of his servants.

No reply.

He dashed to the phone on the sherry table by the
wing chairs tastefully arranged around the fireplace.
The phone was dead. He banged on it, but it remained dead. The fireplace burst into cheery flames,
startling him so badly that he nearly fell over the
sherry table.

Glancing at his wristwatch, Jason saw that it was
precisely seven-thirty. The house's computer was
still working, he realized. It turned on the gas-fed
fireplace on time. But the phones are out and the
servants aren't answering me. And there's a sniper
lurking out in the ravine, taking shots at me.

The door to the library opened slowly. Jason's
heart crawled up his throat.

"Wixon, it's you!"

Jason's butler was carrying a silver tray in his

gloved hands. "Yes sir," he replied in his usual self-effacing whisper.

"Why didn't you answer me when I called for you? Somebody took a shot at me and—"

"Yes sir, I know. I had to go out to the ravine and deal with the man."

"Deal with him?"

"Yes sir," whispered the butler. "He was a professional assassin, hired by your third wife."

"By Jessica?"

"I believe your former wife wanted you killed before your new will is finalized," said the butler.

"Ohhh." Jason sagged into the wing chair. All the strength seemed to evaporate from him.

"I thought you might like a whisky, sir." The butler bent over him and proffered the silver tray. The crystal of the glass caught the firelight like glittering diamonds. Ice cubes tinkled in the glass reassuringly.

"No thanks," said Jason. "I fixed one for myself when I came in."

"Wouldn't you like another, sir?"

"You know I never have more than one." Jason looked up at the butler's face. Wixon had always looked like a wax dummy, his face expressionless. But at the moment, with the firelight playing across his features, he seemed—intent.

"Shouldn't we phone the police?" Jason asked. "I mean, the man tried to kill me."

"That's all taken care of, sir." Wixon edged the tray closer to Jason. "Your drink, sir."

"I don't want another drink, dammit!"

The butler looked disappointed. "I merely thought, with all the excitement . . ."

Jason dismissed the butler, who left the drink on the table beside him. Alone in the library, Jason stared into the flames of the gas-fed fireplace. The crystal glass glittered and winked at him alluringly. Maybe another drink is what I need, Jason told himself. It's been a hard day.

He brought the glass to his lips, then stopped. Wixon knows I never have more than one drink. Why would he . . . ?

Poison! Jason threw the glass into the fireplace, leaped up from the chair and dashed for the garage. They're all out to get me! Five wives, five children, ten sets of lawyers, bankers, the IRS—I'm a hunted man!

Once down in the dimly lit garage he hesitated only for a moment. They might have rigged a bomb in the Ferrari, he told himself. So, instead, he took the gardener's pickup truck.

As he crunched down the long gravel driveway to the main road, all the library windows blew out in a spectacular gas-fed explosion.

By the time he reached his brother's rectory, it was almost midnight. But Jason felt strangely calm, at peace with himself and the untrustworthy world that he would soon be departing.

Jason pounded on the rectory door until Michael's housekeeper, clutching a house robe to her skinny frame, reluctantly let him in.

"The monsignor's sound asleep," she insisted, with an angry frown.

"Wake him," Jason insisted even more firmly.

She brought him to the study and told him to wait there. The fireplace was cold and dark. The only light in the room came from the green-shaded lamp on Michael's desk. Jason paced back and forth, too wired to sit still.

As soon as Michael padded into the study, in his bedroom slippers and bathrobe, rubbing sleep from his eyes, Jason started to pour out his soul.

"Give your entire estate to the Church?" Michael sank into one of the leather armchairs.

"Yes!" Jason pulled the other chair close to his brother, and leaned forward eagerly. "With certain provisions, of course."

"Provisions."

Jason ticked off on his fingers, "First, I want the Church to oversee the maintenance of my frozen body. I want the Church to guarantee that nobody's going to pull the plug on me."

Michael nodded warily.

"Second, I want the Church to monitor medical research and decide when I should be revived. And by whom."

Nodding again, Michael said, "Go on."

"That's it."

"Those are the only conditions?"

Jason said. "Yes."

Stirring slightly in his chair, Michael asked, "And what does the Church get out of this?"

"Half my estate."

"Half?" Michael's eyebrows rose.

"I think that's fair, don't you? Half of my estate to the Church, the other half waiting for me when I'm revived."

"Uh . . . how much is it? I mean, how large is your estate?"

With a shrug, Jason said, "I'm not exactly sure. My personal holdings, real estate, liquid assets—

should add up to several billion, I'd guess."

"Billion?" Michael stressed the *b*.

"Billion."

Michael gulped.

Jason leaned back in the bottle green chair and let out a long breath. "Do that for me, and the Church can have half of my estate. You could do a lot of good with a billion and some dollars, Mike."

Michael ran a hand across his stubbly chin. "I'll have to speak to the cardinal," he muttered. Then he broke into a slow smile. "By the saints, I'll probably have to take this all the way to the Vatican!"

When Jason awoke, for a startled instant he thought that something had gone wrong with the freezing. He was still lying on the table in the lab, still surrounded by green-coated doctors and technicians. The air felt chill, and he saw a faint icy mist wafting across his field of view.

But then he realized that the ceiling of the lab had been a blank white, while the ceiling above him now glowed with colors. Blinking, focusing, he saw that the ceiling, the walls, the whole room was decorated with incredible Renaissance paintings of saints and angels in beautiful flowing robes of glowing color.

"Where am I?" he asked, his voice a feeble croak. "What year is this?"

"You are safe," said one of the green-masked persons. "You are cured of your disease. The year is *anno domini* two thousand fifty-nine."

Half a century, Jason said to himself. I've done it! I've slept more than fifty years and they've awakened me and I'm cured and healthy again! Jason slipped into the sweetest sleep he had ever known.

The fact that the man who spoke to him had a distinct foreign accent did not trouble him in the slightest.

Over the next several days Jason submitted to a dozen physical examinations and endless questions by persons he took to be psychologists. When he tried to find out where he was and what the state of the twenty-first-century world might be, he was told, "Later. There will be plenty of time for that later."

His room was small but very pleasant, his bed comfortable. The room's only window looked out on a flourishing garden, lush trees and bright blossoming flowers in brilliant sunlight. The only time it rained was after dark, and Jason began to wonder if the weather was somehow being controlled deliberately.

Slowly he recovered his strength. The nurses wheeled him down a long corridor, its walls and ceilings totally covered with frescoes. The place did not look like a hospital; did not smell like one, either. After nearly a week, he began to take strolls in the garden by himself. The sunshine felt good, warming. He noticed lots of priests and nuns also strolling in the garden, speaking in foreign languages. Of course, Jason told himself, this place must be run by the Church.

It wasn't until he saw a trio of Swiss Guards in their colorful uniforms that he realized he was in the Vatican.

"Yes, it's true," admitted the youthful woman who was the chief psychologist on his recovery team. "We are in the Vatican." She had a soft voice and spoke English with a faint, charming Italian accent.

"But why—?"

She touched his lips with a cool finger. "His Holiness will explain it all to you."

"His Holiness?"

"*Il Papa.* You are going to see him tomorrow."

The Pope.

They gave Jason a new suit of royal blue to wear for his audience with the Pope. Jason showered, shaved, combed his hair, put on the silky new clothing and then waited impatiently. I'm going to see the Pope!

Six Swiss Guardsmen, three black-robed priests and a bishop escorted him through the corridors of the Vatican, out into the private garden, through doors and up staircases. Jason caught a glimpse of long lines of tourists in the distance, but this part of the Vatican was off-limits to them.

At last they ushered him into a small private office. Except for a set of French windows, its walls were covered with frescoes by Raphael. In the center of the marble floor stood an elaborately carved desk. No other furniture in the room. Behind the desk was a small door, hardly noticeable because the paintings masked it almost perfectly. Jason stood up straight in front of the unoccupied desk as the Swiss Guards, priests and bishop arrayed themselves behind him. Then the small door swung open and the Pope, in radiant white robes, entered the room.

It was Michael.

Jason's knees almost buckled when he saw his brother. He was older, but not that much. His hair had gone white, but his face seemed almost the same, just a few more crinkles around the corners of his eyes and mouth. Mike's light blue eyes were still clear, alert. He stood erect and strong. He looked a hale and vigorous sixty or so, not the ninety-some that Jason knew he would have to be.

"Mike?" Jason felt bewildered, staring at this man in the white robes of the Pope. "Mike, is it really you?"

"It's me, Jace."

For a confused moment Jason did not know what to do. He thought he should kneel to the Pope, kiss his ring, show some sign of respect and reverence. But how can it be Mike, how can he be so young if fifty years have gone by?

Then Pope Michael I, beaming at his brother, held out his arms to Jason. And Jason rushed into his brother's arms and let Mike embrace him.

"Please leave us alone," said the Pope to his entourage. The phalanx of priests and guards flowed out of the room, silent except for a faint swishing of black robes.

"Mike? You're the Pope?" Jason could hardly believe it.

"Thanks to you, Jace." Mike's voice was firm and strong, a voice accustomed to authority.

"And you look—how old are you now?"

"Ninety-seven." Michael laughed. "I know I don't look it. There've been a lot of improvements in medicine, thanks to you."

"Me?"

"You started things, Jace. Started me on the road that's led here. You've changed the world, changed it far more than either of us could have guessed back in the old days."

Jason felt weak in the knees. "I don't understand."

Wrapping a strong arm around his brother's

shoulders, Pope Michael I led Jason to the French windows. They stepped out onto a small balcony. Jason saw that they were up so high it made him feel a little giddy. The city of Rome lay all around them; magnificent buildings bathed in warm sunshine beaming down from a brilliant clear blue sky. Birds chirped happily from the nearby trees. Church bells rang in the distance.

"Listen," said Michael.

"To what?"

"To what you don't hear."

Jason looked closely at his brother. "Have you gone into Zen or something?"

Michael laughed. "Jace, you don't hear automobile engines, do you? We use electrical cars now, clean and quiet. You don't hear horns or people cursing at each other. Everyone's much more polite, much more respectful. And look at the air! It's clean. No smog or pollution."

Jason nodded numbly. "Things have come a long way since I went under."

"Thanks to you," Michael said again.

"I don't understand."

"You revitalized the Church, Jace. And Holy Mother Church has revitalized Western civilization. We've entered a new age, an age of faith, an age of morality and obedience to the law."

Jason felt overwhelmed. "I revitalized the Church?"

"Your idea of entrusting your estate to the Church. I got to thinking about that. Soon I began spreading the word that the Church was the only institution in the whole world that could be trusted to look after freezees—"

"Freezees?"

"People who've had themselves frozen. That's what they're called now."

"Freezees." It sounded to Jason like an ice-cream treat he had known when he was a kid.

"You hit the right button, Jace," Michael went on, grasping the stone balustrade of the balcony in both hands. "Holy Mother Church has the integrity to look after the freezees while they're helpless, and the endurance to take care of them for centuries, millennia, if necessary."

"But how did that change everything?"

Michael grinned at him. "You, of all people, should be able to figure that out."

"Money," said Jason.

Pope Michael nodded vigorously. "The rich came to us to take care of them while they were frozen. You gave us half your estate, many of the others gave us a lot more. The more desperate they were, the more they offered. We never haggled; we took whatever they were willing to give. Do you have any idea of how much money flowed into the Church? Not just billions, Jace. Trillions! Trillions of dollars."

Jason thought of how much compound interest could accrue in half a century. "How much am I worth now?" he asked.

His brother ignored him. "With all that money came power, Jace. Real power. Power to move politicians. Power to control whole nations. With that power came authority. The Church reasserted itself as the moral leader of the Western world. The people were ready for moral leadership. They needed it and we provided it. The old evil ways are gone, Jace. Banished."

"Yes, but how much—"

"We spent wisely," the Pope continued, his eyes glowing. "We invested in the future. We started to rebuild the world, and that gained us the gratitude and loyalty of half the world."

"What should I invest in now?" Jason asked.

Michael turned slightly away from him. "There's a new morality out there, a new world of faith and respect for authority. The world you knew is gone forever, Jace. We've ended hunger. We've stabilized the world's population—*without* artificial birth control."

Jason could not help smiling at his brother. "You're still against contraception."

"Some things don't change. A sin is still a sin."

"You thought temporary suicide was a sin," Jason reminded him.

"It still is," said the Pope, utterly serious.

"But you help people to freeze themselves! You just told me—"

Michael put a hand on Jason's shoulder. "Jace, just because those poor frightened souls entrust their money to Holy Mother Church doesn't mean that they're not committing a mortal sin when they kill themselves."

"But it's not suicide! I'm here, I'm alive again!"

"Legally, you're dead."

"But that—" Jason's breath caught in his throat. He did not like the glitter in Michael's eye.

"Holy Mother Church cannot condone suicide, Jace."

"But you benefit from it!"

"God moves in mysterious ways. We use the money that sinners bestow upon us to help make the world a better place. But they are still sinners."

A terrible realization was beginning to take shape in Jason's frightened mind. "How . . . how many freezees have you revived?" he asked in a trembling voice.

"You are the first," his brother answered. "And the last."

"But you can't leave them frozen! You promised to revive them!"

Pope Michael shook his head slowly, a look on his face more of pity than sorrow. "We promised to revive you, Jace. We made no such promises to the rest of them. We agreed only to look after them and maintain them until they could be cured of whatever it was that killed them."

"But that means you've got to revive them."

A wintry smile touched the corners of the Pope's lips. "No, it does not. The contract is quite specific. Our best lawyers have honed it to perfection. Many of them are Jesuits, you know. The contract gives the Church the authority to decide when to revive them. We keep them frozen."

Jason could feel his heart thumping against his ribs. "But why would anybody come to you to be frozen when nobody's been revived? Don't they realize—"

"No, they don't realize, Jace. That's the most beautiful part of it. We control the media very thoroughly. And when a person is facing the certainty of death, you would be shocked at how few questions are asked. We offer life after death, just as we always have. They interpret our offer in their own way."

Jason sagged against the stone balustrade. "You mean that even with all the advances in medicine you've made, they still haven't gotten wise?"

"Despite all our medical advances, people still die. And the rich still want to avoid it, if they can. That's when they run to us."

"And you screw them out of their money."

Michael's face hardened. "Jace, the Church has scrupulously kept its end of our bargain with you. We have kept watch over you for more than half a century, and we revived you as soon as your disease became curable, just as I agreed to. But what good does a new life do you when your immortal soul is in danger of damnation?"

"I didn't commit suicide," Jason insisted.

"What you have done—what all the freezees have done—is considered suicide in every court of the Western world."

"The Church controls the courts?"

"All of them," Michael replied. He heaved a sad, patient sigh, then said, "Holy Mother Church's mission is to save souls, not bodies. We're going to save your soul, Jace. Now."

Jason saw that the six Swiss Guards were standing by the French windows, waiting for him.

"You've been through it before, Jace," his brother told him. "You won't feel a thing."

Terrified, Jason shrieked, "You're going to murder me?"

"It isn't murder, Jace. We're simply going to freeze you again. You'll go down into the catacombs with all the others."

"But I'm cured, dammit! I'm all right now!"

"It's for the salvation of your soul, Jace. It's your penance for committing the sin of suicide."

"You're freezing me so you can keep all my money! You're keeping all the others frozen so you can keep their money, too!"

"It's for their own good," said Pope Michael. He nodded to the guards, who stepped onto the balcony and took Jason in their grasp.

"It's like the goddamned Inquisition!" Jason yelled. "Burning people at the stake to save their souls!"

"It's for the best, Jace," Pope Michael I said as the guards dragged Jason away. "It's for the good of the world. It's for the good of the Church, for the good of your immortal soul."

Struggling against the guards, Jason pleaded, "How long will you keep me under? When will you revive me again?"

The Pope shrugged. "Holy Mother Church has lasted more than two thousand years, Jace. But what's a millennium or two when you're waiting for the final trump?"

"Mike!" Jason howled. "For God's sake!"

"God's a lot smarter than both of us," Michael said grimly. "Trust me."

(With special thanks to Michael Bienes.)

Introduction to
"Risk Assessment"

This one was written for Jack Williamson.

Jack is probably the most beloved writer in the science-fiction field, the dean of us all, whose first short story was published in 1928. He is a truly gentle man and a fine writer.

To celebrate his more than sixty years as a published writer, Jack's friends put together an anthology of stories, all written on themes that Jack himself has used in his long and productive career.

I was asked to contribute a story to the anthology, and "Risk Assessment" is the result. If you are unfortunate enough to be unfamiliar with Jack Williamson's work, all I can say (aside from urging you to read his fiction) is that he was among the very earliest writers to deal with antimatter, which he called "contraterrene" matter, or seetee. This was at a time when the concept of antimatter was a new and startling idea to theoretical physicists such as P.A.M. Dirac, Fermi, Einstein, and that crowd.

Two stories about Jack:

For many years, Jack was a professor of English at the University of Eastern New Mexico, in Portales. When he reached retirement age, he retired. Not surprising, you might think. But I received a nearly frantic phone call from a group of his students (I was editing Analog *magazine in New York then) who told me that they thought the university's administration was "forcing" Professor Williamson into retirement, and they wanted me to do something about it!*

The first thing I did was to call Jack. "Forcing me?" Jack laughed. "Goodness no. I'm very happy to retire from teaching. Now I can write full-time."

How many professors have been so revered by their students that the students don't want them to retire?

Second story:

Barbara and I visited Jack in Portales one year during the time for the spring calf roundup. We drove out to the ranch where the roundup was taking place that weekend, and watched the local cowhands and teenagers at work. It was a hot, bloody, dusty scene. The calves were separated from their mothers, dehorned, the males deballed, all of the calves branded and shot with about a quart of penicillin apiece. Their was bleating and mooing and horses and roping and the stench of burnt hides and lots of blood, toil, tears, and sweat.

As we leaned against the corral railing, watching all this hard work and suffering, Jack nudged me in the ribs. "See why I became a writer?" he asked softly.

I nodded. I'd much rather sweat over a keyboard than rope a calf, any day.

RISK ASSESSMENT

They are little more than children, thought Alpha One, self-centered, emotional children sent by their elders to take the responsibilities that the elders themselves do not want to bother with.

Sitting at Alpha One's right was Cordelia Thomasina Shockley, whom the human male called Delia. Red-haired and impetuous, brilliant and driven, her decisions seemed to·be based as much on emotional tides as logical calculation.

The third entity in the conference chamber was Martin Flagg, deeply solemn, intensely grave. He behaved as if he truly believed his decisions were rational, and not at all influenced by the hormonal cascades surging through his endocrine system.

"This experiment *must* be stopped," Martin Flagg said firmly.

Delia thought he was handsome, in a rugged sort of way. Not terribly tall, but broad in the shoulder and flat in the middle. Nicely muscular. Big dimple in the middle of his stubborn chin. Heavenly deep blue eyes. When he smiled his whole face lit up, and somehow that lit up Delia's heart. But it had been a long time since she'd seen him smile.

"Why must the experiment be stopped?" asked the robot avatar of Alpha One.

It folded its mechanical arms over its cermet chest, in imitation of the human gesture. Its humanform face was incapable of showing any emotion, however. It merely stared at Martin Flagg out of its optical sensors, waiting for him to go on.

"What Delia's doing is not only foolish, it's wasteful. And dangerous."

"How so?" asked Alpha One, with the patience that only a computer possessed.

The human male was almost trembling with agitation. "You don't think a few hundred megatons of energy is dangerous?"

Delia said coolly, "Not when it's properly contained, Marty. And it *is* properly contained, of course."

Alpha One knew that Delia had two interlinked personality flaws: a difficulty in taking criticism seriously and an absolute refusal to accept anyone else's point of view. Like her auburn hair and opalescent eyes, she had inherited those flaws from her mother. From her father she had inherited one of the largest fortunes in the inner solar system. He had also bequeathed her his incredibly dogged stubbornness, the total inability to back away from a challenge. And the antimatter project.

Marty was getting red in the face. "Suppose you lose containment?" he asked Delia. "What then?"

"I won't."

Turning to the robot, Marty repeated, "What if she loses containment?"

Alpha One's prime responsibility was risk assessment. Here on the Moon it was incredibly easy for a mistake to kill humans. So the computer quickly ran through all the assessments it had made to date of C. T. Shockley's antimatter project, a task that took four microseconds, then had its robot avatar reply to Flagg.

Calmly, Alpha One replied, "If the apparatus loses containment, then our seismologists will obtain interesting new data on the Moon's deep structure." Its voice was a smooth computer synthesis issuing from the horizontal grill where a human's mouth would be.

Martin Flagg was far from pleased. "Is that all that your germanium brain cares about? What about the loss of human life?"

Alpha One was totally unperturbed. Its brain was composed mainly of optical filaments, not germanium. "The nearest human settlement is at Clavius," it said. "There is no danger to human life."

"*Her* life!"

Alpha One turned to see Delia's reaction. A warm flush colored her cheeks, an involuntary physical reaction to her realization that Flagg was worried about her safety.

The human form of the robot was a concession to human needs. The robot was merely one of thousands of avatars of Alpha One, the master computer that monitored every city, every habitat, every vehicle, factory and mining outpost on the Moon. Almost a century ago the pioneer lunar settlers had learned, through bitter experience, that the computer's rational and incorruptible decisions were far sounder—and safer—than the emotionally biased decisions made by men and women.

But the humans were unwilling to allow a computer, no matter how wise and rational, to have complete control over them. The Lunar Council, therefore, was founded as a triumvirate: the Moon was ruled by one man, one woman, and Alpha One. Yet, over the years, the lunar citizens did their best to avoid the duty of serving on the Council. The task was handed to the young, those who had enough idealism to serve, or those who did not have enough experience to evade the responsibility.

Children, Alpha One repeated to itself. As human life spans extend toward the two-century mark, their childhoods lengthen also. Physically they are mature adults, yet emotionally they are still spoiled children.

Martin Flagg was the human male member of the triumvirate. C. T. Shockley was the female. Marty was the youngest human ever elected to the triumvirate. Except for Delia.

The three of them were sitting in the plush highbacked chairs of the Council's private conference room, in the city of Selene, dug into the ringwall mountains of the giant crater Alphonsus. Flagg glared at Delia from his side of the triangular table. Delia smiled saucily at him. She knew she shouldn't antagonize him, but she couldn't help it. Delia did not want to be here; she wanted to be at her remote laboratory in the crater Newton, near the lunar south pole. But Marty had insisted on her physical appearance at this meeting: no holographic presence, no virtual-reality attendance.

"This experiment must be stopped," Flagg repeated. He was stubborn, too.

"Why?" asked the robot, in its maddeningly calm manner.

Obviously struggling to control his temper, Flagg leaned forward in his chair and ticked off on his fingers:

"One, she is using valuable resources—"

"That I'm paying for out of my own pocket." But the pocket was becoming threadbare, she knew. The Shockley family fortune, big as it might have been, was running low. Delia knew she'd have to succeed tomorrow or give it all up.

Flagg scowled at her, then turned back to the robot. "Two, she is endangering human life."

"Only my own," Delia said sweetly.

The robot checked its risk assessments again and said, "She is entirely within her legal rights."

"Three, her crazy experiment hasn't been sanctioned by the Science Committee."

"I don't need the approval of those nine old farts," Delia snapped.

The robot seemed to incline its head briefly, as if nodding. "Under ordinary circumstances it would be necessary to obtain the Science Committee's permission for such an experiment, that is true."

"Ah-hah!" Flagg grinned maliciously.

"But that is because researchers seek to obtain funding grants from the Committee. Shockley is using her own money. She needs neither funding nor permission, so long as she does not present an undue risk to other humans."

Flagg closed his eyes briefly. Delia thought he was about to admit defeat. But then he played his trump.

"And what about her plans to use *all* the power capacity of *all* the solar collector systems on the Moon? Plus *all* the sunsats in cislunar space?"

"I only need their output for one minute," Delia said.

"What happens if there's an emergency during that one minute?" Flagg demanded, almost angrily. "What happens if the backups fail at Clavius, or Copernicus, or even here in Selene? Do you have any idea of how much the emergency backup capacity has lagged behind actual power demand?"

"I have those figures," Alpha One said.

"So?"

"There is a point-zero-four probability that the backup system at Selene will be unable to meet all the demands made on it during that one minute that the solar generators are taken off-line. There is a point-zero-two probability that the backup system at Copernicus—"

"All right, all right," Flagg interrupted impatiently. "What do we do if there's a failure of the backup system while the main power grid is off-line?"

"Put the solar generators back on-line immediately. The switching can be accomplished in six to ten milliseconds."

Delia felt suddenly alarmed. "But that would ruin the experiment! It could blow up!"

"That would be unfortunate, but unavoidable. It is a risk that you must assume."

Delia thought it over for all of half a second, then

gritted her teeth and nodded. "Okay, I accept the risk."

"Wait a minute," Flagg said to the robot. "You're missing the point. Why does she need all that power?"

"To generate antiprotons, of course," Delia answered. Marty knew that, she told herself. Why is he asking the obvious?

"But you already have more than a hundred megatons worth of antiprotons, don't you?"

"Sure, but I need thirty tons of them."

"Thirty tons?" Marty's voice jumped an octave. "Of antiprotons? Thirty tons by *mass*?"

Delia nodded nonchalantly while Alpha One restarted its risk assessment calculations. Thirty tons of antiprotons was a new data point, never revealed to the Council before.

"Why do you need thirty tons of antiprotons?" Alpha One asked, even while its new risk assessment was proceeding.

"To drive the starship to Alpha Centauri and back," Delia replied, as it were the most obvious fact in the universe.

"You intend to fly to Alpha Centauri on a ship that has never been tested?" Alpha One asked. "The antimatter propulsion system alone—"

"We've done all the calculations," Delia interrupted, annoyance knitting her brows. "The simulations all check out fine."

If Alpha One could have felt dismay or irritation at its own limitations, it would have at that moment. Shockley intended to fly her father's ship to Alpha Centauri. This was new data, but it should have been anticipated. Why else would she have been amassing antimatter? A subroutine in its intricate programming pointed out that it was reasonable to assume that she would want to test the antimatter-propulsion system first, to see that it actually performs as calculated before risking the flight. After all, no one had operated an antimatter drive as yet. No one had tried for the stars.

"What's thirty tons of antiprotons equal to in energy potential?" Flagg asked.

Instantly, Alpha One calculated, "Approximately one million megatons of energy."

"And if that much energy explodes?"

Alpha One was incapable of showing emotion, of course. But it hesitated, just for a fraction of a second. The silence was awesome. Then the robot's head swivelled slowly toward Delia, levelling its dark glassy optical sensors at her.

"An explosion of that magnitude could perturb the orbit of the Moon."

"It could cause a moonquake that would destroy Clavius, at the very least," Flagg said. "Smash Selene and even Copernicus, wouldn't it?"

"Indeed," said Alpha One. The single word stung Delia like a whip.

"Now do you see why she's got to be stopped?"

"Indeed," the robot repeated.

Delia shook her head, as if to clear away the pain. "But there won't be any explosion," she insisted. "I know what I'm doing. All the calculations show—"

"The risk is not allowable," Alpha One said firmly. "You must stop your experiment."

"I will not!" Delia snapped.

It took Alpha One less than three milliseconds to check this new data once again, and then compare it against the safety regulations that ruled every decision-making tree, and still again check it against the consequences of Delia's project if it should be successful. Yet although it weighed the probabilities and made its decision that swiftly, it did not speak.

Alpha One had learned one thing in its years of dealing with humans: the less they are told, the less they have to argue about.

And the two humans already had plenty to argue over.

Running a hand through the flowing waves of his golden hair, Flagg grumbled, "You're not fit to be a triumvir."

"I was elected just the same as you were," Delia replied tartly.

"Your father bought votes. Everybody knows it."

Delia's own temper surged. Leaning across the triangular table to within inches of Flagg's nose, she said, "Then everybody's wrong! Daddy wouldn't spend a penny on a vote."

"No," he snarled, "he spent all his money on this crazy starship, and you're spending still more on an experiment that could kill everybody on the Moon!"

"It's my experiment, and I'm going to go ahead with it. It'll be finished tomorrow."

"It is finished now," said the robot. "Your permission to tap power from the lunar grid is hereby revoked. Safety considerations outweigh all other factors. Although the risk of an explosion is small, the consequences are so great that the risk is not allowable."

All the breath seemed to gush out of Delia's lungs. She sank back in her chair and stared at the unmoving robot for a long, silent moment. Then she turned to Flagg.

"I hate you!"

"You're not fit to be a triumvir," Flagg repeated, scowling at her. "There ought to be a sanity requirement for the position."

Delia wanted to leap across the table and slap his face. Instead, she turned to Alpha One's robotic avatar.

"He's being vindictive," she said. "He's acting out of personal malice."

The robot said impassively, "Triumvir Flagg has brought to the attention of the Council the safety hazards of your experiment. That is within his rights and responsibilities. The only personal malice that has been expressed at this meeting has come from you, Triumvir Shockley."

Flagg laughed out loud.

Delia couldn't control herself any longer. She jumped to her feet and didn't just slap Marty, she socked him as hard as she could with her clenched fist, right between the eyes. In the gentle gravity of the Moon, he tilted backward in his chair and tumbled to the floor ever so slowly, arms weakly flailing. She could watch his eyes roll up into his head as he slowly tumbled ass over teakettle and slumped to the floor.

Satisfied, Delia stomped out of the conference chamber and headed back to Newton and her work.

Then she realized that the work was finished. It was going to be aborted, and she would probably be kicked off the triumvirate for assaulting a fellow Council member.

If she let Marty have his way.

*   *   *

Delia stood naked and alone on the dark airless floor of the crater Newton. Even though she was there only in virtual reality, while her real body rested snugly in the VR chamber of her laboratory, she revelled in the freedom of her solitude. She could virtually feel the shimmering energy of the antiprotons as they raced along the circular track she had built around the base of the crater's steep mountains.

More than 350 kilometers in circumference, the track ran past the short lunar horizon, its faint glow scintillating like a giant luminescent snake that circled Delia's naked presence.

The track was shielded by a torus of pure diamond. Even in the deep vacuum of the lunar surface there were stray atoms of gases that could collide with the circling antiprotons and set off a flash of annihilative energy. And cosmic particles raining down from the Sun and deep space. She had to protect her antiprotons, hoard them, save them for the moment when they would be needed.

She looked up, toward the cold and distant stars that stared down at her out of the dark circle of sky, unwavering, solemn, like the unblinking eyes of some wary beast watching her. The rim of the deep crater was ringed with rectennas, waiting to drink in the energy beamed from the Moon's own solar-power farms and from the sunsats orbiting between the Earth and the Moon. Energy that Marty and Alfie had denied her.

In the exact center of the crater floor stood the ungainly bulk of the starship, her father's masterpiece, glittering softly in the light of the stars it was intended to reach.

But it will never get off the ground unless I produce enough antiprotons, Delia told herself. For the thousandth time.

The crater Newton was not merely far from any other human settlement. It was *cold*. Close to the lunar south pole, nearly ten kilometers deep, Newton's floor never saw sunlight. Early explorers had broken their hearts searching Newton and the surrounding region for water ice. There was none to be found, and the lunar pioneers had to manufacture their water out of oxygen from the regolith and hydrogen imported from Earth.

But even though any ice originally trapped in Newton had evaporated eons ago, the crater was still perpetually cold, cryogenically cold all the time, cold enough so that when Delia built the ring of superconducting magnets for the racetrack she did not have to worry about cooling them.

Now the racetrack held enough antiprotons, endlessly circling, to blow up all the rocky, barren landscape for hundreds of kilometers. If all went well with her experiment, it would hold enough antiprotons to send the starship to Alpha Centauri. Or rock the Moon out of its orbit.

The experiment was scheduled for midnight, Greenwich Mean Time. The time when the sunsats providing power to Europe and North America were at their lowest demand and could most easily squirt a minute's worth of their output to Delia's rectennas at Newton. The Moon kept GMT, too, so it would have been easy for the lunar grid to be shunted to Newton for a minute, also. If not for Marty.

Midnight was only six hours away.

Delia's father, Cordell Thomas Shockley, scion of a brilliant and infamous family, had taken it into his stubborn head to build the first starship. Earth's government would not do it. The Lunar Council, just getting started in his days, could not afford it. So Shockley decided to use his own family fortune to build the first starship himself.

He hired the best designers and scientists. Using nanomachines, they built his ship out of pure diamond. But the ship sat, gleaming faintly in the starlight, in the middle of Newton's frigid floor, unable to move until some thirty tons of antiprotons were manufactured to propel it.

Delia was born to her father's purpose, raised to make his dream come true, trained and educated in particle physics and space propulsion. Her first toys were model spacecraft; her first video games were lessons in physics.

When Delia was five years old her mother fled back to Earth, unable to compete with her husband's monomania, unwilling to live in the spartan underground warrens that the Lunatics called home. She divorced C. T. Shockley and took half his fortune away. But left her daughter.

Shockley was unperturbed. He could work better without a wife to bother him. He had a daughter to train, and the two of them were as inseparable as quarks in a baryon. Delia built the antiproton-storage ring, then patiently began to buy electrical energy from the Lunar Council, from the sunsats orbiting in cislunar space, from anyone and everyone she could find. The energy was converted into antiprotons; the antiprotons were stored in the racetrack ring. She was young, time was on her side.

Then her father was diagnosed with terminal cancer, and she realized that both her time and her money were running out. The old man was frozen cryonically and interred in a dewar in his own starship. The instructions in his will said he was to be revived at Alpha Centauri, even if he lived only for a few minutes.

So now Delia's virtual presence walked across the frozen floor of Newton, up to the diamond starship gleaming faintly in the dim light of the distant stars. She peered through its crystal hull, toward the dewar where her father rested.

"I'll do it, Daddy," she whispered. "I'll succeed tomorrow, one way or the other."

Grimly she thought that if Marty was right and the antimatter exploded, the explosion would turn Newton and its environs into a vast cloud of plasma. Most of the ionized gas would be blasted clear of the Moon's gravity, blown out into interplanetary space. Some of it, she supposed, would eventually waft beyond the solar system. In time, millions of years, billions, a few of their atoms might even reach Alpha Centauri.

"One way or the other," she repeated.

Delia stirred in the VR chamber. Enough self-pity, she told herself. You've got to *do* something.

She pulled the helmet off, shook her auburn hair annoyedly, and then peeled herself out of the skintight VR suit. She marched straight to her bathroom and stepped into the shower, where she always did her best thinking. Delia's father had always thought of water as a luxury, which it had been when he had first come to the Moon. His training still impressed Delia's attitudes. As the hot water sluiced along her skin, she luxuriated in the warmth and let her thoughts run free.

They ran straight to the one implacable obstacle that loomed before her. Martin Flagg. The man she thought she had loved. The man she knew that she hated.

In childhood Delia had no human playmates. In fact, for long years her father was the only human companion she knew. Otherwise, her human acquaintances were all holographic or VR presences.

She first met Martin Flagg when they were elected to the triumvirate. Contrary to Marty's nasty aspersions, Delia had not lifted a finger to get herself elected. She had not wanted the position, the responsibility would interfere with her work. But her father, without telling her, had apparently moved heaven and Earth—well, the Moon, at least—to make her a triumvir.

"You need some human companionship," he told her gruffly. "You're getting to an age where you ought to be meeting other people. Serving on the Council for a few years will encourage you to . . . well, meet people."

Delia thought she was too young to serve on the Council, but once she realized that handsome Martin Flagg was also running, she consented to all the testing and interviewing that passed for a political campaign on the Moon. Most of the Lunatics cared little about politics and did their best to avoid serving on the Council. The only reason for having two human members on the triumvirate was to allay the ancient fears that Alpha One might someday run amok.

Once she was elected, C. T. Shockley explained his real reason for making her run for the office. "The Council won't be able to interfere with our work if you're on the triumvirate. You're in a position now to head off any attempts to stop us."

So she had accepted the additional responsibility. And it did eat into her time outrageously. The triumvirate had to deal with everything from people whining about their water allotments to deciding how and when to enlarge the underground cities of the Moon.

And the irony of it all was that nobody cared about Shockley's crazy starship project or Delia's work to generate enough antiprotons to propel the ship to Alpha Centauri. Nobody except her fellow triumvir, Marty Flagg. If Delia hadn't been elected to the triumvirate with him, if they hadn't begun this love-hate relationship that neither of them knew how to handle, she could have worked in blissful isolation at Newton without hindrance of any sort.

But Marty made Delia's heart quiver whenever he turned those blue eyes of his upon her. Sometimes she quivered with love. More often with fury. But she could never look at Marty without being stirred.

And he cared about her. She knew he did. Why else would he try to stop her? He was worried that she would kill herself.

Really? she asked herself. He's really scared that I'm going to kill *him*, and everybody else on the Moon.

Delia's only experience with love had come from VR romance novels, where the heroine always gets her man, no matter what perils she must face along the way. But she did not want Marty Flagg. She hated him. He had stopped her work.

A grimace of determination twisted Delia's lips as she turned off the shower and let the air blowers dry her. Marty may think he's stopped me. But I'm not stopped yet.

She slipped into a comfortable set of coveralls and strode down the bare corridor toward her control center. Alpha One won't let me tap the lunar grid, she thought, but I still have all the sunsats. The Council doesn't control them. As long as I can pay for their power, they'll beam it to me. Unless Alpha One's tried to stop them.

It wouldn't be enough, she knew. As she slid into her desk chair and ordered her private computer to show her the figures, she knew that a full minute of power from all the sunsats between the Earth and the Moon would not provide the energy she needed.

She checked the Council's communications log. Sure enough, Alpha One had already notified the various power companies that they should renege on their contracts to provide power to her. Delia told her computer to activate its law program and notify the power companies that if they failed to live up to their contracts with her, the penalties would bankrupt them.

She knew they would rather sell the power and avoid the legal battle. Only a minute's worth of power, yet she was paying a premium price for it. They had five and a half hours to make up their minds. Delia figured that the companies' legal computer programs needed only a few minutes' deliberation to make their recommendations, one way or the other. But then they would turn their recommendations over to their human counterparts, who would be sleeping or partying or doing whatever lawyers do at night on Earth. It would be hours before they saw their computers' recommendations.

She smiled. By the time they saw their computers' recommendations, she would have her power.

But it wouldn't be enough.

Where to get the power that Marty had denied her? And how to get it in little more than five hours?

Mercury.

A Sino-Japanese consortium was building a strip of solar-power converters across Mercury's equator, together with relay satellites in orbit about the planet to send the power earthward. Delia put in a call to Tokyo, to Rising Sun Power, Inc., feeling almost breathless with desperation.

It was past nineteen hundred hours in Tokyo by the time she got a human to speak to her, well past quitting time in most offices. But within minutes Delia was locked in an intense conference with stony-faced men in Tokyo and Beijing, offering the last of the Shockley fortune in exchange for one minute's worth of electrical power from Mercury.

"The timing must be exact," she pointed out, not for the first time.

The director-general of Rising Sun, a former engineer, allowed a faint smile to break through his polite impassivity. "The timing will be precise, down to the microsecond," he assured her.

Delia was practically quivering with excitement as the time ticked down to midnight. It was going to happen! She would get all the power she needed, generate the antiprotons the ship required, and be ready to lift off for Alpha Centauri.

In less than half an hour.

If everything went the way it should.

If her calculations were right.

Twenty-eight minutes to go. What if my calculations are off? A sudden flare of panic surged through her. Check them again, she told herself. But there isn't time.

Then a new fear struck her. What if my calculations are right? I'll be leaving the Moon, leaving the only home I've ever known, leaving the solar system. Why? To bring Daddy to Alpha Centauri. To fulfill his dream.

But it's not my dream, she realized.

All these years, ever since she had been old enough to remember, she had worked with monomaniacal energy to bring her father's dream to fruition. She had never had time to think about her own dream.

She thought about it now. What is my own dream? Delia asked herself. What do I want for myself?

She did not know. All her life had been spent in the relentless pursuit of her father's goal; she had never taken the time to dream for herself.

But she knew one thing. She did not want to fly off to Alpha Centauri. She did not want to leave the solar system behind her, leave the entire human race behind.

Yet she had to go. The ship could not function by itself for the ten years it would take to reach Alpha Centauri. The ship needed a human pilot, and she had always assumed that she would be that person.

But she did not want to go.

Twenty-two minutes.

Delia sat at the control console, watching the digital clock clicking down to midnight. Her vision blurred, and she realized that her eyes were filled with tears. This austere laboratory complex, this remote habitat set as far away from other human beings as possible, where she and her father had lived and worked alone for all these years—this was *home*.

"Delia!"

Marty's voice shocked her. She spun in her chair to see him standing in the doorway to the control room. Wiping her eyes with the back of a hand, she saw that he looked puzzled, worried. And there was a small faintly bluish knot on his forehead, between his eyes.

"The security system at your main airlock must be off-line. I just opened the hatch and walked in."

Delia tried to smile. "There isn't any security system. We never have any visitors."

"We?" Marty frowned.

"Me, I," she stuttered.

He strode across the smooth concrete floor toward her. "Alpha One monitored your comm transmissions to the power companies," Marty said, looking grim. "I'm here to shut down your experiment."

She almost felt relieved.

"You'll have to call the power companies and tell them you're cancelling your orders," he went on. "And that includes Rising Sun, too."

Delia said nothing.

"Buying power from Mercury. I've got to hand it to you, I wouldn't have thought you'd go that far." Marty shook his head, half-admiringly.

"You can't stop me," Delia said, so softly she barely heard it herself.

But Marty heard her. Standing over her, scowling at the display screens set into the console, he said, "It's over, Delia. I can't let you endanger all our lives. Alpha One agrees with me."

"I don't care," Delia said, one eye on the digital clock. "I'm not endangering anyone's life. You can have Alpha One check my calculations. There's no danger at all, as long as no one interferes with the power flow once—"

"I can't let you do it, Delia! It's too dangerous!"

His face was an agony of conflicting emotions. But all Delia saw was unbending obstinacy, inflexible determination to stop her, to shatter her father's dream.

Wildly, she began mentally searching for a weapon. She wished she had kept a gun in the laboratory, or that her father had built a security system into the airlocks.

Then her romance videos sprang up in her frenzied memory. She did have a weapon, the oldest weapon of all. The realization almost took her breath away.

She lowered her eyes, turned slightly away from Marty.

"Maybe you're right," Delia said softly. "Maybe it would be best to forget the whole thing." Nineteen minutes before midnight.

There was no other chair in the control room, so Marty dropped to one knee beside her and looked earnestly into her eyes.

"It will be for the best, Delia. I promise you."

Slowly, hesitantly, she reached out a hand and brushed his handsome cheek with her fingertips.

The tingle she felt along the length of her arm surprised her.

"I can't fight against you anymore," Delia whispered.

"There's no reason for us to fight," he said, his voice as husky as hers.

"It's just . . ." Eighteen minutes.

"I don't want you to go," Marty admitted. "I don't want you to fly off to the stars and leave me."

Delia blinked. "What?"

"I don't want to lose you, Delia. Ever since I met you, I've been fighting your father for your attention. And then your father's ghost. You've never really looked at me. Not as a person. Not as a man who loves you."

"But Marty," she gasped, barely able to speak, "I love you!"

He pulled her up from her chair and they kissed and Delia felt as if the Moon had indeed lurched out of its orbit. Marty held her tightly and she clutched at him, at the warm tender strength of him.

Then she saw the digital clock. Fifteen minutes to go.

And she realized that more than anything in the universe she wanted to be with Marty. But then her eye caught the display screen that showed the diamond starship sitting out on the crater floor, with her father in it, waiting, waiting.

Fourteen minutes, forty seconds.

"I'm sorry, Marty," she whispered into his ear. "I can't let you stop us." And she reached for the console switch that would automate the entire power sequence.

"What are you doing?" Marty asked.

Delia clicked the switch home. "Everything's on automatic now. There's nothing you can do to stop the process. In fourteen minutes or so the power will start flowing—"

"Alpha One can stop the power companies from transmitting the energy to you," Marty said. "And he will."

Delia felt her whole body slump with defeat. "If he does, it means the end of everything for me."

"No," Marty said, smiling at her. "It'll be the beginning of everything—for us."

Delia thought of life together with Marty. And the shadow of her father's ghost between them.

She felt something like an electric shock jolt through her. "Marty!" she blurted. "Would you go to Alpha Centauri with me?"

His eyes went round. "Go—with you? Just the two of us?"

"Ten years one way. Ten years back. A lifetime together."

"Just the two of us?"

"And Daddy."

His face darkened.

"Would you do it?" she asked again, feeling all the eagerness of youth and love and adventure.

He shook his head like a stubborn mule. "Alpha One won't allow you to have the power."

"Alfie's only got one vote. We've got two, between us."

"But he can override us on the safety issue."

"Maybe," she said. "But will you at least *try* to help me outvote him?"

"So we can go off to Alpha Centauri together? That's crazy!"

"Don't you want to be crazy with me?"

For an endless moment Delia's whole life hung in the balance. She watched Marty's blue eyes, trying to see through them, trying to understand what was going on behind them.

Then he grinned, and said, "Yes, I do."

Delia whooped and kissed him even more soundly than before. He's either lying or kidding himself or so certain that Alfie will stop us that he doesn't think it makes any difference, Delia told herself. But I don't care. He's going to *try*, and that's all that matters.

Twelve minutes.

Together they ran down the barren corridor from the control room to Delia's quarters and phoned Alpha One. The display screen simply glowed a pale orange, of course, but they solemnly called for a meeting of the Council. Then Delia moved that the Council make no effort to stop her experiment and Marty seconded the motion.

"Such a motion may be voted upon and carried," Alpha One's flat expressionless voice warned them, "but if the risk assessment determines that this experiment endangers human lives other than those willingly engaged in the experiment itself, I will instruct the various power companies not to send the electrical power to your rectennas."

Delia took a deep breath and, with one eye on Marty's face, solemn in the glow from the display screen, she worked up the courage to say, "Agreed."

Nine minutes.

"Alpha One won't let the power through," Marty said as they trudged back to the control room.

Delia knew he was right. But she said, "We'll see.

If Alfie's checking my calculations we'll be all right."

"He's undoubtedly making his own calculations," said Marty gloomily. "Doing the risk assessment."

Delia smiled at him. One way or the other we're going to share our lives, either here or on the way to the stars.

Two minutes.

Delia watched the display screens while Marty paced the concrete floor. I've done my best, Daddy, she said silently. Whatever happens now, I've done the very best I could. You've got to let me go, Daddy. I've got to live my own life from now on.

Midnight.

Power from six dozen sunsats, plus the relay satellites in orbit around Mercury, poured silently, invisibly into the rectennas ringing Newton's peaks. Energy from the sun was transformed back into electricity and then converted into more antimatter than the human race had ever seen before. Thirty tons of antiprotons, a million megatons of energy, ran silently in the endless racetrack of superconducting magnets and diamond sheathing along the floor of the crater.

The laboratory seemed to hum with their energy. The very air felt vibrant, crackling.

Delia could hardly believe it. "Alfie let us have the power!"

"What happens now?" Marty asked, his voice hollow with awe.

She spun her little chair around and jumped to her feet. Hugging him tightly, she said, "Now, my dearest darling, we store the antiprotons in the ship's crystal lattice, get aboard and take off for Alpha Centauri!"

He gulped. "Just like that?"

"Just like that." Delia held her hand out to him and Marty took it in his. Like a pair of children they ran out of the control room, to head for the stars.

The vast network of computer components that was known as Alpha One was incapable of smiling, of course. But if it could congratulate itself, it would have.

Alpha One had been built to consider not merely the immediate consequences of any problem, but its long-term implications. Over the half century of its existence, it had learned to look farther and farther into the future. A pebble disturbed at one moment could cause a landslide a hundred years later.

Alpha One had done all the necessary risk assessments connected with headstrong Delia's experiment, and then looked deep into the future for a risk assessment that spanned all the generations to come of humanity and its computer symbiotes.

Spaceflight had given the human race a new survival capability. By developing self-sufficient habitats off-Earth, the humans had disconnected their fate from the fate of the Earth. Nuclear holocaust, ecological collapse, even meteor strikes such as those that caused the Time of Great Dying sixty million years earlier—none of these could destroy the human race once it had established self-sufficient societies off-Earth.

Yet the Sun controlled all life in the solar system, and the Sun would not last forever.

Looking deep into future time, Alpha One had come to the conclusion that star flight was necessary if the humans and their computers were to disconnect their fate from the eventual demise of their Sun. And now they had star flight in their grasp.

As the diamond starship left the crater Newton in a hot glow of intense gamma radiation, Alpha One perceived that Delia and Marty were only the first star travellers. Others would certainly follow. The future of humanity was assured. Alpha One could erase its deepest concern for the safety of the human race and its computer symbiotes. Had it been anywhere near human, it would have sat back with a satisfied smile to wait with folded hands for the return of the first star travellers. And their children.

Introduction to "Delta Vee"

❖

You meet a lot of people over the years, and as a writer's career advances, some of those people become close friends, no matter how geographically distant they may be.

One of my closest friends—even though he lives a three hours' drive from me—is Rick Wilber. Rick is a fellow writer (as you will soon see), a teacher of journalism at Florida Southern University, and editor of the Tampa Tribune Fiction Quarterly.

The fourth edition of 1995's Fiction Quarterly was scheduled to be published on Sunday, the thirty-first of December. Rick asked me to contribute a story with a New Year's Eve theme.

"Delta Vee" is the result. By the way, if you detect a faint hint of Cinderella in this tale, it was an unconscious influence that I myself didn't see until the first draft of the story was finished. Something about that old clock striking a midnight deadline must have, well, struck a chime in my subconscious mind.

DELTA VEE

❖

It was going to be the last New Year's Eve. Forever.

Six months after the last hydrogen bomb was dismantled, a Japanese amateur astronomer discovered the comet. It was named after him, therefore: Comet Hara.

For more than thirty years special satellites and monitoring stations on both the Earth and the Moon had kept a dedicated watch for asteroids that might endanger our world. Sixty-five million years ago, the impact of an asteroid some ten miles wide drove the dinosaurs and three-fourths of all the living species on Earth into permanent oblivion.

Comet Hara was 350 miles long, and slightly more than 100 miles wide, an oblong chunk of ice slowly tumbling through space, roughly the size of the state of Florida minus its panhandle.

It was not detected until too late.

While asteroids and many comets coast through

the solar system close to the plane in which the planets themselves orbit, Comet Hara came tumbling into view high in the northern sky. The guardian battery of satellites and monitoring stations did not see it until it was well inside the orbit of Saturn.

It came hurtling, now, out of the dark vastness of the unknown gulfs beyond Pluto, streaking toward an impact that would destroy civilization and humanity forever. It was aimed squarely at Earth, like the implacable hand of fate, due to strike somewhere in North America between the Great Lakes and the Front Range of the Rockies.

Comet Hara was mostly ice, instead of rock. But a 350-mile-long chunk of ice, moving at more than seven miles per second, would explode on Earth with the force of millions of H-bombs. Megatons of dirt would be thrown into the air. Continentwide firestorms would rage unchecked, their plumes of smoke darkening the sky for months. No sunlight would reach the ground anywhere. Winter would freeze the world from pole to pole, withering crops, killing by starvation those who did not die quickly in the explosion and flames. The world would die.

Desperate calculations showed that Comet Hara would strike the Earth on New Year's Eve. No one would live to see the New Year.

Unless the comet could be diverted.

"It's too much delta vee," said the head of the national space agency. "If we had spotted it earlier, maybe then we'd have had a chance. But now . . ."

The president of the United States and the secretary-general of the United Nations were the only two people in the conference room that the former astronaut recognized. The others were leaders of other nations, he knew; twenty of them sitting around the polished mahogany table like twenty mourners at a funeral. Their own.

"What's delta vee?" asked the president. She had been a biochemist before entering politics. None of the men and women around the table knew much about astronautics.

"Change in velocity," he said, knowing it explained nothing to them. "Look—it's like this . . ."

Using his hands the way a pilot would, the former astronaut showed the comet approaching Earth. Any rocket vehicle sent out to intercept it would be going in the opposite direction from the comet.

"It takes a helluva lot of rocket thrust to get that high above the plane of the ecliptic," he said, moving his two hands together like a pair of airplanes rushing into a head-on collision.

"That's the plane in which the planets orbit?" asked the prime minister of Italy.

"More or less," the ex-astronaut replied. "Anyway, you need a huge jolt of thrust to get a spacecraft out to the comet, but when it gets there it's going the wrong way!"

"Then it will have to turn around," said the American president impatiently.

The space chief nodded unhappily. "Yes, ma'am. But it isn't all that easy to turn around in space. The craft has to kill its forward velocity and then put on enough speed again to catch up with the comet."

"I don't see the difficulty."

"Those maneuvers require rocket thrust. Lots of it. Rocket thrust requires propellants. Tons and tons of propellants. We just don't have spacecraft capable of doing the job."

"But couldn't you build one?"

"Sure. In a year or two."

"We only have five months," said the secretary-general, sounding somewhere between miffed and angry.

"That's the problem," admitted the space chief.

Hovering weightlessly in the cramped little cubbyhole that passed for the bridge of her spacecraft, Cindy Lundquist stared at the communications screen. The image was grainy and streaked with interference, but she could still see the utterly grim expression on the face of Arlan Prince.

". . . and after a thorough analysis of all the available options," the handsome young man was saying, "they've come to the conclusion that yours is the only spacecraft capable of reaching the comet in time."

Arlan was the government's coordinator of operations for all the mining ships in the Asteroid Belt, a job that would drive a lesser man to madness or at least fits of choler. There were dozens of mining ships plying the Belt, each owned and operated by a cantankerous individualist who resented any interference from some bureaucrat back on Earth.

But Arlan Prince did not descend into madness or even choleric anger. He smiled and patiently tried to help the miners whenever he could. Cindy dreamed about his smile. It was to die for.

"I don't want to mislead you, Cindy," he was saying, very seriously. "It's a tricky, dangerous mission."

Grease my monkey! she thought. He wants me to go out and catch a comet? They must be in ultimate despair if they expect this creaking old bucket of bolts to catch anything except terminal metal fatigue.

Cindy's aged spacecraft was coasting along the outer fringe of the Asteroid Belt, well beyond the orbit of Mars, almost four times farther from the Sun than the Earth's orbit. Since she was on the opposite side of the Sun from Earth's current position, it took thirty-eight minutes for a communications signal to reach her lonely little mining craft.

That meant that she couldn't have a conversation with Arlan Prince. She could talk back, of course, but it would be more than half an hour before the man heard what she had to say.

So he didn't wait for her response. He just went right on talking, laying the whole load on her shoulders.

"I know it's a lot to ask, but the entire world is depending on you. Yours is the only spacecraft anywhere in the solar system that has even a slight chance of catching up with the comet and diverting it."

He's not going to give me a chance to say no, Cindy realized. I either do it or the world gets smashed.

A thousand questions flitted through her mind. Why can't they just send some missiles out to the comet and blast it into ice cubes? No missiles and no H-bombs, she remembered. They've all been dismantled.

Do I have enough propellant to get to the comet? That's a whole mess of delta vee we're talking about. While Arlan droned on lugubriously, she flicked her fingers across her computer keypad. The numbers told her she could reach the comet, just barely. If nothing at all went wrong.

Which was asking a lot from this ancient wheeze of a mining ship she had inherited from her father. The old man had died brokenhearted out here among the asteroids that orbited between Mars and Jupiter. Looking for a mountain of gold floating in the dark emptiness of space.

All he ever found were chunks of nickel-iron or carbon-rich rock. Just enough to keep him going. Just enough to get by and raise his only child out in the loneliness of this cold, dark frontier.

Cindy couldn't remember her mother at all. She had died when Cindy was still an infant, killed by a tiny asteroid no bigger than a bullet that had punctured her spacesuit while she worked outside the ship alongside her husband.

Her father had died of cancer only a few months ago. An occupational hazard, he had joked feebly, for anyone who spends as much time exposed to the radiation of space as an asteroid miner has to.

So now all she had was the old spacecraft, so tiny and tight that you had to go into the airlock to have enough room to sneeze. It was all the home that Cindy had ever known, and all she ever would know, yet it felt more like a prison to her.

Cindy knew she would spend her life alone in this ship, plying the vast empty spaces of the asteroid belt. Miners were few and very far between. Born and raised in the weightlessness of zero gravity, her delicate bones could never hold her up on the surface of Earth, or even the Moon.

Arlan was still talking earnestly about saving the

Earth from certain doom. "According to our figures, you won't have enough propellant to return once you've matched velocities with the comet, therefore we will send a drone tanker to your expected position . . ."

Drone tanker, Cindy thought. And if I miss it I'll go sailing out of the solar system forever. I'll die all alone, farther from Earth than anyone's flown before.

So what? a voice sneered at her. You're all alone now, aren't you? You'll always be alone.

Wedged amid consoles and control boards like a key in a slot, Cindy turned to the laser control console and pecked at its faded color-coded keys. Power okay. Focusing optics needed work, but she could bring them in and spruce them up during the couple of months it would take to reach the comet.

She turned off the sound of Arlan's somber voice and spoke into her comm unit's microphone. "Okay, I'll do it. Track me good and have that tanker out there."

The truth was, she could not have refused anything that Arlan Prince asked of her, even though they had never met face-to-face. In fact, they had never been closer to each other than fifty million miles.

The comet was *huge*. Cindy had never seen anything so big. It blotted out the sky, a massive overpowering expanse of dirty gray-white. She was so close that she couldn't see all of it, any more than a butterfly hovering near a flower can see the entire garden.

Cindy floated weightlessly to the ship's only observation port and craned her neck, gaping at the monumental stretch of dust-filmed ice. The port's crystal surface felt cold to her touch. There was nothing outside except frigid emptiness, her fingers reminded her.

In one corner of her control console, a display screen showed how the comet looked from Earth: a big bright light in the sky, trailing a long blue-white plume that stretched halfway across the sky. It was beautiful, really, but every word she had heard from Earth was trembling with fear. The comet was pointed like the finger of doom, growing larger in Earth's sky every night, getting so near and so bright that it could be seen even in daylight.

Other screens scattered across her console scrolled graphs and numbers. Cindy had slaved the laser control to the computer calculations beamed up from Earth. When the moment came she wouldn't even have to press a button. It would all happen automatically.

If her laser worked.

The tanker was nowhere in sight, but Arlan Prince kept assuring her that it was on its way and would be at the rendezvous point on time.

Or else I'm dead, Cindy thought. And that voice inside her head scoffed, You're dead anyway. You've been more dead than alive ever since your father left you.

The thundering howl of the power generator startled her. Looking through the narrow observation port, she saw a sudden jet of glittering white vapor spurt from the comet's surface, like the spout of a gigantic whale's breath blowing into the dark vacuum of space.

Cindy clapped her hands over her ears and stared at the readouts on her display screens. The laser had never run this long, and she feared that it would break down long before its job was finished.

When it finally shut off, Cindy glanced at the master clock set into the console above her head. Its digital numbers told her that the laser ran a full two minutes. Exactly 120 seconds, as programmed.

Was it enough?

Hours passed. The comet was drifting away, slowly at first, but as Cindy stared out through the observation port it seemed to gather speed and leave her farther and farther behind.

Not even the bleeding comet wants to be near me, she thought. She waved to it, a great oblong chunk of grayish white, still spurting a glistening plume of icy vapor. Good-bye, she called silently, knowing that she was alone once again.

When the call from Earth came on her comm screen, it was the secretary-general of the United Nations. The woman had tears in her eyes.

"You've done it," she said, solemnly, like a worshiper thanking a god. "You've saved the world."

Cindy's spacecraft was so close to Earth now that they could talk with only a half minute's delay.

"You diverted it into a trajectory that's pulling it toward the Sun," the secretary-general said, trying to smile. "It will break up into fragments and then fall into the Sun, if it doesn't melt completely first."

"You mean I killed it?" Cindy felt a pang of regret, remorse. The comet had been beautiful, in its way.

"You've saved the world," the secretary-general said gratefully.

Cindy fished around for something to say, but nothing came to mind.

The secretary-general had more, though.

"The tanker..." The woman's voice faltered. With an obvious effort, she went on, "The tanker... isn't going to be at the rendezvous point. One of its rocket engines failed..."

"It won't be there?" Cindy asked, surprised that her voice sounded so high, so frightened.

"I'm afraid not," said the secretary-general.

Cindy felt her entire body slump with defeat. Numbers were scrolling on her data screens. The tanker would pass near the rendezvous point, but too far away for Cindy to reach it. She had no propulsion fuel left, only a bit of maneuvering thrust, nowhere near enough to chase down the errant tanker.

"Then I'll continue on my current trajectory," she said to the screens.

"Which is the same as the comet's original path," the secretary-general pointed out. She waited a decent interval, then added, "We don't want you to crash into the Earth, of course."

"Of course," said Cindy, as she turned off her communications system. The secretary-general's oh-so-sad face winked out.

Cindy knew that her little ship was no threat to the world. It would burn to cinders once it hit the atmosphere. Maybe I can jink it a little so I'll blaze through the atmosphere like a falling star, she thought. I'll be cremated, and my ashes will scatter all across the world.

But then she thought, no, I'll use the last of my maneuvering thrust to move out of Earth's way altogether. I'll just sail out of the solar system forever. I'll be the first human to reach the stars—in a couple-three million years.

New Year's Eve.

All across the world people celebrated not only the beginning of a new year, but the end of the fear that had gripped them. Comet Hara was gone. The world had been saved.

Cindy Lundquist floated alone in her little space-craft as it streaked safely beyond the Earth and speeded out toward the cold darkness of infinite space. For days her communications screen had been filled with gray-headed persons of importance, congratulating her on her heroic and self-sacrificing deed.

Now the screen was blank. The world was celebrating New Year's Eve, and she was alone, heading toward oblivion.

Precisely at midnight, on her ship's clock, the comm screen chimed once and the blond, tanned face of Arlan Prince appeared on it, smiling hand-somely.

"Hi," he said brightly. "Happy New Year."

Cindy didn't have the heart to smile back at him, handsome though he was.

"I've been put in charge of your rescue opera-tion," he said.

"Rescue operation?"

Nodding, he explained, "Since we weren't able to get the tanker to you, we decided to send out a res-cue mission."

"But I'm heading out of the solar system now."

"We know." His smile clouded briefly, then lit up

again. "It's going to take us at least six months to build the ship we need, and another six months to reach you."

"You're going to come out after me?"

"Certainly! You saved the world. We can't let you drift off and leave us. You're a celebrity now."

"Oh," said Cindy, dumbfounded.

"But it'll take a year before we get to you," he said, apologetically. "Do you have enough supplies on your ship to last that long?"

Cindy nodded, thinking that she'd have to skimp a lot, but losing a few pounds wouldn't hurt, especially if . . .

"Will you personally come out to get me?" she asked.

"Yes, of course," he replied. "When they asked me to head up the rescue mission, I insisted on it."

"A year from now?"

"Exactly one year from today," he said confidently.

"Then we can celebrate New Year's Eve together, can't we?" Cindy said.

"Indeed we will."

Cindy smiled her best smile at him. "Happy New Year," she said sweetly.

Introduction to
"Lower the River"

I worked for a dozen years at Avco Everett Research Laboratory, in Massachusetts. In many ways, it was the best experience of my life. I was living a science-fiction writer's dream, surrounded by brilliant scientists, engineers, and technicians working on cutting-edge research in everything from high-power lasers to artificial hearts.

We got involved in developing superconducting magnets in the early 1960s. Superconductors can generate enormously intense magnetic fields, and once energized they do not need to be continuously fed electrical power, as ordinary electromagnets do.

But they only remain magnetized if they are kept below a certain critical temperature. For the superconductors of the 1960s, the necessary temperature was a decidely frosty −423.04° Fahrenheit, only a few degrees above absolute zero. The coolant we used was liquified helium.

In the 1980s, "high-temperature" superconductors were discovered: they work at the temperature of liquid nitrogen, −320.8°F. Whoopee.

The search for a room-temperature superconductor, one that will remain superconducting at a comfortable 70°F *and therefore would not need cryogenic coolants, is being pushed in many labs.*

In the meantime, business colleges have sent their graduates into all sorts of industries. What would happen, I wondered, if one of these MBAs tried to use the management techniques of goal-setting and negative incentives on a physicist who is laboring to produce a room-temperature superconductor?

"Lower the River" is the result.

LOWER THE RIVER

❖

Jackson Klondike did not look like a world-class physicist. He was a shaggy bear of a man with a gruff manner and a ferocious sense of humor. Yet he was the unchallenged leader of the Rockledge Research Laboratory's bright and quirky scientific staff.

William Ratner did not look like a research lab director. He was astonishingly young, astoundingly handsome, and incredibly vapid. Yet he held a master's degree in business administration, and the Rockledge corporate officers (including his uncle Sylvester) had handed him the directorship of the lab.

With one single demand: Get results!

Klondike was smolderingly unhappy as he sat in front of Ratner's desk. It was obvious that he felt the time spent in the director's office was wasted; he wanted to be back in his own rat's nest of a lab where he could do some creative work.

Ratner had peeked into Klondike's lab only once. It looked like a chaotic mess, wires dangling from the ceiling, insulated tubing snaking everywhere, and vats of some mysterious stuff boiling and filling the chamber with steam that somehow felt cold instead of hot.

Klondike was the resident genius, though. His specialty was solid-state physics. For years he had been experimenting on superconducting magnets.

"I have a directive here from corporate headquarters in New York," Ratner said, as sternly as he could manage, rattling the single sheet of paper in one hand.

Across his desk Klondike sat straddling a chair he had turned backward, leaning his beefy arms on the chair's back, his chin half-buried in their hair, his eyes glowering at Ratner.

"A directive, huh?" Klondike vouchsafed.

Sitting up as straight as he could, Ratner said, "I know you don't think much of me, but I've been studying this superconductivity business for several weeks now."

"Have you?" Klondike's voice rumbled from somewhere deep in his chest, like distant thunder.

"Yes I have," Ratner said. "Superconducting magnets could be a major product line for this corporation, if it weren't for the fact that you need to keep them cold with liquid oxygen."

"Liquid nitrogen," reverberated Klondike.

"Nitrogen. That's what I meant."

"Used to be worse. When I first started in this game, we hadda use mother-lovin' liquid helium for cooling the coils. Liquid nitrogen's easy."

"But it's still a problem, as far as practicality is concerned, isn't it?"

"Nah. The real problem's the ductility of—"

"Never mind!" Ratner snapped, unwilling to allow Klondike to snow him with a lot of technical jargon.

Klondike glared at him, but shut up.

"I know what we need, and I made the suggestion to corporate management. They agree with me." He rattled the paper again.

Klondike remained in scowling silence.

"What we need is a superconductor that works at ordinary temperature, so we won't have to keep it cold with liquid—uh, nitrogen."

Klondike lifted his chin off his shaggy arms. "You mean we oughtta produce a room-temperature superconductor?"

"That's exactly right," said Ratner. "And the corporate management agrees with me. This directive *orders* you to produce a room-temperature superconductor."

Barely suppressing his disdain, Klondike replied, "Orders me, huh? And when do they want it? This week or next?"

Ratner smiled shrewdly. "I'm not a neophyte at this, you know. I understand that breakthroughs can't be made on a preconceived schedule."

Klondike glanced ceilingward, as if giving swift thanks for small mercies.

"Any time this fiscal year will do."

"This fiscal year?"

"That gives you nearly six months to get the task done."

"Produce a room-temperature superconductor in less than six months."

"Yes," said Ratner. "Or we'll have to find someone else who can."

Five months and fourteen days went by.

In all that time Ratner hardly saw Klondike at all. The man had barricaded himself in his lab, working night and day. His weekly reports were terse to the point of insult:

Week 1: Working on room-temperature superconductor.

Week 7: Still working on r-t s.

Week 14: Continuing work on rts.

Week 20: Making progress on rts.

Week 21: Demonstration of rts scheduled for next Monday.

Ratner had been worried, at first, that Klondike was simply ignoring his instruction. But once he saw that a demonstration was being set up, he realized that his management technique had worked just the way they had told him it would in business school. Set a goal for your employees, then make certain they reach your goal.

"So where is it?" Ratner asked. "Where is the demonstration?"

Klondike had personally escorted his boss down hallways and through workshops from the director's office to his own lab, deep in the bowels of the building.

"Right through there," Klondike said, gesturing to the closed door with the sign that read: ROOM-TEMPERATURE SUPERCONDUCTOR TEST IN PROGRESS. ENTRY BY AUTHORIZED PERSONNEL ONLY!

Feeling flushed with triumph, Ratner flung open the insulated door and stepped into—

A solid wall of frozen air. He banged his nose painfully and bounced off, staggering back into Klondike's waiting arms.

Eyes tearful, nose throbbing, he could see dimly through the frozen-solid air a small magnet coil sitting atop a lab bench. It was a superconductor, of course, working fine in the room temperature of that particular room.

Klondike smiled grimly. "There it is, boss, just like management asked for. I couldn't raise the bridge so I lowered the river."

Introduction to "Remember, Caesar"

One little phrase, "What if . . . ?" has been the beginning of many a science-fiction story.

Wars are started by old men (and sometimes old women) who sit at home and direct their troops. They are fought by young men (and sometimes young women) who do the bleeding and the dying.

But what if the dangers, the risks, the terror of battle could be brought home to the leaders who can sit out a war in a bombproof bunker, far from the fighting front?

And what if modern technology could produce a suit that makes its wearer invisible?

A "cloak of invisibility" is not terribly far from our current technological capabilities. Could that second "What if . . . ?" be used to answer the first one?

REMEMBER, CAESAR

We have never renounced the use of terror.
— VLADIMIR ILYICH LENIN

She was alone and she was scared.

Apara Jaheen held her breath as the two plain-clothes security guards walked past her. They both held ugly, deadly black machine pistols casually in their hands as they made their rounds along the corridor.

They can't see you, Apara told herself. You're invisible.

Still, she held her breath.

She knew that her stealth suit shimmered ever so slightly in the glareless light from the fluorescents that lined the ceiling of the corridor. You had to be looking for that delicate little ripple in the air, actively seeking it, to detect it at all. And even then you would think it was merely a trick your eyes played on you, a flicker that was gone before it even registered consciously in your mind.

And yet Apara froze, motionless, not daring to breathe, until the two men—smelling of cigarettes and after-shave lotion—passed her and were well down the corridor. They were talking about the war, betting that it would be launched before the week was out.

Her stealth suit's surface was honeycombed with microscopic fiber-optic vidcams and pixels that were only a couple of molecules thick. The suit hugged Apara's lithe body like a famished lover. Directed by the computer built into her helmet, the vidcams scanned her surroundings and projected the imagery onto the pixels.

It was the closest thing to true invisibility that the Cabal's technology had been able to come up with. So close that, except for the slight unavoidable glitter when the sequinlike pixels caught some stray light, Apara literally disappeared into the background.

Covering her from head to toe, the suit's thermal absorption layer kept her infrared profile vanishingly low and its insulation subskin held back the minuscule electromagnetic fields it generated. The only way they could detect her would be if she stepped into a scanning beam, but the wide-spectrum goggles she wore should reveal them to her in plenty of time to avoid them.

She hoped.

Getting into the president's mansion had been ridiculously easy. As instructed, she had waited until dark before leaving the Cabal's safe house in the miserable slums of the city. Her teammates drove her as close to the presidential mansion as they dared in a dilapidated, nondescript faded blue sedan that would draw no attention. They wished her success as she slipped out of the car, invisible in her stealth suit.

"For the Cause," Ahmed said, almost fiercely, to the empty air where he thought she was.

"For the Cause," Apara repeated, knowing that she might never see him again.

Tingling with apprehension, Apara hurried across the park that fronted the mansion, unseen by the evening strollers and beggars, then climbed onto the trunk of one of the endless stream of limousines that entered the grounds. She passed the perimeter guardposts unnoticed.

She rode on the limo all the way to the mansion's main entrance. While a pair of bemedaled generals got out of the limousine and walked crisply past the saluting uniformed guards, Apara melted back into the shadows, away from the lights of the entrance, and took stock of the situation.

The guards at the big, open double doors wore splendid uniforms and shouldered assault rifles. And were accompanied by dogs: two big German shepherds who sat on their haunches, tongues lolling, ears laid back.

Will they smell me if I try to go through the doors? Apara asked herself. Muldoon and his technicians claimed that the insulated stealth suit protected her even from giving off a scent. They were telling the truth, as they knew it, of course. But were they right?

If she were caught, she knew her life would be over. She would simply disappear, a prisoner of their security apparatus. They would use drugs to drain her of every scrap of information she possessed. They would not have to kill her afterward; her mind would be gone by then.

Standing in the shadows, invisible yet frightened, she tongued the cyanide capsule lodged between her upper-right wisdom tooth and cheek. This is a volunteer mission, Muldoon had told her. You've got to be willing to give your life for the Cause.

Apara was willing, yet the fear still rose in her throat, hot and burning.

Born in the slums of Beirut to a mother who abandoned her and a father she never knew, she had understood from childhood that her life was worthless. Even the name they had given her, Apara, meant literally "born to die."

It was during her teen years, when she had traded her body for life itself, for food and protection against the marauding street gangs who raped and murdered for the thrill of it, that she began to realize that life was pointless, existence was pain, the sooner death took her the sooner she would be safe from all fear.

Then Ahmed entered her life and showed her that there was more to living than waiting for death. Strike back! he told her. If you must give up your life, give it for something worthwhile. Even we who are lost and miserable can accomplish something with our lives. We can change the world!

Ahmed introduced her to the Cabal, and the Cabal became her family, her teacher, her purpose for breathing.

For the first time in her short life, Apara felt worthwhile. The Cabal flew her across the ocean, to the United States of America, where she met the pink-faced Irishman who called himself Muldoon and was entrusted with her mission to the White House. And decked in the stealth suit, a cloak of invisibility, just like the magic of old Baghdad in the time of Scheherazade and the Thousand and One Nights.

You can do it, she told herself as she clung to the shadows outside the White House's main entrance. They are all counting on you: Muldoon and his technicians and Ahmed, with his soulful eyes and tender dear hands.

When the next limousine disgorged its passengers, a trio of admirals, Apara sucked in a deep breath and walked in with them, past the guards and the dogs. One of the animals perked up its ears and whined softly as she marched in step behind the admirals, but other than that heart-stopping instant she had no trouble getting inside the White House. The guard shushed the animal, gruffly.

She followed the trio of admirals out to the west wing, and down the stairs to the basement level and a long, narrow corridor. At its end, Apara could see, was a security checkpoint with a metal detector like the kind used at airports, staffed by two women in uniform. Both of them were African-Americans.

She stopped and faded back against the wall as the admirals stepped through the metal detector, one by one. The guards were lax, expecting no trouble. After all, only the president's highest and most trusted advisors were allowed here.

Then the two plainclothes guards walked past her, openly displaying their machine pistols and talking about the impending war.

"You think they're really gonna do it?"

"Don't see why not. Hit 'em before they start some

real trouble. Don't wait for the mess to get worse."

"Yeah, I guess so."

They walked down the corridor as far as the checkpoint, chatted briefly with the female guards, then came back, passing Apara again, still talking about the possibility of war.

Apara knew that she could not get through the metal detector without setting off its alarm. The archwaylike device was sensitive not only to metals, but sniffed for explosives and x-rayed each person stepping through it. She was invisible to human eyes, but the x-ray camera would see her clearly.

She waited, hardly breathing, until the next clutch of visitors arrived. Civilians, this time. Steeling herself, Apara followed them up to the checkpoint and waited as they stopped at the detector and handed their wristwatches, coins and belts to the women on duty, then stepped through the detector, single file.

Timing was important. As the last of the civilians started through, holding his briefcase in front of his chest, as instructed, Apara dropped flat on her stomach and slithered across the archway like a snake speeding after its prey. Carefully avoiding the man's feet, she got through the detector just before he did.

The x-rays did not reach the floor, she had been told. She hoped it was true.

The alarm buzzer sounded. Apara, on the farside of the detector now, sprang to her feet.

"Hold it, sir," said one of the uniformed guards. "The metal detector went off."

He looked annoyed. "I gave you everything. Don't tell me the damned machine picked up the hinges on my briefcase."

The woman shrugged. "Would you mind stepping through again, sir, please?"

With a huff, the man ducked back through the doorway, still clutching his briefcase, and then stepped through once more. No alarm.

"Satisfied?" he sneered.

"Yes, sir. Thank you," the guard said tonelessly.

"Happens now and then," said her partner as she handed the man back his watch, belt and change. "Beeps for no reason."

"Machines aren't perfect," the man muttered.

"I guess," said the guard.

"Too much iron in your blood, Marty," joked one of the other men.

Apara followed them down the corridor, feeling immensely relieved. As far as her information went, there were no further security checkpoints. Unless she bumped into someone, or her suit somehow failed, she was safe.

Until she tried to get out of the White House. But that wouldn't happen until she had fulfilled her mission. If they caught her then, she would simply bite on the cyanide capsule, knowing that she had struck her blow for the Cause.

She followed the civilians into a spacious conference room dominated by a long, polished mahogany table. Most of the high-backed leather chairs were already occupied, mainly by men in military uniforms. There were more stars around the table than in a desert sky, Apara thought. One bomb in here and the U.S. military establishment would be decapitated, along with most of the cabinet heads.

She pressed her back against the bare wall next to

the door as the latest arrivals went around the table, shaking hands.

They chatted idly for several minutes, a dozen different conversations buzzing around the long table. Then the president entered from the far door and they all snapped to their feet.

"Sit down, gentlemen," said the president. "And ladies," she added, smiling at the three female cabinet members who sat together at one side of the table.

The president looked older in person than she did on television, Apara thought. She's not wearing so much makeup, of course. Still, the president looked vigorous and determined, her famous green eyes sweeping the table as she took her chair at its head. For an instant those eyes looked directly at Apara, and her heart stopped. But the moment passed. The president could not see Apara any more than the others could.

The president's famous smile was absent as she sat down. Looking directly at the chairman of the joint chiefs, she asked the general, "Well, are we ready?"

"In twenty-four hours," he replied crisply. "Troop deployment is complete, the naval task force is on station and our full complement of planes is on site, ready to go."

"Then why do we need twenty-four hours?" the president demanded.

The general's silver eyebrows rose a centimeter. "Logistics, ma'am. Getting ammunition and fuel to the front-line units, setting our communications codes. Strictly routine, but very important if we want the attack to come off without a hitch."

The president was not pleased. "Every hour we delay means more pressure from the U.N."

"And from the Europeans," said one of the civilians. Apara recognized him as the secretary of defense.

"The French are complaining again?"

"They've never stopped complaining, Madam President. Now they've got the Russians joining the chorus. They've asked for an emergency meeting of NATO."

"Not the General Assembly?"

The secretary of defense almost smiled. "No, ma'am. Even the French realize that the U.N. can't stop us."

A murmur of suppressed laughter rippled along the table. Apara felt anger. These people use the United Nations when it suits them, and ignore the U.N. otherwise.

The secretary of state, sitting at her right hand, was a thickset older man with a heavy thatch of gray hair that flopped stubbornly over his forehead. He held up a blunt-fingered hand and the table fell silent.

"I must repeat, Madam President," he said in a grave, dolorous voice, "that we have not yet exhausted all our diplomatic and economic options. Military force should be our *last* choice, after all other possibilities have been foreclosed, not our first choice."

"We don't have time for that," snapped the secretary of defense. "And those people don't respect anything but force, anyway."

"I disagree," said state. "Our U.N. ambassador

tells me that they are willing to allow the United Nations to arbitrate our differences."

"The United Nations," the president muttered.

"As an honest broker—"

"Yeah, and we'll be the honest brokee," one of the admirals wisecracked. Everyone around the table laughed.

Then the president said, "Our U.N. ambassador is a well-known weak sister. Why do you think I put him there in New York, Carlos, instead of giving him your portfolio?"

The secretary of state was not deterred. "Invading a sovereign nation is a serious decision. American soldiers and aircrew will be killed."

The president glared at him. "All right, Carlos, you've made your point. Now let's get on with it."

One of the admirals said, "We're ready with the nuclear option, if and when it's needed."

"Good," snapped the president.

And on it went, for more than an hour. The fundamentalist regime of Iran was going to be toppled by American military power. Its infiltration of other Moslem nations would end, its support of international terrorism would be wiped out.

Terrorism, Apara growled silently. They speak of using nuclear weapons, and they call the Iranians terrorists.

And what am I? she asked herself. What is the Cabal and the Cause we fight for? What other weapons do we have except terror? How can we struggle for a just world, a world free of domination, unless we use terror? We have no armies, no fleets of ships or planes. Despite the lies their media publish, we have no nuclear weapons, and we would not use them if we did.

Apara felt sure of that. The guiding precept of the Cause was to strike at the leaders of oppression and aggression. Why kill harmless women and children? Why strike the innocent? Or even the soldiers who merely carry out the orders of their leaders?

Strike the leaders! Put terror in *their* hearts. That was the strategy of the Cabal, the goal of the Cause.

Brave talk, Apara thought. Tonight we will see if it works. Apara glided along the wall until she was standing behind the president. She looked down at the woman's auburn hair, so perfectly curled and tinted. The president's fingernails were perfect, too: shaped and colored beautifully. She's never chipped a nail by doing hard work, Apara thought.

I could kill her now and it would look to them as if she had been struck down by God.

But her orders were otherwise. Apara waited.

The meeting broke up at last with the president firmly deciding to launch the attack within twenty-four hours.

"Tell me the instant everything's ready to go," she said to the chairman of the joint chiefs.

"Yes, ma'am," he said. "We'll need your positive order at that point."

"You'll get it."

She rose from her chair, and they all got to their feet. Like a ghost, Apara followed the president through the door into a little sitting room, where two more uniformed security guards snapped to attention.

They accompanied her down the corridor to the main section of the mansion and left her at the ele-

'vator that went up to the living quarters on the top floor. Apara climbed the stairs; the elevator was too small. She feared the president would sense her presence in its cramped confines.

Unseen, unsensed, Apara tiptoed through the broad upstairs hallway with its golden carpet and spacious windows at either end. There were surveillance cameras discreetly placed up by the ceiling, but otherwise no obvious security up at this level—except the electronic sensors on the windows, of course.

The president lived alone here, except for her personal servants. Her husband had died years earlier, during her election campaign, in an airplane crash that won her a huge sympathy vote.

Apara loitered in the hallway, not daring to rest on one of the plush couches lining the walls, until a servant bearing a tray with a silver carafe and bottles of pills entered the president's bedroom. Apara slipped in behind her.

The black woman turned her head, frowning slightly, as if she heard a movement behind her or felt a breath on the back of her neck. Apara froze for a moment, then edged away as the woman reached for the door and closed it.

The president was showering, judging by the sounds coming from the bathroom. Legs aching from being on her feet for so many hours, Apara went to the far window and glanced out at the darkened garden, then turned back to watch the servant deposit the tray on the president's night table and leave the room, silent and almost as unnoticed as Apara herself.

There was one wooden chair in the bedroom, and

Apara sat on it gratefully, knowing that she would leave no telltale indentation on its hard surface. She felt very tired, sleepy. The adrenaline had drained out of her during the long meeting downstairs. She hoped the president would finish her shower and get into bed and go to sleep quickly.

It was not to be. The president came out of the bathroom soon enough, but she sat up in bed and read for almost another hour before finally putting down the paperback novel and reaching for the pills on the night table. One, two, three different pills she took, with sips of water or whatever was in the carafe the servant had left.

At last the president sank back on her pillows, snapped her fingers to turn off the lights, and closed her eyes. Apara waited the better part of another hour before stirring off the chair. She had to be certain that the president was truly, deeply asleep.

Slowly she walked to the side of the bed. She stared at the woman lying there, straining to hear the rhythm of her breathing through the insulated helmet.

Deep, slow breaths. She's really sleeping, Apara decided. If the thought of invading another country and killing thousands of people bothered her, she gave no indication of it. Maybe the pills she took help her to sleep. She must have *some* qualms about what she's going to do.

Apara realized she was the one with the qualms. I can leave her here and get out of the mansion undetected, she told herself.

And the Cause, the purpose of her life, would evaporate like dew in the hot desert sun. Muldoon would be despairing, Ahmed so furious that he would never speak to her again. They would know she was unreliable, a risk to their own safety.

Strike! she told herself. They are all counting on you. Everything depends on you.

She struck.

By seven-fifteen the next morning the White House was surrounded by an armed cordon of U.S. Marines. No one was allowed onto the grounds, no one was allowed to leave the mansion.

Apara had already left; she simply walked out with the cleaning crew, a few minutes after 5:00 A.M.

The president summoned her secretary of state to the oval office at eight sharp. It was early for him, and he had to pass through the gauntlet of Marines as well as the regular guards and Secret Service agents. He stared in wonder as more Marines, in their colorful full-dress uniforms, stood in place of the usual servants.

"What's going on?" he asked the president when he was finally ushered into the oval office.

She looked ghastly: her face was gray, her eyes darting nervously. She clutched a thin scrap of paper in one hand.

"Never mind," the president said curtly. "Sit down."

The secretary of state sat in front of her desk. He himself felt bleary-eyed and rumpled, this early in the morning.

Without preamble, the president asked, "Carlos, do you seriously think we can settle this crisis without a military strike?"

The secretary of state looked surprised, but he quickly regained his wits. "I've been trying to tell you that for the past six weeks, Alicia."

"You think diplomacy can get us what we want."

"Diplomacy and economic pressures, yes. We can even get the United Nations on our side, if we call off this military strike. It's not too late, you know."

The president leaned back in her chair, fiddling with that scrap of paper, trying to keep her hands from trembling. Unwilling to allow her secretary of state to see how upset she was, she swivelled around to look out the long windows at the springtime morning. Birds chirped happily among the flowers.

"All right," she said, her mind made up. "Tell Muldoon to ask for an emergency session of the Security Council. That's what he's been after all along."

A boyish grin broke cross the secretary of state's normally dour face. "I'll phone him right now. He's still in New York."

"Do that," said the president. Then she added, "From your own office."

"Yes, ma'am!"

The secretary of state trotted off happily, leaving the president alone at her desk in the oval office. With the note still clutched in her shaking hand.

I'll put the entire White House staff through the wringer, she said to herself. Every damned one of them. Interrogate them until their brains are fried. I'll find out who's responsible for this . . . this . . .

She shuddered involuntarily.

They got into my bedroom. My own bedroom! Who did it? How many people in this house are plotting against me?

They could have killed me!

I'll turn the note over to the Secret Service. No,

they screwed up. If they were doing their job right this would never have happened. The attorney general. Give it to the FBI. They'll find the culprit.

Her hands were shaking so badly she could hardly read the note.

Remember Caesar, thou art dust.

That's all the note said. Yet it struck terror into her heart. They could have killed me. This was just a warning. They could have killed me just as easily as leaving this warning on my pillow.

For the first time in her life, she felt afraid.

She looked around the Oval Office, at the familiar trappings of power, and felt afraid. It's like being haunted, she said to herself.

In his apartment in New York, the U.S. ambassador to the United Nations nodded as he spoke to the president's secretary of state.

"That's good news, Carlos!" said Herbert Muldoon, with a hint of Irish lilt in his voice. "Excellent news. I'm sure the president's made the right choice."

He cut the connection with Washington and immediately punched up the number of the U.N.'s secretary general, thinking as his fingers tapped on the keyboard:

It worked! Apara did the job. Now we'll have to send her to Tehran. And others, too, of course. The mullahs may be perfectly willing to send young assassins to their deaths, but I wonder how they'll react when they know they're the ones being targeted.

We'll find out soon.

Introduction to
"The Babe, the Iron Horse, and Mr. McGillicuddy"

❖

As I mentioned in the introduction to "Delta Vee," Rick Wilber is a writer, as well as an editor and teacher. A very fine writer, as a matter of fact; one of the few true literary stylists in today's science-fiction field.

Rick is also, like me, a baseball fan. He comes to this genetically, being the son of Del Wilber, a big-league catcher for many years. Thus, when he writes about baseball Rick adds an insider's knowledge to his formidable writing skills. My knowledge of baseball is strictly from the grandstand seats, rooting for the tragedy-prone Boston Red Sox.

One day we got talking about baseball and, as writers will, we were soon plotting a story that involved Babe Ruth, Lou Gherig (baseball's "Iron Horse") and Cornelius McGillicuddy, known to the world as Connie Mack, long-time owner and manager of the Philadelphia Athletics.

This story is pure fantasy, of course. I only hope that you have as much fun reading it as Rick and I had writing it.

THE BABE, THE IRON HORSE, AND MR. McGILLICUDDY

The Iron Horse uncoiled, bringing the hips through first and then following with the shoulders, those quick wrists, that snap as the bat hit the ball.

It was just batting practice, but Lou felt wonderful, like a kid again, with no pain, with the body doing what it had always done so well. He had no idea what was going on, how he'd gotten here, what had happened. He almost didn't want to think about it, for fear it might all be some hallucination, some death dream, his mind going crazy in the last moments, trying to make the dying easier for him.

There was a sharp crack as he sent a towering shot toward the center-field wall in Yankee Stadium, over the wall for sure, sailing high and deep. He stood there and watched this one go. It would be nearly five hundred feet before it landed, he guessed.

But the Negro ballplayer roaming around out in center shagging flies did it again, turned his back to the plate and raced away, heading straight toward the wall, full tilt. There was, surprisingly, a lot of room now in center, and the Negro had blazing speed. He somehow managed to nearly catch up with the ball, and then, amazingly, reached straight out in front to make a basket catch over his shoulder. It was a beautiful catch, an amazing one, really, the large number 24 on the man's back all that Lou could see for a moment as the ball was caught.

Then the Negro turned and fired a strike toward second, where Charlie Gehringer waited for it, catching it on one long hop and sweeping the bag as if there were a runner sliding in. Gehringer whooped as he made the tag, as impressed as everyone else with the centerfielder's arm. Then he rolled the ball in toward the batting practice pitcher.

On the mound, taking a ball out of the basket and pounding it into his catcher's mitt, Yogi just smiled. Like everyone else, he didn't understand how this was happening, how they all came to be here—but he really didn't care. When he let that last pitch go he'd have sworn he was in Yankee Stadium somehow, but then, looking at Willie chase it down in dead center, it looked for all the world like the Polo Grounds, with Coogan's Bluff in the background.

It didn't make any kind of sense, but Yogi just decided he wasn't going to worry about it. He and the other fellows were having a good time, that was all. And he'd been right, he figured with pride. It wasn't over till it was over.

He took a quick look around. There was Willie Mays out there in center, and Gehringer at second, and Ted out in left. Next to the cage, swinging a couple of bats, getting loose to hit next, was Scooter himself, happy as a clam. There were great players everywhere, and more showing up all the time, walking in from the clubhouse or just suddenly out there, in the field, taking infield or shagging flies.

Yogi counted heads. Where, he wondered, was the Babe? You'd think he'd be here. Then Yogi went into a half-wind, took a short stride toward the plate, making sure to get the pitch up over that open corner of the screen that protected him from shots up the middle, and threw another straight ball in to Lou. Imagine, he thought, me, throwing bp to Gehrig. The line drive back at him almost took his head off.

In the stands, up a dozen rows near the back of the box seats, an old, fat, sad-faced Babe Ruth sat in a wide circle of peanut shells. He was eating hot dogs now, and drinking Knickerbocker beer, watching batting practice, not saying much. He knew a few of the guys out there, but couldn't place the others. There was a sharp clap of thunder, and the Babe wondered if the day might be rained out. Low dark clouds circled the field, swirling and rumbling with menace.

Next to him sat white-haired, saintly Connie Mack, producing hot dog after hot dog as the Babe shoved them into that maw and chewed them down. Amazing, really, this fellow's capacity. Ruth was perspiring in a heavy flannel suit. Mack, slim as a willow, looked coolly comfortable in his customary dark suit, starched collar, and straw boater.

"George," Mack said, "isn't that about enough for now?"

Ruth never stopped chewing, but managed to say

"Mr. Mack, I ain't got any idea how long it's been since I sat in a ballyard and ate a hot dog, and I also ain't got any idea how long this is gonna' last. Them clouds move in and this thing'll be a rain-out. I'm eating while I can, you know?"

"George, I understand. Truly I do. But I really don't think it will rain, and I'd hoped that you might want to get out there and take a few cuts, meet the other fellows. There are some very fine players out there."

Mack pointed toward the infield. "That fellow there at third is Brooks Robinson, as fine a glove man as you'll ever see at that position. And at short-stop, that young, lanky fellow is Marty Marion, one of the slickest men to ever play short. And there, in the outfield, is Willie Mays, the Negro who just caught that ball. Next to him, in left, is Ted Williams..."

"I know him, the Williams kid," said the Babe between bites. "Helluva young hitter. Got a real future."

"Indeed," said Mack. "And at second is Charlie Gehringer, you know him, too. And there are others showing up all the time. Look, there's Dominic DiMaggio, and Hoot Evers. These are good men, Babe, all of them, good men. You really should make the decision to join them, before it's too late."

"Who's that catching?"

"Fellow named Wilber. Del Wilber. A journeyman, but with a fine mind, Babe. He'll make a fine manager someday, and he has a good, strong arm. He'll cut people down at second if we need him to play."

"And pitching?"

"That's a coach throwing batting practice, Yogi Berra. Another good catcher, too, in his day. He can help us if it comes to that. And warming up out there in the bullpen is Sandy Koufax, he's our starter. You should see his curveball, George, it's really something.

"You know," Mack said, "you belong out there. You really do. You should be loosening up a bit, running around out in the outfield, a few wind sprints perhaps, instead of"—he handed the Babe a napkin—"this."

The Babe shook his head. "I gave all that up a few years back. I appreciate it, Mr. Mack. But the thing is, it's like this, I hung 'em up, Mr. Mack, and that's all there is to it. Now if you need a manager . . ."

Mack smiled. "I'm afraid that the managerial position is filled for now, George. But, there *is* a roster spot for you, I'd love to have you on my team. You could play in the outfield for us, or even pitch. I think you'd enjoy it."

The Babe held out his hand, and Mack started to shake it, thinking the deal was done, and quite early, too. Then he realized what the Babe really wanted, sighed to himself, and obligingly placed another hot dog into it. Incredible capacity, really.

"Maybe in a little while, Mr. Mack," Ruth said, taking a huge first bite. "But right now, if you don't mind, I'd like to just sit and watch Lou and these other guys. The Dutchman, he looks fine, don't he? Always was a sweet hitter, got those wrists, you know? Snap on that ball and away she goes."

There was another sharp crack as Gehrig sent one deep to center. Mays drifted under this one, waited, then made a basket catch to some general laughter from the other players. What a showboat, that Mays.

"He's something, ain't he, that nigger?" said the Babe. "Remember Josh Gibson, Mr. Mack? Now, there was a ballplayer. Boy, I tell you, he could hit that thing a ton. Played against him once or twice in exhibitions."

But Mack wasn't listening to the Babe, who, Mack figured, would just have to make his decision later. For now, Mack had heard the clatter of a dying engine out in the parking lot and rose to head out that way, excusing himself absentmindedly and leaving six more hot dogs with Ruth—enough, Mack hoped, to tide the Babe over for a few minutes.

Although he carried a cane, the elderly Mack seemed almost to float along the row of seats and out to the steps that led up from the box seats. He was a quiet man, and despite the peanut shells everywhere, there was no crunching, no sound at all, really, as he left, moving up to the back ramp of the stadium, from where he watched the old 1937 Ford bus clang its way into the empty parking lot. There was a cloud of blue smoke and a loud bang as the engine finally seized up entirely and the bus shuddered to a stop.

Mack frowned slightly, then watched with interest as the front door of the bus creaked open halfway. A hand reached out and tugged, tugged again, and the door banged open another foot or so. People started to emerge.

First off the bus was Leo Durocher, scowling and cursing, five o'clock shadow already darkening his jaw. Pushing him from behind was Pete Rose, who in turn was being pushed by Ty Cobb, who threatened to spike Rose if he didn't hurry it up.

A quiet, scared-looking Joe Jackson got off next, looking around anxiously for any kids ready to ask troublesome questions. Then came Billy Martin, Buck Weaver, Bill Terry, John "Bad Dude" Sterns, Carl Mays, Eddie Stanky, Sal Ivars, Bill Lee, Bob Gibson, Rogers Hornsby, Thurman Munson. This was a tough bunch of guys.

Charlie Comiskey was driving the bus, and still on it, arguing with someone while the others stood around outside, waiting.

"Damn it, we're here. You have to get off now, all right? We can settle all this later."

"*Merde*," said a voice from the back, enveloped in a cloud of cigar smoke. "You are all the same, always, you colonialists, always demanding that we do your bidding. Well, I tell you this, I will get off when I am damn well ready to get off, and no sooner. *Comprende?*"

"Get your ass out here, Fidel," shouted Rose. Then he turned to Durocher, and added, "Damn commies. All the same, I swear."

Durocher nodded, but added, "I played winter ball down there in Cuba a couple of times, Petey. Great times. Food was good, women were fast, and the players were pretty damn decent. They're not too bad, you know. But this guy? Shit. Nothing but bitching for twenty miles of bumpy roads getting here."

Durocher looked over at the ballpark. "Where the hell is 'here,' anyway?"

"We're in Fostoria, Ohio, Leo," said Comiskey, giving up on Castro for the moment and stepping down from the bus. "Nice little park. Seats about a thousand. Built in the early twenties. Two showerheads. Cold water. A few nails to hang your street clothes on. You'll love the accommodations."

"Oh, Christ," said Bill Terry. "I played in this park. It's got a godforsakin' skin infield, and some fucking mountains in the outfield. What a hole. Jesus, the Ohio State League. I don't fuckin' believe it. This is hell, just hell."

Comiskey just smiled and pointed toward the door that said "Visitors" in faded black paint. The players headed that way, all except for Castro, who still wouldn't budge.

"Hey, Fidel," said Rose, "I hear Lou Gehrig's in there taking batting practice. If you can move your fat Cuban ass outta there, you can pitch to him today. Wouldn't that be something, striking out Gehrig?"

There was a rustle from the back of the bus, and then Castro's head appeared out the top half of one cracked window. "Gehrig? Is this true?"

"Swear to god, Fidel. Swear to god. The Iron Horse himself. And in his prime."

Fidel looked at Comiskey, who simply nodded. It was true. And so, a few minutes later the President for Life and the Black Sox owner walked side by side toward the clubhouse through the dusty parking lot. Castro's expensive Italian shoes left a perfect outline in the dust, aimed toward the ballpark and a chance to pitch to the Iron Horse. And next to them, filling in quickly even in the lightest of breezes, were other prints, narrower prints, almost round ones, like hoofprints with a sharp indentation.

Above, in the stands, Connie Mack watched them open the clubhouse door and walk through. He sighed. So, he thought, it was time.

He looked out across the field, seeing stately old Shibe Park with its double-decked stands out in left field and the deep, deep center field and the long high wall in right. Bobo Newsome was throwing batting practice pitches to Stan Musial. Walter Johnson was warming up in the home-team bullpen. Roberto Clemente had just arrived and was trotting out to join Ted Williams in the outfield.

Mack looked up. The dark clouds still swirled by, but he knew the rain would hold off for as long as he needed to get the game in. Otherwise, the setting was perfect.

There was a long, low rumble of thunder, and Mack looked down to see Charlie Comiskey, fat and grunting and sweating, climbing the concrete steps toward him. No, Mack saw. Comiskey was heading for the Babe. By the time Mack got back to the box— littered with peanut shells and hot-dog wrappers— Comiskey had peeled off his woolen jacket and was sitting next to the Babe, laughing and wheezing away.

Mack took a seat behind them.

"Why, Cornelius McGillicuddy, as I live and breathe!" Comiskey said, with mock good cheer. "The Babe tells me you won't let him manage your team."

"And you won't allow him to manage yours, either, will you Charles?" Mack replied.

"Well," Comiskey drew out the word tantalizingly. "I don't exactly know about that. You do well on the field, Babe, get the rest of my men to look up to you, maybe I'll step aside and let you take over as manager."

Mack gave his rival a wintry smile. "But not for today's game."

Comiskey scowled and squinted at Mack. "No, that's right. I've got to be manager for today. That's in the agreement we signed." Then he added, almost growling, "In blood."

"That," said Mack, "was your idea, Charles. Not mine."

"I did all the playin' I intend to do," Ruth said, looking around for more hot dogs. "There's nothing left for me to do on a ball field that I ain't already done. But they never let me manage a club. I coulda' been a good manager. You know, if things had worked out better in '35 . . ."

Comiskey reached into the jacket he had tossed over the back of the empty seat next to him and pulled out a hot dog. It looked cold and soggy, flecked with lint here and there, but the Babe took it and munched away hungrily.

"Don't they have any more beer around here?" he asked, through a mouthful of hot dog.

"Down in the visitors' clubhouse," Comiskey answered quickly. "We brought barrels of beer. Good stuff, too."

"Well, then," said the Babe, putting his hands on the rail in front of his seat to help pull his bulk up and out of the tight fit of the chair.

"George. Here," said Mack, miraculously producing another bottle of Knickerbocker and handing it to Ruth.

"Why, thanks, Mr. Mack, thanks very much," said the Babe, taking a long swig and then turning away from both managers to look at the field.

"Say, look at those guys coming out of the visitors' dugout," he said suddenly, pointing with the brown bottle of Knickerbocker toward the first-base line.

"Say!" he said, again, excited, rising from his seat. "Why, that's Ty Cobb, and poor old Joe Jackson, and . . . Why, there's a whole team full of 'em. Look at that." And he slumped back into his seat, stunned by what he was seeing.

"Why, I guess you two *are* going to have a game today, aren't ya. And it's gonna be a helluva game, too, I can tell you that. A hell of game. That's some of the best fellows out there that has ever played hardball. I mean it, the best."

"Yes, George," said Mack, kindly. "Yes, it is going to be a very fine game, played by some of the best the game has ever produced."

"And my team is going to win it, McGillicuddy," snarled Comiskey. "You can bet on it." And he chuckled. "As if you'd ever bet on anything."

Mack just looked at Comiskey, shook his head slightly, then turned to speak to Ruth.

"George, you just relax here for now, all right?" and he handed the Babe a few more hot dogs and another beer. "Enjoy the game. And if you ever decide you'd like to play, for one team or the other, you just let us know, all right?"

"Sure, Mr. Mack. Sure. I'll let the two of you know, right away," said the Babe. "But y'know, I'm not sure this is enough beer," and he turned to face the two men to request a bit more, figuring one of them would come through, for sure.

But they were gone. Both of them. And when the Babe turned back to look at the field, Sandy Koufax was warming up on the mound, Pete Rose was at the plate, leading off, and the game was about to begin.

It was a battle, right from the outset. Koufax was blazing fast, and his curve looked as if it was dropping off a table. But Ty Cobb chopped one of those curves into the dirt along the third-base line and beat it out for a single. Then Rogers Hornsby slapped a Texas Leaguer that dropped between Gehrig, Gehringer, and Aaron for a double while Cobb raced home with the first run. Koufax then fanned Ducky Medwick and Bill Terry, to end the inning with Hornsby stranded on second.

As the players trooped in from the dugout, Gehrig saw the Babe sitting alone and forlorn in the box seat. He waved to his old teammate, then ducked into the shadow of the dugout and sat next to Connie Mack.

"What's this all about, Mr. Mack?" he asked, as he sat next to the frail-looking old man.

"What do you mean, Louis?"

Phil Rizzuto led off for Mack's team. Carl Mays scowled at the diminutive shortstop, then threw a wicked underhand fastball at the Scooter's head. Rizzuto hit the dirt as Bill Klem calmly called ball one.

"This game, the guys here." Gehrig's handsome face was truly troubled. "I mean, I *died*, Mr. Mack. There was a lot of pain, and I was in the hospital, and my wife was crying and ... all of a sudden, I'm here."

"I died, too, Louis," said Mack, as Rizzuto danced away from another fastball aimed at his ear. "Everyone dies."

Gehrig stared at him. "Then . . . where are we?"

Mack smiled gently. "That all depends, Louis. It all depends on this game. And that big fellow sitting up there in the stands."

"The Babe?"

Mack nodded as Rizzuto slapped weakly at a curve and popped it toward Eddie Stanky at second base. The Scooter trudged halfway down the base path, then turned toward the dugout, looking glad to be out of range of Mays' beanballs.

Gehrig scanned the infield. "Wait a minute, where's Hornsby? Who's that little fellow out at second?"

Connie Mack sighed unhappily. "The other team has a certain amount of flexibility in the rules," he said.

"They can take players in and out of the lineup whenever they want to?"

With an even deeper sigh, Mack admitted, "That was just one of the provisions that Mr. Comiskey insisted upon, Louis. There are others changes, too. Now and again you'll see them playing on an artificial surface, a kind of fake grass. It helps the singles hitters immensely. You'll see their Rose fellow take special advantage of that, I suspect. And if this threatening weather actually turns to rain, they'll play indoors, in a ballpark with a roof over it."

Gehrig gaped at the thought.

"And they even have what they call a designated hitter, Louis, a fellow who just steps up to the plate and hits for the pitcher. He never has to play any defense."

"Free substitution?" Gehrig shook his head in surprise. "Fake grass? A roof, for God's sake? Full-time hitters? That just doesn't seem like baseball to me, Mr. Mack.''

"There are a lot of us who feel that way, Louis, but those are today's rules."

"And we can't get our own roof, or use a permanent hitter if we want?''

Mack took off his straw hat, used the back of his hand to mop his brow and put the hat back on. "Well, Louis, it's more that we choose not to. It just doesn't seem right to me. We are, after all, on the side of the angels, Louis. I thought we ought to play the game the way it's meant to be played."

And Lou nodded in agreement, then turned to look up into the box seats, where the Babe sat, watching.

To the Babe's credit, by the bottom of the first he was pretty much done with the hot dogs and beer and was limiting himself to an occasional peanut, carefully squeezing the shell to crack it, then breaking off the top half of the shell and tossing the nuts, nestled there in the bottom half, into his mouth.

But that was all, just the peanuts. Oh, and a sip of beer once in a while to wash them down. And just one more hot dog now and again.

But he was slowing down on the eating because, in truth, the game was beginning to bother him. He knew it was just some sort of exhibition, and so they were being a little easy on the rules and all, but not only were Comiskey's guys substituting right and left, coming in and then out of the game whenever they seemed to want to, they were also playing a mean, vicious brand of ball.

In the top of the second, for instance, Ty Cobb, at

the plate again even though he'd hit in the first and wasn't due up, slashed a line drive into the gap in right that had stand-up double written all over it. The black kid in right, though, got a good jump on the ball and chased it down on the third hop, before it got to the warning track. Then he turned and fired to second, and it was suddenly a close play as the ball and Cobb approached the bag at the same time.

And damned if Ty didn't come in with those spikes up high, trying to move the shortstop, that Rizzuto guy, off the bag or cut him if he stayed in. Rizzuto, to his credit, stood his ground, catching Aaron's throw on the first hop and bringing the glove down in front of Cobb's right foot as it approached the bag. Out.

But the left foot, up high, caught Rizzuto on the right calf, tearing right through the baggy flannel and cutting open a good six-inch gash that bled badly until the trainer, Bob Bauman from the Cardinals, trotted out from the dugout to get enough pressure on it to stop the flow.

Rizzuto limped off the field under his own power, but he was obviously in pain. Marty Marion, tall and lanky for a shortstop, came out to replace him. Cobb, glaring defiantly, watched it all, hands on hips, until Rizzuto left, then trotted into the Comiskey dugout to a few handshakes and back slaps from his teammates.

And in the bottom of the second Carl Mays hit two of Mack's players. First he put a fastball into Aaron's ribs, then he followed that up with another heater that caught Brooks Robinson on the left wrist. If Brooks hadn't gotten that hand up in the way, the ball might have caught him in the face. There was an audible gasp from Mack's dugout as the dull thwack of the ball hitting flesh echoed through the park. Then there were angry shouts, but Mays, imperious on the mound, ignored them, and Klem, behind the plate, bade the game go on.

The Babe, munching peanuts, scowled as he sat in the stands. It wasn't right. One side not only seemed to get special rules but also played a really mean brand of ball. He was starting to get downright mad about it. Okay, it wasn't like Comiskey's guys were a bunch of choirboys, they were rough, tough players, by God, and everybody knew it; but the Babe thought this game was meant to be for fun, for the love of the game and all that. Those guys shouldn't be cutting each other up out there. They're playing like it was a World Series, like their lives depended on it.

They took Mays out after Charlie Gehringer whacked a double down the right-field line. The Babe stared, wide-eyed, at Comiskey's new pitcher. The guy had a beard! Must be from the House of David team. He was a southpaw, in to face Williams and then Lou.

Williams walked. Lou swung and missed a really wicked curve ball. The bearded lefthander grinned on the mound and yelled something the Babe couldn't understand. Hebrew, maybe.

He tried his curve again. Wrong move. Lou smashed it 'way, 'way out there, so high and deep the ball disappeared into the bright sky. Three-run homer. That was all for the bearded lefthander.

But Comiskey's guys started hitting, too. And slashing any infielder who got in their way. Durocher barrelled into Charlie Gehringer at second on a routine double-play ball, knocked him flat. It was such a cheap shot that the Babe jumped out of his seat and yelled at Durocher as he trotted in from the field. Leo glanced up at the only man in the stands and seemed to look—embarrassed? The Babe sat down again, stunned at that.

The game went on, seesawing back and forth. The Babe would roar whenever Comiskey's guys pulled one of their lousy stunts. It felt real good, in fact, to let the anger explode, tell those cheap-shot bums what bush-league bastards they were, get the juices flowing again like they hadn't in a long, long time.

"By God," the Babe muttered to himself, "if I wasn't so old, if I wasn't in such rotten shape, I'd go out there and teach those sonsabitches a lesson they wouldn't forget."

But he was old and fat and useless. And he knew it.

Then came the sixth inning.

A chunky righthander named Wynne was pitching for Comiskey now. Lou was at the plate, and the Babe was thinking about all the good years he and Gehrig had put in together.

Truth be known, the Babe had always had mixed feelings about Lou. On the one hand, he envied the Dutchman a bit, that tight focus on the game, the way he always kept himself in shape, the reputation he had as a nice guy and a smart one, a real gentleman. In a lot of ways, the Babe wished he could have been a gentleman.

But, on the other hand, the Babe thought that Lou had always been so busy being nice that a lot of times he didn't seem to be having much fun. The booze, the women, the high life—it was all part of the fun, and if the game wasn't fun, why play? My god, it ought to be fun, that was the whole point. Lou had always seemed so damned serious about everything, and that was too bad.

That was part of what was making the Babe so mad right now about these other fellows, these guys playing for Comiskey. The way they were playing was too low, too mean, for it to be any fun. They had forgotten what the game was about. It wasn't life and death, it was baseball, for Christ's sake, the joy of hitting, of catching and throwing the ball, or rounding third on a home-run trot, of sliding into second with a double, of just knocking the dirt off the cleats with the handle of the bat.

Ah, yes, the bat. Watching Lou take two balls low and away, then swing and hit a long foul ball out into the right-field seats for a 2-1 count, the Babe could almost feel the way it was to hold his old Louisville Slugger, to swing it and make contact. He leaned back in his seat and stretched his arms out, opening and closing those meaty hands, tightening the arm muscles, feeling good in doing it.

He brought his hands together, made fists, placed the left fist over the right as if holding a bat, and brought the two fists back into a stance, as if he were waiting for a pitch, a good fastball out over the plate, rising, begging to be hit. He felt good doing it, real good, like a kid again, having fun.

"Damned if it wouldn't feel good. Just one more time," he said aloud, to no one in particular. "Damned if it wouldn't."

It was calming, thinking about that. The Babe almost forgot how infuriated he'd been by the rough play, when Wynne changed all that, almost forever.

First he came inside on Lou for ball three, and then, while the Babe watched horrified, Wynne—despite the count—brought in a rising fastball, high and tight, that caught Lou just above the ear and laid him out cold in the dirt.

It looked for a second like maybe Lou had gotten his hand up to block it, but then, the Babe heard the awful *chunk* of ball hitting flesh and the Iron Horse just lay there. Babe knew it was serious. As Lou lay still in the dirt the Babe rose from his seat.

"You god-damned sonsabitches," he yelled, and started walking down toward the diamond. "You bunch a' shitheaded bastards," he yelled again, taking the wide concrete steps two at a time. "That ain't baseball, that ain't the way it's supposed to be played."

He reached the low gate that was next to the dugout, but didn't bother to open it, just vaulted over the rail instead and landed on the field.

And in doing that he realized there had been some changes. He felt good, he felt really good. He looked down at himself, expecting to see the man he'd become, that rounded belly, the toothpick legs, the arms with the flesh on them loose, hanging down, like the jowls on his face. Damn age. He hated it, hated getting old, hated knowing he couldn't hit anymore, hated having to live the game through memories.

And what he saw instead was the Babe he'd been at twenty-five, his first year in the outfield for the Yankees. Solid, tight, firm. The legs were strong, he could feel that. And the arm felt good, real good. He brought his hands to his face, felt the youth there.

He hustled over to where Lou lay there, barely

conscious, the trainer working on him, talking to him in low tones, trying to bring him out of it.

"Lou," the Babe said, leaning over to look at Gehrig. "Lou, it was a damn cheap shot, a rotten lowdown no-good thing."

Gehrig, his eyes focusing as Ruth watched, smiled. "Yeah, Babe, it was a little inside, wasn't it?"

"A little inside?" Babe snorted. "He *meant* to bean you, Lou. That dirty little coward. He did it on purpose, I tell you."

"Babe," said Lou, slowly sitting up. "Babe, you look good, you look ready to play." And he started to try and stand, first coming to a kneel.

"Lou. I sure wished he hadn't thrown at you like that, that's all. He could've killed you."

"No, no," said Gehrig, waving away the help and sympathy. "No, I'll be all right. I'll . . ." And he nearly collapsed, giving up on the idea of standing and then falling back to one knee. "Shoot, I'm a little woozy, I guess."

Connie Mack, standing next to Lou, patted his star on the back. "You just take it easy, Louis. We'll get a pinch runner for you. There's plenty of talented players left around here, you just don't worry about it."

"Mr. Mack," said the Babe, reaching down to help Lou to his feet as Gehrig tried again to rise. "I'd like to be that runner, if it's all right with you. I think I'd like to get into this game after all."

"Well, that's fine, George, of course," said Mack, as he and the Babe helped Gehrig walk slowly toward the dugout. "You'll be hitting fourth, then, in Lou's spot. We'll put you out in right, in Henry's spot, and bring in Gil Hodges. And we're sure glad to have you on the team."

The Babe trotted out to first, not bothering to loosen up at all, feeling too good to need it. Somehow he was in uniform now, instead of the suit he'd been wearing.

The next fellow up for Mack's team was Willie Mays and he went with the first pitch from Wynne, a fastball low and away, and took it to the opposite field, sending it into the corner in right. The Babe, off at the crack of the bat, was making it to third standing up, but that wasn't good enough, not after what had been going on here.

Instead of easing into third, he ignored the stop sign from Yogi, the third-base coach, and barrelled right on through, pushing off the bag with his right foot and heading toward home.

Out in right, Joe Jackson had chased down the ball and came up expecting to see men on second and third, but there was Ruth already rounding third and heading home. Shoeless Joe took one hop step and fired toward Thurman Munson at the plate.

Munson had the plate blocked, and was reaching up with that big mitt to catch the throw as the Babe came in, shoulder down, determined to plow right through him and score.

The collision raised a cloud of dust, and for a long second Bill Klem hesitated over making the call. Then, with a smile and long, slow deep-throated growl, he yanked his thumb toward the sky and called the Babe out.

The Babe was in a fury. He leaped to his feet, started screaming bloody murder at Klem.

"Out? How the hell could you call me out? He dropped the goddamned ball! Can't you see anything, you dumb—"

The umpire silenced him with the jab of a finger. "You just got into the game, Babe," Klem snapped. "You wanna get tossed out so soon?"

Growling, holding in the anger, the Babe slowly dusted off his uniform, staring at Klem the whole time. Klem stared back, hands on hips. Then, shaking his head, fists clenched, the Babe trudged over to the dugout.

Munson shakily got up on one knee, reached over to pick up the ball from where it had trickled away, gave Klem a puzzled glance, and then flipped the ball out to Wynne. In all the commotion Mays had moved up to third, and there was still a game to play. Munson adjusted his chest protector, pulled the mask down firmly, and crouched behind the plate as Wynne went through the usual fidgeting and finally stood on the rubber and looked in for the signal. The game went on.

The Babe had calmed down a bit in the dugout when Gehrig, still pale, came over to chat with him.

"Tough call, Babe," Lou said, slapping him on the back.

"Yeah. Tough, all right. Say, Dutch, you feeling OK now?"

Gehrig ran his right hand through his hair. There was an ugly bluish lump rising behind his ear. He saw Ruth notice the bruise, touched at it gingerly, then smiled, nodded, said "Yeah, sure, better, Babe, better," he said. "You just keep that temper under control out there, right? You always did have a problem with that. We need you thinking straight, Babe, OK?"

"Sure, Lou, sure," said the Babe, and gave Lou a puzzled look as the Iron Horse walked away.

The sixth ended with Mack's team still a run ahead, but in the seventh Comiskey's team used a walk, an outrageously bad call at first, and a sharp single up the middle from Rose to tie the game at five apiece. Mack's team threatened in the bottom but couldn't get a run across even with the bases full and just one out.

Then, in the top of the eighth, Bill Terry hit a sharp grounder to Hodges at first, who moved away from the bag to get a glove on it, then flipped to Robin Roberts, Mack's pitcher. Roberts had to reach to catch the toss while stepping on the bag, and Terry ran him down. There was a tangle of arms and legs rolling in the chalk and dust, and when it all settled, Terry was safe at first and Roberts was done for the day, his ankle badly spiked.

There were other pitchers available, of course, but Connie Mack had something particular in mind, some kind of purpose, and waved out to right, to the Babe. And so, for the first time since a brief appearance in 1933, Babe Ruth came in to pitch.

He had his best stuff, a blazing fastball that he could place accurately. It was the Babe Ruth of 1916 on the mound, the Ruth who won twenty-three games and had an E.R.A. of 1.75. The Ruth who pitched twenty-nine straight scoreless innings in World Series play.

Comiskey's guys would have had a tough time getting to the Babe in any event, but now, his anger really seething, the Babe was viciously untouchable, high and tight fastballs threatening skulls, everything working inside, his ire obvious to every hitter who stepped into the box.

"Stay on your toes, wise-ass," he bellowed at Cobb, throwing close enough to shave his chin.

And at the plate he was just as angry, though he had to control it some. In the bottom of the eighth, he came to the plate again with one out and nobody on. Bob Gibson, pitching in relief, wasn't at all afraid to play even-up, and came in with one under Ruth's chin on the first pitch, and then broke off a curve low and away for ball two, before throwing something in the strike zone, a blazing fastball low and inside, an unhittable pitch. For anybody else.

The Babe golfed it, reached down to make contact and drove the ball up and out, deep to right, twenty rows up, a towering home run. As he rounded the bases he muttered under his breath as he passed each of Comiskey's players, cursing them quietly, so the umps wouldn't hear, but swearing to get each and every one of them the next time up.

They all looked shocked. The Babe? Swearing vengeance? Rollicking, fun-loving Babe Ruth, threatening to bean them, calling them the foulest names they'd ever heard? They looked like whipped little boys, scared and ashamed.

They deserve it, the Babe said to himself as he trotted into the dugout. They deserve whatever I dish out to them, the dirty bastards.

Then he looked across the infield to the other team's dugout and saw Comiskey grinning from ear to ear, like he was perfectly satisfied with the way the game was developing.

It stopped being a baseball game and turned into

a war. Every batter who faced the Babe had to dive
into the dirt. The Babe wasn't throwing warning
pitches; he was trying to break skulls. He fired his
hardest, especially at Cobb and Durocher. Klem, of-
ficiating behind the plate, gave him a few hard
stares, but let the mayhem go on.

The Babe expected the other guys to come charg-
ing out to the mound after him. He was ready for a
real fight. Spoiling for one, in fact. But they just took
their turns at bat, dived to the ground when the Babe
zinged a fastball at their heads, and meekly popped
up or grounded out. Vaguely, through his haze of
anger, the Babe saw that they all looked scared. Terrified. Good, he thought. Serves 'em right.

In the top of the ninth Rose worked up the nerve
to stand in there and one of the Babe's fastballs
nailed him in the shoulder. Hal Chase went in to run
for him. The Babe tried twice to pick him off first,
couldn't do it, and then, angry as hell, came in with
a high, hard one to Shoeless Joe, who slapped it out
into short right field, putting men on first and third.
Cobb's fly ball to center, three pitches later, gave
Comiskey's men the tie before the Babe could pitch
out of the jam.

Babe trudged off the field, more furious than ever
that he'd let them tie the score. His teammates shied
away from him. They're sore at me, Babe grumbled
to himself. Connie Mack just shook his head, looking
distressed. Even Lou seemed unhappy, disappointed
in him.

So what? the Babe thought. So they got a lucky
run off me. At least they're not beaning and spiking
anybody now. They're whipped, and they know it.

In the bottom of the ninth the Babe was hitting

fourth and just hoping to get an at-bat. Marty Marion, leading off, smacked a grounder up the middle that looked like a sure single, but Durocher came behind the bag and made a hell of a play to get him. Charlie Gehringer fouled off four pitches and finally drew a walk, but then Lefty Grove came in to get Ted Williams on a long fly to deep right, so that brought the Babe up with two outs and one on.

The Babe knew all about Grove. He was a fastball pitcher all the way, with a good curve that he didn't bother with much since he had so much heat. Somebody said once that Grove could throw a lamb chop past a wolf. We'll see about that, the Babe thought.

The Babe figured he could wait him out a pitch or two and then take him deep and end this game. That would feel good, real good. He was so mad that he wanted to do more than just win, he wanted to really hurt these guys, teach them a lesson, humiliate them.

But the Babe didn't figure he'd get a chance to do anything like that, much as he wanted to. Instead, he'd just sit back a bit, let Grove have a little rope, and then crush one. End the game in real Babe Ruth style and leave the damned bastards standing there on the field, cowed for good.

But it wasn't Grove on the mound when the Babe stepped into the batter's box. Instead, as he settled in, digging a spot for the left foot to brace, and looked up, it was Charley Root.

Where the hell had Root come from? Then the Babe smiled. This was typical. Of course Comiskey would pull a stunt like this. In 1932, in the third game of the World Series, the Babe had gotten even with the Cubs by showing up Root, pointing at the spot in the stands where he planned to hit his home run and then doing it. He called his shot, and it became part of baseball's legend.

Root said it never happened that way, experts analyzed old home movies of the moment and tended to agree. But the Babe knew better, he'd gotten even with Root back then and he would do it now, just the same way.

First, he wanted to let a few pitches go by, just to get another good look at Root's stuff, and to let the moment build up a bit.

The first pitch came right at his head, and the Babe had to fight the instinct to hit the dirt, getting away from it. Instead, he just leaned back and let the pitch go by his eyes, inches away. Gehringer, on first, could see how Root had his attention focused on the plate, and took off as the pitcher started his windup. Munson pegged it down to second, but never had a chance, and Gehringer was on second with an easy steal.

The Babe, laughing as the ball came back to the mound, stepped back out of the box and looked back at the catcher.

"That the best you guys can do? You sons of bitches, give me a strike in here now and I'll ride the thing right out of here."

Munson just shook his head, said nothing.

The second pitch came even closer, aimed at the Babe's ribs. It was another fastball, a good one with a lot of movement aimed high and tight. The Babe didn't flinch, and the ball came so close to him that Klem, umping behind the plate, hesitated for a moment, wondering if it hadn't clipped the Babe's jersey.

Sensing the hesitation, the Babe turned to face

Klem, and said loudly "It didn't touch me, and you
know it. You and me got some history, Klem, but
this ain't your fight here. Just let it go, you hear me?
Let it go."

Klem stared back at Ruth. "You're showing me
up, Babe, and I don't like it. That's not your style. I
don't know what's eating you, but just get back in
there and play."

"What's eating me," growled the Babe as he dug
in again, "is a bunch of snotty little goddamned
bushers playing dirty ball. That's what eating me."

"And what've you been doing, Babe?" Klem
snapped.

Munson, looking toward Root on the mound,
pulled down his face mask, and added: "Hey Babe,
some of us don't have a choice out here, so don't
take it out on us, huh?"

"No choice, hell. You guys play rough and then
when I give you a dose of your own medicine you
start crying," the Babe said.

Munson shook his head, and muttered, "You still
don't get it, do you, Babe?"

"Play ball," Klem ordered.

Root pounded the ball into his glove nervously
and glared toward the plate. The Babe stepped back
out of the box, lifted his bat toward the right-field
seats, and pointed it.

"You got that?" the Babe yelled out to the pitcher.
There was no doubt about it this time, nothing un-
sure. This was meant. "You got that? Right out there,
Charlie, right out there, maybe ten rows up."

Root glared at him, and then, as the Babe stepped
back in, went into his windup and brought in the
next pitch, a good fastball down low for a strike.

The Babe just watched it go by, full of confidence, not bothering with the pitch because it wasn't where he wanted it. By God, he wanted to show these guys up, every one of them. They'd put some good men out of the game, especially poor old Lou, and the Babe was going to get even, going to win this thing in fine style.

The next pitch started out low and away, way out of the strike zone, and then tailed off into the dirt as Root tried to get the Babe to go after a bad one. But the Babe didn't move, and the ball got by Munson, who couldn't even get a glove on it as it skipped by.

Gehringer, on second, made it easily to third while Munson chased it down.

The count was 3 and 1 now, with a man on third and two outs. The Babe started to step back in, then hesitated.

He stared at Root and saw a look of utter hopelessness in the pitcher's face. Root knew the Babe was going to hammer him, blast the ball out of sight, just the way he'd done in '32. The infielders all looked like whipped dogs, too. Hell, even Durocher had that hangdog look about him. That's not like Lippy, he'd always been a scrapper.

What had the catcher said? *You still don't get it, do you, Babe?* And before that: *Some of us don't have a choice out here.*

Damn, he wanted to get even with these guys, he really did. But . . . something really weird was going on here.

And the Babe remembered. Remembered his own cancer, remembered Lou being so sick and frail and—the Dutchman had died. I went to his funeral, for God's sake. I died! The Babe looked around the field again. Cobb, Hornsby, Joe Jackson.

"Time out," he said to Klem. And he went over to the dugout, trailing his big brown Louisville Slugger in the dust.

Connie Mack came halfway up the dugout steps. "Something wrong, George?"

Feeling perplexed, not really believing what his own mind was telling him, the Babe asked, "Mr. Mack, this ain't just another ball game, is it?"

Mack's blue eyes seemed to sparkle. "No, George, it certainly is not an ordinary game."

Lou came over and joined them, holding an ice bag to his head. "It's a special game, Babe. We've got to win it."

"But we've got to win it in the right way," Mack said. "It won't matter if we win the game but you end up playing with Mr. Comiskey's team."

The Babe felt startled. "You'd trade me?"

Mack shook his head. "No, George. Up here the players make their own decisions about which side they want to be with."

"Well, I sure don't want—" The Babe hesitated. "You mean all those guys, Leo and Cobb and Shoeless Joe and all, they *chose* to play for Comiskey?"

"They didn't realize it at the time, but, yes, they chose the wrong team."

"They didn't mean to, though, did they?" Gehrig asked.

The ghost of a smile played across Mack's bloodless lips. "I'm sure that if they knew then what they know now, they would have acted differently."

The Babe frowned with concentration. This was a lot to think about, a lot to figure out.

"Are we playing a ball game here or not?" Klem

bellowed from home plate. "Get back in the box, Babe, or I'll forfeit the game."

"Okay, Klem, okay," the Babe hollered back. He started back toward the plate, his mind churning. These other guys have *got* to play for Comiskey, whether they want to or not? They got no choice?

Abruptly he turned and yelled to Mack, "If we win this game, it's for all of 'em. Get me? Not just for me. *All* of the others, too!"

Lou grinned happily at him. Mack seemed to hesitate for a moment, as if holding a private conversation with himself. Then he, too, smiled, and tipped his straw boater to Ruth, agreeing to the terms.

And the Babe dug in at the batter's box, cocked his Louisville Slugger, looked ready to cream Root's next pitch.

But that's what they all expect, he thought. They're waiting for me to crush it, waiting for me to show them how much better I am than any of them.

"Pride, George." He remembered Brother Dominic telling him, time and again at the orphanage in Baltimore. "Pride will be your undoing, unless you learn to control it, use it for good."

He took a deep breath. As Root stepped onto the rubber and checked Gehringer, leading off third, the Babe pointed with his bat again toward the right-field seats. "Maybe twenty rows up," he taunted.

Root scowled, went into an abbreviated windup, and threw a wicked fastball at the Babe's ear. He hit the ground. The ball thwacked into Munson's mitt.

"Strike two!" called Klem.

The Babe leaped to his feet, bat in hand. Klem stared at him from behind his mask.

Then, with a childish grin, the Babe got back into

the batter's box. "Come on, chickenshit," he yelled to Root, hoisting the bat over his shoulder. "Put one over the plate."

Root did. Another fastball, low and away this time. The Babe knew Klem would call it strike three if he let it pass.

He didn't. He squared his feet and tapped the ball toward third base, as neat a bunt as ever laid down the line. The infield had been playing 'way back, of course. The outfielders, too. Everybody knew that the Babe was going to swing for the fences.

And here's this bunt trickling slowly down the third-base line, too far from the plate for Munson to reach, too slow for Tabor at third to possibly reach it. Gehringer streaked home with the winning run while the Babe laughed all the way to first base.

The game was over.

And the other guys were laughing, too! Tabor picked the ball off the grass near third and twirled it in his hand. As the fielders headed in for the visitors' dugout, Durocher cracked:

"Twenty rows up, huh, Babe?"

Cobb gave a huff. "You're stealing my stuff now, Babe. Using your head out there."

Even old Charlie Root just shook his head and grinned at the Babe. "Who'd a thought it?" he said, true wonderment in his eyes. "Who'd a thought it?"

On impulse, the Babe reached out his hand. Root looked startled, then he took it in a firm ballplayer's grip.

"I was afraid you'd strike me out, Charlie," said the Babe.

Root actually laughed. "Yeah. Sure. Like I did in Chicago."

And he followed his teammates into the shadows of the dugout, where Charlie Comiskey stood glaring hotly at them.

The Babe trotted to his own dugout. Lou and the other guys slapped his back and congratulated him on the big winning blast. One of the black players, Mays, raised his hand up above his head, palm outward. The Babe didn't know what to do.

Hank Aaron, looking slightly embarrassed, demonstrated a high five with Mays. The Babe grinned and tried it.

"Okay!" he laughed.

About an hour later, Connie Mack and Charlie Comiskey stood on the mound, staring out toward left, talking it over. Both men were in a good mood. Mack had proven his point, and said so to Comiskey.

"I told you he'd do the right thing, Charles. You wouldn't believe me, of course, but I was confident."

"Oh, that's all right, McGillicuddy, that's all right," said Comiskey with a wave of his hand. "I never thought he'd bunt, but it's turned out all right for me. Some of my fellows proved they really belong on my team, you might say."

Mack smiled. "Well, I suppose that's true, Charles. But you do remember what George said just before he went back to bat."

"What he said?"

"Well. Yes. You heard him. He said he wasn't doing it merely for himself. It was for all of them."

Comiskey scratched his jowly jaw. "Yeah, I remember. What'd he mean by that?"

"What he meant," said Mack, "was that he wants

all the players—yours as well as mine—to be free to choose which team they want to be with from now on."

"All the players? Mine? *My* players?" Comiskey sputtered. "Never! He can't do that! It's against our rules. Each player is bound to the team that owns him. The reserve clause—"

"The reserve clause is ancient history, Charles," said Mack patiently.

"What in hell do you mean?"

"I've already spoken to the Commissioner. The reserve clause that you insisted upon has been stricken from each player's contract."

Comiskey just gaped at Cornelius McGillicuddy. "You can't! You—it's not fair! Dammit to hell, it's not fair! Those players signed their lives away. To me!"

Mack shook his head ever so slightly. "Those poor souls are free, Charles. The Commissioner agreed to the terms George requested. And with that bunt, the Babe freed them."

Comiskey's face was redder than fire. "You engineered this, McGillicuddy! You *knew*—"

"I hoped, Charles," replied Mack softly. "And the Babe came through for me. And for all of them."

Stamping his cloven feet in fury, Comiskey snarled, "This isn't the end of it! You'll see!"

"Oh, goodness gracious, yes, I know. You'll make an offer that some of the players can't refuse, Charles. Some of them will want to stay on your team, of course. That's up to them."

Comiskey shook his fist under Mack's nose. "Wait till next year, McGillicuddy. Wait till next year!"

Connie Mack smiled. "Next year the Babe will be

managing my club. I'm being moved . . . eh, up-stairs." And Mack began to shimmer, his form slowly losing its solidity, becoming transparent.

"Oh, and Charles," he added while slowly fading away. "It's my understanding that you've been moved to a new assignment, too, something a little slower paced; cricket, I believe. And if you do well there, then, perhaps, next year you'll be back to face the Babe. I *do* hope so, really, for your sake." And he was gone.

Comiskey, furious but helpless, could only stamp his foot in anger and shake his fist at the sky, where the dark clouds that had rumbled and threatened rain all day were now, finally, blowing clear and letting the late-afternoon sun shine through.

PERMISSIONS

❖

AVON EOS

RISING STARS

Meet great new talents
in hardcover at a special price!

$14.00 U.S./$19.00 Can.

Hand of Prophecy

by Severna Park
0-380-97639-0

Child of the River: The First Book of Confluence

by Paul J. McAuley
0-380-97515-7